S FUCKING STORIES

STORIES SELECTED BY
SEAN FERRARI
KATIE DEEREST
KEVIN STRANGE

EDITED BY
SEAN FERRARI

STRANGEHOUSE BOOKS

WWW.STRANGEHOUSEBOOKS.COM

Strangehouse Books Catalog:

Strange Sex: A Strange Anthology
Robamapocalypse by Kevin Strange
Tales of Questionable Taste by John Bruni (stories)
Cotton Candy by Kevin Strange
The Last Gig on Planet Earth by Kevin Strange (stories)
Zombie! Zombie! Brain Bang! A Strange Anthology
Vampire Guts in Nuke Town by Kevin Strange
Strange Vs Lovecraft: A Strange Anthology
McHumans by Kevin Strange
Dinner at the Vomitropolis by Jesse Wheeler
Alien Smut Peddlers from the Future by Kent Hill
Damnation 101 by Kevin Sweeney
A Very Strangehouse Christmas: A Strange Anthology
The Humans Under the Bed by Kevin Strange
Re-Animated States of America by Craig Mullins and Andrew Ozkenel (stories)
Strange Fucking Stories: A Strange Anthology
Hamsterdamned! by Adam Millard

StrangeHouse Books
P.O. Box 592
Wood River, IL
62095
www.strangehousebooks.com

ISBN-13: 978-1494995973
ISBN-10: 1494995972

TABLE OF CONTENTS

¡NTRoDUCTioN

When I started StrangeHouse Books in late 2011, I didn't know exactly what I wanted it to be. I knew it would be a vehicle for my fiction and a home for anthologies that showcased up-and-coming (as well as veteran) voices of the weird, but that's still a very vague picture. I knew the logo would be a big ugly Frankenstein head with a house on top of it and that our very first book would be an extreme horror/sex-themed anthology, but I didn't have a clue what kind of stories would actually end up in the book. I took it on faith that our publishing house would build itself, as long as we kept pushing it forward.

And now, as I sit here in the Crow's Nest of SHB HQ, looking down at all that we've accomplished in the short time we've existed, I smile, knowing that's exactly what has happened. StrangeHouse Books is a thing that exists. If I have a coronary tomorrow, it could conceivably continue to churn out Strange Fiction for decades to come. It requires less and less of my guiding hand. Authors now know exactly what kind of books and stories to submit to us for publication.

SHB Editor Sean Ferrari and our submission readers Katie Deerest, John Bruni and Joel Blair have as much of a hand in shaping our releases as I ever have. We all share a vision of the weird, schlocky B-movie type fiction that we've come to be known for. With classics like *Strange Sex*, *Dinner at the Vomitropolis*, the upcoming *Hamsterdamned!* or our Zombie anthology *Zombie! Zombie! Brain Bang!* people know what they're getting into when they see the ugly head with the house on it.

But along the way, we never really put together a flagship anthology. We do lots of different themes, for sure, from Christmas to Lovecraft to our upcoming Oz-themed anthology, but we don't have a standout "here is the BEST of Strange Fiction" type of book that showcases our talented authors on their own merit without being tied down to a particular theme.

Strange Fucking Stories is the first of what I hope will be many anthologies that forgo themes of plot in favor of the simple theme of Strange.

This collection is as diverse as they come, with stories about football, the monster apocalypse, blow up doll western towns, suits made of human skin, caterpillar portals and so, so much more. You'll read stories here from veteran SHB anthology authors like Rich Bottles Jr. and K.M. Tepe as well as brand new voices crying out to be counted among the Strange elite. This anthology series is where the future authors of StrangeHouse Books will get their start, and veterans hone their craft. This is quintessential StrangeHouse, gang. Enjoy.

-Kevin Strange 1/10/2014 12:46am SHB HQ

HEARTS AND CATERPiLLARS

MP Johnson

At the tip of Percy's fork, a caterpillar crawled from chunks of lettuce and grated carrots, stretched its pale emerald body high and waved its tiny black legs, as if to say, "Get me the fuck out of here."

"Um, did you wash these veggies, Em?" Percy asked.

"Yes!" Emily shouted, throwing her fork down and slapping her palm against the table. "Are you saying your fucking salad is dirty?"

"It's not that it's dirty," Percy replied, holding out his pointer finger for the caterpillar to climb onto. "It's just that I found this little guy."

"So? Kill the fucking worm and eat your salad."

"It's a caterpillar, Em, and I'm not going to kill it."

A single plant—a hibiscus—lived on the sill of the one window in Percy's apartment. He had named it Cussy. It flowered every morning like clockwork. Just one flower at a time, though; no more. He set his finger against one of its leaves and the caterpillar tickled away, excited for its new home.

Emily stomped across the hardwood floor in her Mary Janes, which she always refused to take off at the door. "I'm going to squish it."

Percy grabbed her and pulled her in for a hug. She squirmed away, trying to get past him to Cussy and the caterpillar. When she realized he wasn't going to let her pass, she stepped back and crossed her arms over her chest. Her angry face—her most frequently made face—involved her lower lip engulfing her upper lip as if trying to pull her face into her mouth. Her thin brows zigzagged over her tapioca eyes. As usual, Percy tried to kiss the angry face away.

Emily dodged his lips. "You really want to keep that thing?"

"It's just a caterpillar."

"It's gross, Perky. Get rid of it," she ordered gently, poking a French manicured nail into Percy's chest. Her angry face unraveled. Without it, her features—the slashing cheekbones and long eyelashes—created an equation that mathed out to equal totally hot to most men, Percy included.

Percy held his ground—not an easy task when she unleashed the pet names. They had grown increasingly rare now that the two of them had eclipsed the first year of their relationship and were getting down to the nitty gritty of figuring out who made dinner on which nights and at who's place.

"Fine, you keep it then. I'm going to my fucking yoga class."

Percy asked, "Will you be back later?"

"Maybe if I feel like pity fucking you, loser."

"Love you."

"Yeah."

Emily didn't come back that night. Percy sat on the couch, reading. His apartment always got hotter at night, but he didn't feel like turning the air conditioning on. Sweat soaked through the pits of his purple polo shirt, which Em said looked good with his green eyes. She also said it made him look like a fag, but she had said it looked good first, so that's what Percy focused on.

He toyed with his long hair. "What color is that?" Emily once asked. "My mom used to call it root beer. Have you thought of cutting it? It looks kind of faggy. It's longer than mine." Percy thought of her hair—jaw-length and bleached blonde, smelling like oranges or chocolate—and pleasured himself before falling asleep.

The sun shined through the window the next morning, unimpeded by the hibiscus, which had been stripped of all but a single leaf, a surrender flag.

"I thought you'd eat a leaf or two, Cat, not the whole thing. My mom gave me Cussy at my dad's funeral." Percy poked at the remnants, looking for the caterpillar. "Where are you, anyway?"

After scouring his apartment, he found the caterpillar under his bed. The insect had digested and expelled what it had eaten and now writhed in a puddle of what looked like granola. The caterpillar had doubled in size.

Percy returned the caterpillar to the carcass of Cussy. "I have to lay down the law here, Cat. You don't go beyond the windowsill. Deal?"

The caterpillar stood on its hind section and waved. Percy took the gesture as a "Yes." With that agreement in place, he went to work at the office, designing websites for dentists, every single one looking exactly the same at the request of his clients: "I want happy people smiling wide! Big shiny teeth!" He always delivered.

After work, he went to a greenhouse and picked up five more hibiscus plants: Cussy Two, Three, Four, Five and Six.

"What's this shit?" Emily asked when she visited again a couple days later, making her angry face at all the chomped-on plants that cramped the windowsill.

"Just wanted more plants," Percy said.

"They're dead."

"I guess I don't have a green thumb, Em."

Emily shrieked. "What the fuck is that?"

The caterpillar climbed to the top of one of the plants, stretching up as if to wave hello. It had grown to be roughly the length of a rat.

"It's just the caterpillar, Em."

She backed toward the door, lower lip quivering. "It's a monster!"

The caterpillar coughed up a stream of half-digested plant matter. The gritty muck dribbled from its mouth onto its underbelly. Its little legs writhed, struggling impotently to wipe the embarrassing mess away.

Emily turned and ran. Percy chased after her, but even in her heels she managed to get out to her car and drive away before he could explain—not that he even knew what he had to explain. What was the big deal?

A month later, Percy sat on his couch, rubbing the corner of his cellphone against his cheek through strands of unkempt root beer hair. He had lost track of which Cussy he was on—thirty-six, maybe—but he did know he had left Emily exactly fifty voicemails. She had not responded to one.

Cat stretched up and pressed against the window, scratching its many black legs across the glass. It had grown to two feet, and as thick around as Percy's thigh. When it slid back down to the windowsill, it shuffled accordion-like, its emerald skin crushing together and then stretching. It turned and looked at Percy.

Cat's puzzle of a face started with a pair of thin lips, spread wide and slathered with the cheap ruby lipstick elderly women gravitated toward. What appeared to be the head of a much more grotesque insect seemed ready to emerge from the lips, diarrhea brown with mandibles and pokers and pus-colored nodules. Two black pits rode on top of the old lady lips. Percy considered those Cat's eyes, although they might have been nostrils or laser-shooters, for all he knew. On the underside of the lips smiled a smaller pair of lips. From these, a steady stream of hibiscus debris drizzled.

"Can she really be that freaked out by you?" Percy asked.

To his surprise, Cat replied, in a voice as shiny as its skin, "She's not freaked out by me. She's using me as an excuse to cheat on you."

When Percy peeled his hand away from his mouth, he said, "You talk?"

Cat took a bite of hibiscus, chewed it slowly and repeated, "She's cheating."

That evening, Percy planned to follow Emily. However, parked a block away from her apartment, he couldn't help but think he was going to get caught. Maybe that's what he wanted. She would confront him and he could tell her he loved her and missed her, all the things he had already elaborated on ad nauseum in his voicemails, which he had begun scripting and also sending in letter form.

When she finally stepped out of her apartment, her attire shocked Percy. She always dressed risqué, with her miniskirts and low-cut tops, but this was straight-up stripper apparel: Clear heels, a leather miniskirt that barely concealed her avalanche of butt flesh, and a pink top with less material than his handkerchiefs. And, strangely, a baseball hat over her bleached blonde hair.

He lowered himself in the driver's seat, but Emily didn't even look his way. She climbed into her car and pulled away without so much as a flash of her blinker. Percy followed, driving faster than he would have preferred, leaving the city and weaving through the chain restaurants and strip malls of the suburbs.

She finally pulled into the parking lot of one of those strip malls, outside of Mega Mattress Warehouse, home of the annual Mega Mattress Meltdown and its companion television ads, featuring a man in a pink armadillo suit lighting mattresses on fire in this very parking lot and bellowing, "Bargains that will melt your mind!"

Percy parked on a side street and hustled back to MMW on foot. On the tips of his toes, with his arms outstretched like a ballerina for balance, he crept through shadows, avoiding the bright parking lot lights.

In front of the store, he dropped to his hands and knees, immediately getting a palm-full of cigarette butts. Wiping the butts away, he moved closer. The facade of Mega Mattress Warehouse (like every store in the strip mall) was all window, with the exception of three feet of tan brick. Percy hunkered down behind the brick.

Lifting his head, he imagined himself as the caterpillar, moving slowly and fluidly, a boneless tube of flexible material. When he could see into the store, he gasped. He covered his eyes to prevent them from popping out of their sockets.

In the darkened store, Emily sprawled out on a California king size mattress. She had already abandoned her little clothing, except her heels and hat. The wrinkly fingertips of a mustachioed man old enough to be her grandfather danced over her tattoo – a rainbow wrapped in barbed wire that ran from her right hip to the fold under her right breast. She opened and closed her legs, teasing, and shoved a finger into the old man's mouth. He sucked it and unbuttoned his shirt.

Outside, Percy puffed out his cheeks, catching his groans of disgust so they could linger on his tongue, letting him savor their charcoal flavor.

The pink armadillo from the commercials rolled out

from a back room on a skateboard. A whip dangled around his neck like an undone tie. The armadillo did an ollie before kicking the board aside. Emily shoved the old man away and reached for the armadillo, who did an awkward frat boy dance before waving his whip overhead as if getting ready to lasso something.

Having seen all he needed to see, all he would ever need to see in his entire life, Percy scurried back to his car.

"You were right," Percy said to the caterpillar as it gorged on grass in the park the next day. Around him, kids threw baseballs at each other's heads and spewed the F-word at a faster pace than Emily. If they were curious about the thing beneath the blanket by Percy's feet, they didn't show it. Percy considered taking the blanket away so Cat could enjoy the sunlight, but didn't want to push his luck.

"Was there any doubt?" Muffled by the blanket, Cat sounded distant.

"I think I knew it all along."

"The question is, what are you going to do about it?"

"What am I going to do about it?" Percy hadn't considered doing anything about it. Now that Cat mentioned it, though, he realized that, at the very least, he had to break up with Emily. That bummed him out. She made him feel safe. When she was around, the only thing that could hurt him was her; and she didn't hurt him too bad. He could handle her making fun of him. Unless they were having sex; then he would get frustrated and lose his drive, which would only make her wrath worse.

He didn't think of that now, though. Instead, he thought about the time at the movie theater when, after standing at the counter far too long trying to decide whether he wanted a slushee or chocolate-covered raisins, the popcorn jockey grinned and asked, "Do you think you'll decide before the movie's over?" Emily responded, "He's distracted by your pimples, cocksucker. Now give us another minute or I'm going to take off my heels and start popping zits my way."

Cat wriggled out from under the blanket. Blades of grass hanging from its little red mouth, it said, "Yeah, what are you going to do about it, man?"

Realizing Cat meant something more drastic than politely severing the relationship, Percy looked to the sky for answers. "I guess I could throw out all the clothes she left at my place. Except her leather jacket; her uncle gave her that jacket when she was a kid. He was in some popular rock band, kind of a one-hit wonder... the Din Lonesomes? I couldn't throw that away."

Cat squirmed back under the blanket. "This grass tastes like piss."

Emily sat at the table in Percy's apartment, arms crossed, face on the verge of being sucked in by her lower lip. Percy hadn't thrown her stuff away. He had spent the previous two days hurling voicemails at her, and his perseverance had paid off. Of course, he had told her he had gotten rid of the caterpillar.

"I made fajitas. I know you love them." Percy slid a plate in front of her.

"They're the only thing you make that doesn't taste like complete shit."

"What have you been up to?" he asked.

Pulling her lips away from her teeth to reveal how intensely she clenched them, she dipped pointer finger and thumb into her food and snatched out a sauce-soaked strand of Percy's hair. Percy's heart kamakazeed straight into his throat, where it melted down into a thick meaty muck that temporarily prevented air from entering. Pinky outstretched, Emily daintily put the strand of hair back into her food and pushed her plate aside. "You want to know what I've been up to?"

Percy nodded, bracing himself for bluntness.

"I just needed some me time, you know?"

"Oh, I know how that goes. I needed some me time too." Percy laughed. Even in the thick of their relationship, he hadn't had any trouble finding "me time." He'd had a lifetime of "me time."

Emily lowered her eyelids. "You have something on your mind."

"You're cheating on me."

She pushed herself back in her chair. "That hurts, Perky. That really hurts."

"I followed you to Mega Mattress Warehouse and saw you doing... things... with an old man and that pink armadillo from the commercials."

She tapped her long nails against the table, louder and louder, until the sound felt like a hammer hitting Percy at the base of his skull. Tap. Tap. Tap.

"You followed me? What are you saying? You don't trust me?"

"It's not that I don't trust you, Em, it's just that..."

"Don't even try to explain, I... I... I... Jesus Fucking Christ!"

The caterpillar had crawled out of the bedroom and now stood a few feet from the table, stretching up as tall as possible, its mouth grinding. Its many black legs slashed the air, pointing accusingly at Emily.

She threw her hairy fajita at it, but missed and the food knocked over Percy's TV. The glass screen shattered and sparks flew, singing the caterpillar's hide. It hissed, leaning forward, closer to Emily, its underside bubbling.

"I'm done with you!" she screamed as she stood to leave. "I'm done with your distrust. I'm done with your faggy fucking hair. I'm done with your freaky fucking caterpillar. And you know what, I'm glad, because you're boring. I told myself you were stable, but you aren't stable at all. You're totally unstable, and you're still boring, and I don't even know how that's possible, but it

15

doesn't matter. I've got a line of people waiting to fuck me. Oh yeah, you followed me, so you saw that."

"No, I didn't see that!" Percy shouted.

"I wish you had. You might have learned something."

Cat whipped forward, shooting a stream of hibiscus-colored ooze that formed a perfect arch as it made its way to its destination: Emily's face. It splattered like pancake batter dumped onto the griddle too fast. Emily screamed, but that only opened the gate for the ooze to go down her throat. She put her hands up, slapping at the stream before it finally stopped. Slipping on the puddle, she ran out the door.

Percy wished Emily had given him one final "fuck you" before leaving. At the very least, she could have reiterated how worthless he was. Just not silence.

Anything but silence.

That night, Percy wandered nearly naked back and forth between the bed and the couch. Neither offered sleep. His bed smelled like the orange and chocolate lotion Emily rubbed on her skin in the evening. His couch smelled like farts.

Mirroring Percy's unrest, Cat moved back and forth on the moonlit windowsill, casting a massive shadow on the opposite wall.

"Why did I have to confront her?" he asked, hooking his thumbs under the waistband of his tighty-whities and running them back and forth around his waist. "Some people might have asked to join in. It's not like she's in love with that old man and that mattress mascot. She's just being sexually adventurous. It's hot."

"It's not hot," Cat said. "It's treacherous."

"Ah, what do you know? This is all your fault."

"Catalyst and cause are two different things."

"I don't know what that means, Cat."

"Go to her."

Percy snapped the waistband of his underwear against his belly. "That's what any other man would do, isn't it?"

"Go to her and kill her. Kill them all." Cat stood tall in front of the window. His shadow looked almost human, minus arms and legs.

"Well I don't know about that, but I can put the fear into them."

Shirtless, he wore his best jeans – the pair Emily said made him look like he had a construction worker butt. He stalked through the strip mall parking lot toward Mega Mattress Warehouse, resting his shower curtain rod on his shoulder. As much as he wished he would have found a baseball bat, he figured this would do the trick. He test-bashed it on a presumably broken-down car. It only bent a little and the shrill ringing sounded appropriately cataclysmic.

The other night, Emily had walked right in, so Percy assumed he'd be able to step through the front door triumphantly and demand that all the monkey business come to an immediate halt. "And the girl's coming home with me," he whispered to himself as he got closer, practicing. She'd respect that.

Unfortunately, he found the door locked. He pressed his face to the glass, scanning the mattress landscape for his targets. When he saw one, he stepped back. The pink armadillo skated to the door, unlocked it and held it open.

"Looking for mattress bargains galore?" the armadillo asked.

"Emily," Percy said, holding the shower curtain rod like a wizard's staff.

From within the store, Emily's voice cut like a razor-edged boomerang. "Let the fucking retard in. I want to hear what he has to say. It'll be a laugh."

The armadillo waved Percy in. As Percy stepped confidently into the store, his rod caught in the doorframe with a cataclysmic clang. Tugged from his grip, it fell to the concrete and rolled into the parking lot. Percy clumsily chased it down, grabbed it and, this time, stepped through the door with a bit more caution.

He followed the armadillo to a tower of mattresses. Emily sat at the top, face hidden beneath her baseball bat, cross-legged with her hands on her knees, one of her yoga poses. "Just talk," she ordered.

"These two guys," Percy said, pointing at the armadillo and the old man, who wore a sheet like a cloak, "they're having an adventure. You're having an adventure too, I get that. Adventure is important. I want you to know that you're my adventure. You're my life's adventure. But you're more than that. You're the love of my life, and that's better than any adventure I can think of."

The old man flung the sheet away, revealing a massive erection rising out of a clump of what looked like steel wool. He clapped furiously and whistled. The armadillo joined in, claps muffled due to his giant pink plush paws.

The applause gave Percy the courage to add boldly, "So you're coming with me."

The clapping stopped suddenly.

"You are really fucking slow, you know that? I have made fun of you and treated you like shit for more than a year. You've treated me to movies and meals at crappy chain restaurants, and you've gotten nothing. Well, you got some good sex. But emotionally, I haven't given you shit. I was doing you a favor by breaking up with you, but then in you march, with your shower curtain rod… hey, what the fuck were you planning to do with that?"

Percy knew she wasn't looking for an answer. She wanted a demonstration. She wanted him to take action, to prove himself. Well, if that was what it was going to take to win her back, then he would damn well do it.

Raising the shower curtain rod over his shoulder

like a spear, he drove its rubber-coated tip into the old man's wrinkly gut. The blow forced the old man backwards to the floor. His boner wobbled like a boxer about to be TKO'ed.

"Whoa, buddy," the armadillo said, paws up in surrender.

Percy swung the shower curtain rod hard, careful to hit the weak spot between the mask and the body of the costume. The blow slid past the plush and hit human neck, sending vibrations through Percy's forearms. The armadillo shouted, "Fuck," grabbed his skateboard and rolled toward the exit.

Emily slid off the pile of mattresses. "You're not saving me, assfuck!"

Now that she stood in front of him, Percy could see the stain left on her face by the caterpillar vomit. The hibiscus flower color wasn't unpleasant, but the emerging whiteheads were. They bubbled up even now, staking their claim to her previously flawless skin. Percy stepped back, surprised.

"Oh, you don't like what your little pet did? This breakout is going to take weeks to clear up. I should go back home with you and make you fuck me with your eyes wide open while I'm on top, popping my zits."

"I'm sorry."

She grabbed the shower curtain rod and pulled. "Give me that!"

Percy held tight. As they fought over the makeshift weapon, the tip hit her in the nose, but her nose didn't break. It sank. It dripped out of the way. The rod slid into her face, an inch deep. Attempting to pull it out, Percy slashed downward. It splashed through her body like an oar in a pond, leaving a gaping chasm from expanding nostrils to her belly button.

Through a plus sign where her minus sign mouth used to be, she said, "Oh God," and puked her organs out. They spewed through her mouth at first, but eventually poured through the entire wound, which widened as she sank to the floor. Her body flopped open like a book.

Having ejected her insides all over the tile floor, where they formed a connect-the-guts puzzle around Percy's feet, her shell was hollow. And it was deep. Percy leaned closer, drawn to a greenish glow emanating from within. He could hardly believe what he saw. There, amidst the still-quivering innards, he found a flight of stairs made out of muscle and bones. When he placed his foot on the first step, he surprised himself. He wasn't the most adventurous person in the world, but here he was, fighting off rapists with a shower curtain rod and climbing into this impossible cavern in the pulse-less body of the love of his life.

"Oh God, Emily!" he cried as he slipped all the way into the body and proceeded down the stairs toward the light. He arrived at the bottom sooner than he expected. As long as space was being manipulated somehow, what with this entire passage jammed into Emily's svelte carcass, he assumed the steps would go on for hours, twisting upside down and right side up like that Escher piece he had been intrigued with in high school. Thankfully, they didn't.

He emerged into rolling dunes of golden sand, sparkling underneath a trio of emerald suns that undulated across the sky. Blackbirds with tentacles instead of beaks swooped overhead, caw-cawing the prettiest caw-caw he had ever heard. A breeze gathered the scent of the dunes and the skies and whisked it to Percy's nostrils. It smelled of candied roses and it breathed deep, gazing around. What had he expected to find? Maybe Emily's heart, so he could hug it back into beating. Perhaps it hid somewhere in the distance, closer to those three suns.

Before he could move toward them, something scurried across his feet. A caterpillar with twisted bristles and yellow bulbs poking out of its tan skin chewed on his shoe. Percy pulled his foot away just in time to avoid the glob of tar-black muck the caterpillar hurled at him.

"Cat's puke," Percy whispered. "That's why Em got messed up."

As soon as he realized the danger at his toes, an army of caterpillars shuffled over the dunes, coming his way. Thousands of them squirmed over each other, desperate to get to him first, to spray him down with their flesh-softening horks. He knew he had no hope of saving Emily. He could only save himself now.

Percy ran up the steps and shoved his way out of Emily's corpse. Before he left, he stomped on the staircase until it ruptured and then crumbled, preventing the caterpillar horde from following him.

"Emily's dead!" Percy shouted, bursting into his apartment and crying great goobery tears that seemed to come as much from his nostrils as his eyes.

Cat balanced atop the foliage free branch of one of the dozens of skeletal hibiscus plants clogging up Percy's apartment. "Of course."

"You killed her! You set this whole thing up!"

"She fed me to you in a salad."

"Maybe I should have eaten you. You know what?" Percy ran into the kitchen, grabbed a dirty fork and said, "I think I'm going to do just that."

Percy charged, jabbing the prongs of his utensil in the air threateningly. The caterpillar reared back. Its midsection expanded suddenly, as if an explosion had taken place somewhere inside. The lump slowly moved up the length of the caterpillar. When the bulge almost at the insect's head, Percy realized what was happening. He whipped the fork at the caterpillar. The tip miraculously stuck into the caterpillar's underbelly, right between its two rows of twitching legs.

At the exact moment of impact, the caterpillar lurched forward, hurling a meteor of hibiscus bark vomit at Percy's bare chest. The wad of muck knocked him back a few feet, but he remained standing, even as the goop ate into his flesh.

"I'm dying," Cat said, gray-green blood pouring from the fork wound, "but my work is done. My brothers have been given a new path."

Percy's chest meat bubbled like gravy left on the burner too long. Flesh dripped to the ground, leaving behind a door like the one in Emily's torso. From inside, the greenish glow of those three suns bathed his apartment.

Percy could feel the steps forming inside, his ribs and sternum expanding, twisting and cracking into new positions, supported by muscles and tendons that manipulated themselves into place like sentient clay. Worse, he could feel the pointy legs of caterpillars making their way up the steps. The sensation made the backs of his teeth itch. He sat on the couch, hung his head and prepared for war.

When the first caterpillar popped through the hole in Percy's chest, looking cautiously from side to side with its purple earmuff face, Percy wrapped his hands around it and squeezed. He kept squeezing until the insect's quivering head slopped through his fingers like grape jelly. He tore the rest of its limp body out of his chest hole and threw it across the room, next to Cat's soon-to-be corpse.

"No! Let them be!" Cat shouted, expelling insect innards with its final words.

Percy sat on the edge of his couch. Every muscle in his body flexed as he crushed one caterpillar after the next – furry ones, slimy ones, bristly ones. He smashed the life out of each of them.

After a while, he stopped bothering to pull the insects out and fling them onto the pile. He let their dead bodies form a barricade at the top of the staircase that led out of him, the gateway to the dune-filled dimension the crawlers came from. The barricade grew so deep he had to reach elbow-deep into himself to claw the face off any caterpillar that dared push against it. Eventually, the barricade plugged the hole in his chest completely, impenetrable even to the strongest caterpillar.

Then he stood, fighting to keep his knees and ankles from buckling under the newfound weight inside him. He felt like he had joined a strongman competition and been harnessed to a bus that he needed to drag forward with every step as his competition grunted beside him. He did move forward, though.

And he kept moving forward.

Over time, Percy's legs grew strong. He grew strong. The barricade of caterpillar corpses in his chest did not decompose or turn to ooze. It hardened like concrete. Best of all, the colors didn't fade. When he took off his shirt in front of the mirror, he saw a torso with a sideways smile filled with a swirl of purple, green, zebra-patterned, furry, glassy and bristly teeth.

And when the next girl sat beside him on his couch, eating fajitas and watching ten-year-old comedies, and asked him sarcastically, "Why are you so boring, Percy?" he put her hand on his chest and said, "I'm not."

WORSE FOR THE WEAR

Matt Kurtz

Arriving home at the crack of dawn, Ron crept through the back door then past his wife, restlessly sleeping on the couch in her bathrobe, phone at her side. He slinked past his daughter's room, praying she wouldn't hear his steps and awaken to see her daddy.

Ducking into the hallway bathroom, he gently closed the door and fumbled with the lock. He shunned the mirror and sat on the edge of the bathtub.

Trembling, he unzipped his jacket and let the large, crumpled, brown paper grocery bag fall to the tiled floor with a thud. He stared at the bloodstained sack for a long beat. His stomach clamped tight, but having already vomited its contents numerous times earlier, there was no need to lift the toilet's lid. He kicked the bag as far away as possible within such a tiny room, until it was wedged between the toilet and far wall.

The damn thing just needed to be out of his sight; at least for now.

He stared down at his shaking hands clutching his thighs. Turning them over, he inspected both palms for any crimson stains. Nothing. Even under his nails were clean.

But they *still* felt dirty.

Ron climbed to his feet, went to the sink, and turned

on the hot water. He waited for the steam then stuck his hands under the facet, rubbing them back and forth. Slowly looking up, he stared at his haggard face until the mirror fogged over and, thankfully, hid his reflection.

* * *

Eleven hours earlier, hunched at the desk in the rear of his dimly-lit tailor shop, Ron jumped from his seat over the sudden explosion of thunder overhead. Thankfully he wasn't threading a needle, or the reflex would've resulted in an impaled, bloody digit. Rather, the unexpected noise caused him to drop the handful of overdue bills across the desktop.

Leaning back in the creaky wooden chair, he peered through the curtains separating the storefront from rear, looked over the counter, and out the window.

Darkness was approaching. So was the storm. Something bad. Fierce.

Ron returned to the stack of bills then glanced at the till taken from the register upfront. It was still a half-hour before closing, but he figured he might as well call it a day since only six dollars and fifteen cents had been made. For a ten hour workday. Using the eraser on his gnawed pencil, he punched some numbers into the calculator beside him, hit enter, and groaned over the depressing fact that he'd worked for sixty-two cents an hour that day. Sounded about right, since, besides replacing two buttons on a blazer for a walk-in, he spent all morning and most of the afternoon dusting and re-organizing his work area full of garments, fabrics, threading, and needles.

He'd kept busy while waiting for all those customers that never seemed to arrive.

So how was he going to take care of the wrinkled papers, damp with his palm sweat and stamped with red ink reading FINAL NOTICE? His eyes clicked over to the framed black and white of his wife, Brenda, and Haley, his little girl.

No, the real question was how was he going to take care of *them*?

A clap of thunder punctuated the graveness of his inquiry. The rain began its downpour, rapping heavy drops upon the rooftop.

His stomach dropped as a wave of nausea rose regarding his fear of being a complete failure. Swallowing it back down, he exhaled and opened the top desk drawer.

Next to the snub-nosed revolver kept for protection, his grandfather's gold pocket watch reflected the light from the desk lamp.

Ron picked up the watch and checked the time. Still accurate.

And it'll buy me some time, he thought (not finding the pun particularly funny), knowing he'd swing by the pawn shop on his way home to sell the precious heirloom.

He went to the front door to lock up. Beyond the window, the rain was falling in heavy sheets, making it damn near impossible to see past a few yards.

Flipping the sign attached to the glass from OPEN to CLOSED, Ron reached to do the same to the deadbolt, but stopped. He squinted at the silhouette materializing out of the grey haze, approaching from across the parking lot.

The figure was dressed in a heavy dark overcoat and fedora, and carried a large, boxy, trial bag briefcase. From the broad shoulders, style of coat, and dress shoes, Ron presumed it to be male. With head tilted downward, the brim of the hat concealed the stranger's face. He moved with a slight limp, splashing through the puddles.

As the man stepped onto the storefront's porch, a shiver slithered up Ron's spine. He couldn't explain his sudden uneasiness and found himself taking a step away from the stranger. The man stood at the door and slowly lifted his chin. A dark wool scarf wrapped around his mouth and nose concealed all features except for vacant black eyes—like those of a Great White—set in wrinkled, sunken sockets.

Seeing those eyes, Ron suddenly understood the reason for his earlier apprehension.

The stranger waved at the tailor and pointed to the doorknob, asking permission to enter. Ron felt his head nod but didn't remember commanding it to do so.

The shrouded man wrapped his pale bony fingers around the handle, gave it a turn, and slowly entered. The brass bell above his head tinkled and the black eyes slid up in the direction of the sound. He shut the door behind him.

"Thank you, kind sir," the man said, shivering. After setting the bulky briefcase at his feet, he locked eyes with Ron. A chuckle escaped from the behind the scarf, and from the way the exposed flesh wrinkled, Ron could tell that the man was smiling. Grinning.

Backing into the counter, Ron flinched and yelped slightly, unaware that he'd even been stepping away from the customer. The stranger was too busy removing his outer garments to notice; first the coat, revealing a tall, wiry body dressed in a vintage three-piece suit that cost a pretty penny from the fabrics alone. The scarf was unwrapped and placed over his forearm. With head bowed, his identity still concealed by the hat's brim, he reached up with long spindly fingers and removed the fedora, exposing a balding, liver-spotted pate with wisps of white hair. Tilting his chin up, Ron finally saw the man's face.

Sickly looking—even for his estimated age of late sixties, early seventies—his wrinkled, sagging skin was pitted like a large orange and discolored in bruised hues of yellow, maroon and blue. His heavy brow sunk over his eyes as if melting from atop his bulbous skull.

Dandruff peppered the shoulders of his dark blazer. He gazed at Ron and smiled, unsheathing a row of stained yellow teeth too small for any adult.

"Hello, dear sir. The name is Drake." For a brief moment, his lips seemed to move slightly out of sync from the raspy voice. "And I'm here this evening to see if you'd like to make a tiny fortune for a mere fraction of your troubles."

An ominous rumble of thunder sounded overhead. Both men looked toward the heavens for a beat, then back to each other. The man forced a smile. Ron glanced down at the briefcase, knowing it was probably full of paperwork for some multi-level marketing Amway scam.

Drake noticed and continued grinning, something Ron wished the man would stop doing since it seemed so fake (not to mention creepy as hell with those little baby teeth).

"Oh, yes. The answer *is* in my briefcase. But only partially. The rest you'll find in your God-given talent." If at all possible, his smile grew. "And, of course, your discretion."

Not in the mood to even humor the man by listening to his sales pitch, Ron raised his hands in mock surrender. "Look, sir. I appreciate the offer, but I was just closing up. And now I'm running late."

Drake hitched a thumb over his shoulder. "But the lettering on the window states your closing time to be six o'clock. That's twenty minutes from now."

Ron sidestepped the man and went to the door, putting his back to the stranger. "Sorry, but I've got something that requires my attention." Opening the front door, he turned around to usher Drake out. "Which is why I have to close—"

Drake snapped a crisp, clean one hundred dollar bill in his bony hands. He placed it on the counter and took a few steps back.

"Yours," he said, motioning to the money with an

exaggerated wave like some two-bit magician after a trick. "For your time. If you'll simply listen to my proposition."

Looking back and forth between the large bill on the counter and the unblinking eyes of the old man, Ron finally closed the door. He walked to the counter and stared down at the currency, refusing to touch it.

"Please, inspect. I can assure you it's not counterfeit. And it now belongs to you."

Ron shot him a look, then guffawed. "What's the catch?"

Drake held up a long index finger and wagged it. "Oh, no. I am a business man much like yourself. And I firmly believe that a man's time is worth money. You're being compensated for allowing me to acquire a little of that precious time. So please, sir. Take it."

Ron eyed him for a long moment then gazed back at the bill. This was stupid. And he knew he was being silly about it. Ron took the bill and flipped it over to see if it was blank on the opposite side. It wasn't.

"Hold it to the light," Drake said, nodding. "Look for that little strip embedded in the paper's fibers to prove its authenticity."

Ron almost did it, but the bill felt real enough. And he didn't want to insult the man any more, especially if there was more cash to follow. If the guy was going to pay him a hundred bucks simply to listen to him, who was he to turn away a fool's money? Maybe the crazy old coot was lonely. Lonely and rich. In any case, he'd made more in the past five minutes than he had all week, and could hold off pawning his grandfather's watch for another day.

"So what can I do for you, sir?" Ron said.

Drake was clutching the large briefcase against his chest like a child with a teddy bear. He was all smiles. Ron shivered over the sight.

"My dear Ronald…"

Ron did a slight double-take at the man. He never gave Drake his name. And his business was called The Little Tailor Shop. So how did the weirdo know...? It really wasn't important. If the guy was any type of salesman, he did some sort of research before stepping through his doorway.

"You stand to make so much more if I can have your complete discretion over my..." Drake patted the briefcase against his chest, "*unique*...choice of wardrobe. I prefer few know that I wear something so...lurid." He giggled slightly. "Some might even consider it shocking."

It took a moment. Then Ron almost laughed out loud. So that was what this was all about? The old guy was probably some fruitcake that got off by dressing in women's clothing or something. A drag queen; probably hiding it from his wife. Or family. Or the employees at the business he's CEO for. Probably just bought some new fancy outfit and needed it adjusted so he can hit the town all dolled up.

But wasn't he a little old to be into such kinky stuff? Ron shook it off, knowing it's always the rich ones that are the most eccentric. Although having a hundred dollars in his pocket already felt good, it now felt right. He had nothing to feel guilty about, owing the man nothing more than what he'd give any other customer. Who was he to judge the old timer? Sure, bring in your whole secret wardrobe! I'll do it all! And please recommend me to all your friends.

Ron ticked his head at the briefcase. "So you need things fitted?"

Drake nodded.

"Sure, not a problem."

The old man grew giddy.

Another clap of thunder rumbled the walls.

"Why don't you show me what we'll be dealing with?" Ron motioned for the briefcase to be placed on the counter.

Drake turned to the large windows of the open storefront. With the shop so bright and such darkness outside, they'd practically be on display like fish in an aquarium to whoever might pull up or pass by.

"Do you think….maybe…?" Drake, looking either nervous or embarrassed (Ron really wasn't sure), nodded to the back.

"Oh, sure. I've got a dressing room there, if you'd prefer. We could get your measurements first."

"That sounds splendid. But first, a gentlemen's agreement about keeping our exchange of business discreet." Drake extended his hand.

The old guy really was paranoid. Maybe he was a bigger fish than originally thought—some politician or something. Now those creeps were the weirdest, equal only to religious fanatics.

Ron shrugged and shook his hand. Upon contact, the cold damp flesh of Drake's palm made his own skin crawl. Afterwards, he fought the urge to wipe his hand on his pant leg.

"Okay, before we get started, let me make a call first," Ron said.

"To inform your wife and little girl that you'll be working late?"

Ron shot him a look. How did he know about—

"The picture," Drake answered, nodding beyond the curtains. "Framed. On your desk." He craned his neck, stretching the turkey waddle hanging below. "I can see them from here. They really are two beautiful young ladies. You're quite a lucky man."

With his black eyes, bad skin, baby teeth, and perverted secret, the thought of this creep knowing anything about his family turned Ron's stomach. He just wanted to get on with it. Get it done. Get paid. Get Drake the hell out of his shop. And go home and hug his wife and hold his little girl.

Though he didn't want to retreat to the back of the

31

shop—hidden from view—with the stranger, Ron knew he had the revolver in the top desk drawer if trouble arose.

"C'mon," he said. "I'll show ya to the dressing room."

After locking the front door, they went into the back and Ron pointed out the changing stall with a rod and thick curtain across it for privacy. Drake smiled and nodded, then slid between the fabric slit, disappearing with his briefcase.

Ron chuckled. Guess the guy and his flashy garments were inseparable.

While Drake got undressed, Ron made a quick call to Brenda to inform her he'd be staying a few hours late. As he hung up and grabbed his tape measure off a workbench, a loud fart sounded from behind the curtain. Ron froze, then turned in the changing room's direction. Had he actually just heard—

Another long, wet fart puttered out.

"Please excuse that flatulence sound, Ronald," Drake disembodied voice said. "Sometimes I get air trapped in strange places."

Ron rolled his eyes. *Sure, it sucks to get old and have your body fall apart*, he thought, *but at least try to practice some damn couth, okay?*

An extended squishy noise came from behind the curtain. For some reason, the bizarre image of Jell-O extruded from a large, wet balloon filled Ron's mind. *Oh, please stop and please, please, don't stink*, Robert thought, regarding the disgusting sounds coming from the stall.

The curtains snapped open and Drake exited, wearing only boxer shorts and black socks pulled up to his knobby knees.

Ron's jaw unhinged over the sight of the man's near naked body.

Pale, bruised flesh gave way to gravity, hanging

loose inches from where it should be. Sagging breasts like an old hound's udders after one too many litters. Dark, puffy nipples pointed down at his feet, swaying like clock pendulums with every step forward. His pot belly lay in rolls, folding into his pubic region. Ron couldn't help but look away to avoid gawking. Maybe the guy had lost a ton of weight and never had the loose skin surgically removed. The last thing Ron wanted to do was to get any closer, see this guy up close and personal. Not to mention all that gas. But the sooner he took measurements and got to work, the sooner he'd be heading home with a pocketful of cash.

Just like ripping a Band-Aid off, right?

"Ready to get started?" Ron said after clearing his throat. He held up the tape measure.

Drake nodded. "Shall I try it on first?" He ducked back behind the curtain, suddenly moving way too agile for such old age. The briefcase split the curtains first as Drake proudly held it outright and made his way to the large worktable in the center of the room, gently setting the case on its wooden surface.

The table's low-hanging overhead lamp made his pale, near-naked body almost blow out in the light.

He flipped the first brass latch open, glanced up at Ron, and eerily smiled.

The man's expression caused an invisible hand to clamp around Ron's gut.

Grinning from ear to ear, Drake giggled and returned his attention to the briefcase. The second latch flipped open, the loud clack causing Ron to jump.

Drake ticked his head down at the case. "Would you mind giving me a hand with it?" He slowly unfolded the overlapping lids, peered inside, and exhaled with excitement.

Ron forced himself forward, feeling queasy over the fact that he locked himself inside the shop with Drake. No one would see if he was in trouble or enter if he needed help. Had greed blinded his better judgment? What if this was some sort of trap? Asking help with the garments to get him closer so Drake could whip a gun from his case and rob him? Ron knew he could easily take the old guy by force, but not if he drew a gun first.

Oh, c'mon, Ron thought. *The guy's standing there in only his underwear and dress socks. If he was going to rob you do ya really think he would've stripped down to his skivvies? As for getting robbed? Ha! Besides the hundred he gave me, good luck finding anything else.*

"If you could gently grab one end and help me lift it out and onto the table," Drake said.

In the shadowy workspace, and at the angle the men stood, what lay deep within the briefcase was hidden from view.

Ron dipped his hand inside, then flinched at what he felt. He pulled back slightly, but still kept his hand in the case.

Drake caught his hesitance. "It's okay," he said, "the material still might be a little damp. Which is why it's so heavy."

Getting a firm grip on the moist spongy fabric, Ron pulled it up.

A matted hairy mass rose from the darkness. Ron let go and jumped back. The case tipped over on its side, flush with the edge of the table. Ron shuffled backwards. Seeing his hand slick with blood, he tripped over his own feet and crashed to the floor.

In exact unison with his ass hitting the ground, the briefcase's contents flopped out and over, hanging from the workbench like a sopping wet towel thrown over a clothesline.

Ron's eyes nearly exploded at the sight of the human flesh. A sheet of it; or moreso, a suit. Like some sort of flesh-colored hooded sweatshirt that swayed in the air, upside down. Only there was no opening on this hood, just a gelatinous, unblemished visage like a slip-over Halloween mask of filleted flesh. The arms, outstretched over its head, swayed back and forth, the nails of its boneless fingers scraping across the floor.

It appeared to be a seamless, perfectly intact, one-piece skin suit of a young, Caucasian male.

Ron spun away and spewed his ham and cheese lunch on the socked feet of the old man standing next to him. He looked up at Drake with glassy, bloodshot eyes and a long strand of spittle hanging from his chin.

Drake cocked his head and leered at him, flashing his baby teeth, now razor sharp. He offered Ron a boneless sleeve of his new wardrobe selection. "Gentlemen's agreement, remember?"

Ron pushed back and flipped onto his belly. Trying to rise, his feet slid in the vomit, then out from under him, sending him crashing back to the floor, knocking the wind from him. Groaning, he pushed to his feet and lumbered to the desk across the room. Though it was a simple straight path, Ron bounced off the wall and workbench like a pinball at full tilt. With mind reeling and heart drumming, it was damn near impossible to keep his balance. It took all his might to stay focused on the desk. A part of him wanted to spin around and see if Drake was in pursuit, but he knew if he whipped his head, he'd lose his balance and tumble back to the floor. Instead, his eyes locked on the framed picture of his wife and daughter. They were his destination. He just had to stay focused.

Ron slammed into the desk, scooting the heavy oak piece back a few inches. His hands clawed at the handle of the top drawer. Ripping it open, he snatched the pistol and spun with weapon raised.

Drake wasn't there. Neither was the skin suit. Only the overturned briefcase dripping blood.

Ron fought to catch his breath. Sweat dripped from his hairline and from under his armpits, rolling over his heaving ribcage. He aimed the gun down with a trembling hand and crouched to look under the worktable.

Shadows; but no one hiding within.

Rising, he felt a hot breath against his nape.

"Shall I try it on?" whispered into his ear.

Shrieking, Ron leapt away and spun around, pointing the gun at Drake.

The old man was on the desk, crouching, perched like a bird, holding up the suit. The flaccid material extended below the waist and included the victim's pubic hair, sex, and dangling legs like empty long john bottoms. Drake offered the flesh again to the tailor, extending it in front of him.

How Drake initially moved past him, undetected, and got on the desk so fast while being so decrepit really wasn't a question Ron cared to ask.

Instead, he fired at the man. The bullets punched two holes in the head of the floppy suit, then Drake's chest exploded twice in an inky mist. Somehow the old man remained balanced, rocking back on his heels upon impact before quickly returning upright on the balls of his feet. Ignoring the black liquid seeping from his wounded chest, Drake was more concerned with the large chunk of flesh missing from the head of his suit.

Upon closer inspection, he saw its upper lip and nose had been blown off.

Glaring at Ron, Drake's black eyes narrowed with rage. "Uselessss…" he hissed and dropped the flesh to the ground with a wet splat.

Ron didn't know if he was talking about the damaged skin or Ron himself. He fired two more shots in response.

The bullets pierced the old man's saggy chest. He reeled back then lunged forward, flying over the large workbench and across the room. Along his path, he hit the low-hanging work light, making it rock on its cord, sending the shadows in the room dancing. The old man crashed into Ron, knocking the gun from his grasp, and pinned him against the wall. Drake throttled Ron into submission with a single, liver-spotted hand.

"I should kill you for that, you hairless ape."

Ron clawed at the long fingers constricting his neck, attempting to pry them loose.

"But your skill has value to me," Drake said.

Ron peered into the eyes of his attacker and saw the black pupils expand until all white vanished. One of Drake's lower eyelids and bottom lip drooped, as if the glue holding it in place had come loose. Behind the façade of the old man's flesh, Ron could make out an inky, writhing mass of muscles rearranging themselves.

It was no man that was slowly choking the life from him, but something from another plane of existence—one only disguised as a man.

Drake looked back to the damaged pile of skin on the floor, shook his head, and squeezed tighter. Ron squeaked in agony.

Drake returned his gaze to Ron's purple face, glaring deep into his bulging, bloodshot eyes.

"You're lucky I always travel with a change of clothes." He smiled, his grin of sharp baby teeth stretching from ear to ear, tearing the cheeks of the old flesh like a snake shedding its skin.

"Sleep now, kind sir," Drake said, "while I go retrieve my spare set and get it prepared."

Drake slammed Ron's head against the wall and let him collapse to the floor. Ron's lids fluttered. He fought to get back up; knew he had to escape. He watched Drake move toward the back door leading to the alleyway. The simple act of rolling over was too much, spending all his energy. Then a wave of black crashed completely over him.

* * *

A flash of lightning. Ron bolted upright in the darkness. He scurried backwards in a crabwalk until slamming into the far wall. His body numb. Mind on fire. Eyes shifting, searching for eminent danger. He sucked in a breath and pushed to his feet.

Then froze.

A white male, probably in his late twenties, early thirties, was on his back, tied spread-eagle to the large workbench in the center of the room. He was pale, naked, slick with sweat, and, from the waist below, lying in a pool of blood.

Ron bobbed his head like a spooked owl, searching the surrounding darkness for any sign of Drake.

Nothing.

He locked eyes with the helpless man, whose pupils were dilated and glazed over. Approaching cautiously, Ron saw the weird symbols painted in blood over the man's chest and thighs. Rather than struggling with his restraints, the captive barely moved his arms and legs, as if waking from a restless sleep. A sloshing sound came from under his chalky skin, which seemed to be slightly larger than his thin frame needed.

Ron searched for the cause of the puddle of blood, but didn't find the wound until moving to the end of the table…between the man's spread legs.

A long, deep incision ran from the calloused sole of each foot, around the inner ankle, and up the calf, stopping mid-thigh. Pumping blood trickled from the wounds like water down the porcelain sides of a overflowing bathtub.

He looked again for Drake. Either he was outside or up front.

Ron made his move. The leather straps binding the man could easily be cut by the large scissors last left on his desk. He spun around and rushed for them. Searching the cluttered desktop, he finally spotted the shears. Lunging for them, he knocked over a large, brown paper grocery sack he'd never seen before. It fell to its side, and a small fortune of loose twenty and one hundred dollar bills spilled across the desk, stopping at the framed picture of his family.

Awestruck, Ron stared at the money, jaw unhinged, and failed to notice the shadowy figure scuttling *down* the wall just over his shoulder.

He ran his fingers through the cash, spreading it out, forcing himself to touch it so his brain would accept its reality. There was so much there. All within his grasp. His eyes clicked over to the picture of his wife. To his little girl.

"You could be their provider again," Drake said.

Ron gave a hissing intake of breath and spun around with the scissors raised. Drake was perched on the edge of the table, at the bound man's waist. The old man looked worse for the wear, his flesh torn and hanging off in parts. The exposed surface underneath was smooth and black as coal. The mouth and eye areas were stretched and drooping like a wax mask on a hot summer day.

"You could be a man again," Drake said. "Never having to worry about the roof over their heads or a hot meal on the table." He nodded at the fortune on the desk. "All that can be yours for a single night's work."

Ron looked at the bound man and slowly shook his head.

"He's already dying," Drake answered without needing to hear the question, "so there should be no guilt felt over his death." He pinched the man's skin and pulled, stretching it like pie dough. Releasing it, the flesh barely snapped back. "So why let such outerwear rot in the earth when it could be put to much better use?" Drake smiled and pushed up his own sagging cheek. "As it has been for millennia."

Ron could only stare at Drake, trying to figure out what the hell he was really looking at.

"Oh, my dear Ronald…my kind and your tradesmen

have been helping one another since the dawn of time. It's a special kind of partnership." He nodded back to the money, "Goods," then down at the man, "for services."

Ron still held the scissors out with trembling hand.

"What do you say, Ronald?"

Taking a few steps aside, Ron's attention fell to the dying man on the table, the perched devil above, and the money beside him.

Then to the framed picture of his family.

Yes, in one night he could fix all his financial woes and start over with a clean slate. Be a man in his wife's eyes. A provider to his family. And not some failure unable to support the people depending upon him.

A long moment passed in complete silence.

He slowly lowered the scissors and gently placed them on the desk.

Drake smiled. "A wise man."

Ron forced his feet forward, moving to the table as Drake untied the straps binding the young man.

Drake beckoned Ron closer with a curled finger that suddenly sported a large, ivory talon. Using the razor-sharp digit, he continued the incisions along each of the man's upper thighs then paused at his crotch.

The prisoner made no sound and barely flinched.

"You see," he lifted the testicular pouch, "this seam along the perineum?" He pointed out the line of skin between balls and anus. "That's evidence of God's little primordial seam when he made you," he said, grinning. "And it's our way in."

Ron fought to focus on what was being said, but his only desire was to get out of this den of depravity and home to his wife and child.

Drake sliced along the seam with the talon. "It's there where your kind was sewn up after He filled you with *alllll* that moist stuffing." He laughed and leapt off the table, strolling to its opposite end.

Drake, now beaming, caressed the young man's

cheek.

"And now," he said, addressing Ron, "for the pièce de résistance." He ran the fingers of both hands between the man's mop of sweaty hair and grabbed firmly.

"One…"

Ron shook his head, unsure (yet terrified) of what was coming next.

"Two…"

"No…" Ron whimpered.

Drake inhaled deeply. "Three!"

In a single, mighty pull of the hair, he ripped the man's flesh from his body like a magician pulling the cloth out from under a fully set table. Blood splashed all four walls as Drake twirled the one-piece skin suit over his head in triumph.

Everything—including Ron, his newly acquired fortune, and the picture of his wife and baby girl—was showered in the warm, crimson fluid. With his mind and body already numb, he barely flinched at the bloody spatter that hit his face.

Drake shuddered in orgasmic glory and held the flesh up, offering it to his new friend and business partner.

"Oh, I do hope you're able to remove bloodstains."

Ron barely registered the maniacal laughter flooding his ears, attacking his sanity.

Then he heard the simple question, "Shall I try it on?" echoing somewhere in the far off distance.

DiCK SiCK

Frank J. Edler

Preston knew he was sick the moment he woke up. He could feel it in the back of his throat and up through his sinuses. He grunted and hocked up to try to loosen the phlegm; nothing came up, but he felt the wad of mucus dislodge a bit. He grabbed for a tissue and began grunting, trying to induce a cough. His body's natural reflexes took hold and expunged a glob of thick fluid from his throat and splattered onto the tissue.

Preston pulled the tissue away from his mouth feeling a great amount of relief already in the back of his throat. He examined the contents splattered into the tissue; the phlegm was a tell-tale yellowish green—infection—he was sick for sure.

There was something curious suspended in the thick, contaminated phlegm. It looked like little sprinkles or ants, but had a more peculiar shape. Preston blink disbelievingly as he held the vile contents of the tissue up closer to his eyes.

No! It couldn't be! his inner voice argued with the unmistakable vision his eyes were telling him he was seeing. *Are those* DICKS *in my snot?!*

There was no denying it; there were tiny penis-shaped things congealed in his tainted boogers. Preston was sicker then he felt. Either he was hallucinating that there were tiny penises in his phlegm, or there was a much more reasonable explanation that he wasn't able to grasp in his weakened state. He wadded up the tissue and tossed it in the waste basket beside his bed.

Preston was already feeling too miserable to lay back down, so he got up out of bed and made his way to the bathroom. He lumbered down the hall, his slippers scraping along the floor with each step because he was too achy to make the effort to lift his feet up as he walked. He flicked on the light and looked at his pathetic self in the vanity mirror. The face that stared back at him was pale and drawn. His nose was puffy and red, a clear indication of the infection now looming within his sinuses.

Preston could feel the pressure building again in the back of his throat. Another round of phlegm was balling up, demanding to be expelled. He leaned over, aiming his mouth into the sink, and began to induce another deep cough that would bring the pollution up. He made a disgusting guttural noise and felt the nasty ball begin to dislodge. The muscles in his throat reacted and triggered another productive cough, which resulted in a runny green wad of scum which he spat out of his mouth. The gooey glob drooled down the side of the white porcelain sink.

Preston examined the mess for more unusually shaped particles within as it oozed down the side of the sink like a slimy slug. Sure enough, there were several solid pieces flowing amongst the infected goop. They were a bit bigger now, too; flesh-toned, about the size of a tic tac, and once again oddly penis-shaped.

You've gotta be shitting me! Preston cursed out in his mind. *What. The. Fuck?!*

He could recall being sick before and seeing chunkier pieces of snot among his phlegm, but never anything solid. When he was a kid, his older brother would try to make Preston laugh as he ate rice or pasta. Occasionally, his brother would succeed in his quest and get Preston to laugh real hard as he swallowed, causing a small piece of food to fly out his nose. His brother's proudest moment was the time he got Preston to laugh out an entire foot long length of linguine. The floppy, wet noodle jettisoned onto the dinner table complete with a big nasty booger attached to it.

The flaccid looking cock particles in his mucus were definitely not food, though. Preston ran the faucet in the sink and washed the mess down the drain. He had no idea what to do or if he should even do anything. He knew he would get progressively sicker as the day went on, but he was hoping the tiny little dicks would clear out the more he hocked up a wad or blew out his nose.

His cell phone rang from within the pocket of his terrycloth robe. Preston moaned aloud, upset that he would have to field a phone call as he was trying to deal with a level of sickness he had never had to deal with before in his life. He knew by the ring—a fifteen second clip of The Stones' *Sympathy For The* Devil—that it was his best friend, Benny. He fished the phone out of his pocket and tried to prepare himself to sound as healthy as possible.

"Hello?" he answered, sounding more like Droopy Dog then Preston Kilmer.

"Fuck dude! You sound like shit. You get the clap from that girl you hooked up with the other night?" Benny joked, at least halfheartedly. Benny's tone sounded like the idea, while farfetched, wasn't entirely out of the scope of possibility.

"No man, at least I don't think so. The clap don't give you a head cold, does it?" Preston asked, now a bit worried about the possibility of gonorrhea that it was brought up. "That shit makes you piss pus, not spit up cocks."

Preston knew he said too much as soon as the words left his lips. He hoped the words would fly through the ear Benny held the phone to and fly straight through the rocks inside his skull and right out the other ear and into the vastness of space, never to be considered again.

"Your spitting up cocks? What the fuck, Prez?!"

Damn it, no such luck. Preston wasn't sure how he was going to explain his way out of that admission. He had no choice. Besides, Benny was just as crazy as he was; if anyone would actually take Preston at face value, it would be Benny.

"Benny man, I dunno dude. I woke up and felt sick. I've been blowing my nose and hocking up phlegm wads and there are dicks in it. Like little dicks, dude. I dunno what the fuck to do, man!" Preston told Benny, already feeling a bit of the weight from the burden of coughing up penises lift somewhat.

"Dude, Prez man, we got that thing tonight. That's the last place you want to be coughing up cock, man!"

"I know, Benny, I know. I dunno what the fuck I'm gonna do, man. You may have to go without me," Preston said, sounding even more depressed now, realizing this cold was cutting into his social life.

"Tell you what, Prez, I'm gonna grab some meds. I think I have some good shit that should knock this stuff outta you for long enough to get through tonight feeling good enough. I'll be over in like an hour, man. Just hang tight. Oh, and Prez?"

"Ya?"

"Don't fucking choke on any cock while you're waiting for me to get there!" Click.

Fucking Benny, always fucking around with him.

The truth was, though, Preston really did hope he wouldn't choke on any dicks for the next hour until Benny arrived. They had gotten a bit bigger the second time around, and he was already feeling a new batch of phlegm tightening up in his throat.

He grabbed for another tissue, but before he could get it, a healthy batch of snot dripped down his throat from the back of his nose. When it hit the ball of phlegm already sitting in his throat, his muscles reflexively caused him to swallow, and he felt the whole lump slide down his throat and into his stomach. Immediately his stomach turned on him, he could feel the gears shift rapidly. This wasn't good.

He threw open the lid of the toilet bowl and took a knee on the cold tile floor. He felt the nausea build up from his stomach to his throat. The system was reversing. He was going to vomit, there was no doubt. He hovered over the bowl, breathing heavy, spitting a bit into the bowl, waiting for the coup de grace.

It would be hard to think of a time a person is more introspective in their lives then in the few brief moments when they come face to face with a porcelain bowl of water that is normally reserved for fluids that expel from the other end of your body. Every human shares that moment at least a few times in their lives. It doesn't matter if you're black or white, young or old, rich or poor, intelligent or imbecilic; we have all faced the bowl. We question what we've done in our lives to get to that position. We make promises to forces greater than ourselves in hopes of averting another experience like this. We marvel at the recognition of an otherwise insignificant brown speck glued to the waterline as actually being the remains of something we ate a few days ago.

Preston delighted in discovering the tiny remnant of a delicious salad he had for lunch two days ago, then out of nowhere his stomach went from zero to sixty in half-a-second. Vomit rocketed up through his digestive track and blasted out of his mouth. It hit the water hard and splattered in all directions. His face was bathed in backwashed vomit and toilet water as puke still poured from his mouth. The first wave stopped after what felt like an eternity, but was barely longer than a second. Then he hiccupped and let loose another wave of vomit.

The upchuck was pink, slimy, and viscous, made up of mostly stomach fluids and phlegm. There were chunks, however. Preston felt as if he ejected whole cocktail weenies out of his throat. He spit out the last tendrils of puke as he caught his breath. He grabbed a cold washcloth and wiped away the filth from around his mouth, still feeling the wicked burn of bile in the back of his throat. He didn't want to, but he knew he had to, so he composed himself as best he could and looked into the bowl.

Cocktail weenies were indeed the appropriate analogy. Preston saw at least a half dozen or so inch-long wieners floating in among the stew of puke. Not the kind of wieners you wrap in croissant dough and call pigs in a blanket, either. It looked like Preston ate a bunch of newborn babies and vomited out their privates before he could digest them.

He flushed the toilet and became mesmerized watching the wee-little penises begin to swirl in the tumult. They swirled in the vortex of water and vomit in a counterclockwise motion, riding the tides down to infinity (or at least the local sewage plant). He bade the odd dicks Godspeed and happy travels.

* + * +

Not long after, Preston heard Benny's car turn into the driveway. He was relieved. Benny had a knack for beating illnesses. Once, Benny came down with the flu.

He drank a half-cup of automotive antifreeze, and the next morning he woke up without so much as a sniffle. Another time, his cousin came down with mono. After teasing her mercilessly about the type of boys she'd been kissing, he whipped her up a concoction of pig cum and a splash of lemon juice. He instructed her to gargle with it every night before bed. Within a few days she was making out with every neighborhood boy who gave her a wink and a nod.

Preston had asked him how he knew pigs semen would do the trick. Benny shrugged and told him he really didn't know, he just wanted to watch his cousin gargle pig jizz so he would have something for the spank bank later. He was shocked when it worked, but told Preston never to underestimate the power of the placebo effect. Preston had no idea what that meant at the time, but it sounded very mystical to him.

Nowadays, Preston knew exactly what the placebo effect was, but that didn't do much to erase his youthful convictions of its secret magical prowess. When they were kids, he looked at Benny as some sort of shaman (nowadays, "holistic healer" would have been the operative word). Right down to Benny's magical smoke weed.

The doorbell rang. Preston answered it, already feeling better just knowing Benny had arrived.

"Hey, Benny, whatcha got for me, man?" Preston said with an emphatic flair through a stuffy nose.

"Easy, Prez. I gotta check out these dicks before I can ascertain what to dispense to you, dude," Benny said, trying (and failing) to sound like some sort of doctor.

Preston lowered his head. He never considered saving a sample. He wasn't too thrilled with the idea of producing more for Benny to examine. He explained to Benny that he hadn't bothered to save any, but if he waited around he was sure, unfortunately, that he would produce some more soon.

"Cool, bro!" Benny slapped Preston on the back. "I got all day, man."

Preston felt a bit relieved that he would no longer have to face this odd disease alone. He felt confident that Benny's knack for apothecary would produce a positive result and he would be feeling fine to go out and party tonight. That placebo effect seemed to be taking hold, he was feeling better already. Benny was the fucking man!

Benny fetched an old fishing tackle box from the trunk of his car. He set it up on the coffee table in the living room and perused its contents while he waited for Preston to puke up some dicks. Each compartment in the box contained a variety of herbs, ground powders, vials of liquid and a few other oddities. One of those oddities was what appeared to be several dozen dried-out mouse eyeballs.

Preston looked on as Benny took stock of his medicinal box. He marveled at the collection Benny had put together. He knew Benny liked to toy around with odd home remedies, but he had not seen his tackle box before, and it was clear by looking at it that Benny was taking this knack for creating cures to the next level. He was impressed with his friend's commitment to something so important. Preston always figured Benny was destined to become a drifter, a stoner, a dead head, wandering the country without direction. Benny's tackle box represented something more concrete in his life.

"Feel anything coming on yet, Prez?" Benny asked.

"Nothing yet. Wait..." Preston felt a grumble in his stomach. Lower than his stomach, actually; something roiled around in his intestines. Preston clinched his butt cheeks suddenly.

"Oh no. I think I just got the shits!" Preston duck-walked as quickly as possible to the bathroom.

Benny stifled a laugh. He couldn't help it; funny was funny.

+ * + *

The urgency grew rapidly. Preston could barely get his pants down around his ankles quickly enough. Before his ass cheeks came to rest on the seat of the bowl, he began to splatter shit out of his asshole. Some splashed on the back of the seat. He was powerless to do anything about it. He would have to deal with it when the contents of his bowels had ceased blasting out of his colon.

This was some bad diarrhea; the type so watery it feels like you're pissing out of your asshole. With one exception: Preston felt a few more solid pieces break the shit stream as it poured out of his ass. He didn't need to wonder what that was all about.

After crunching as hard as he could to be sure that that round was completely out, he began the process of wiping. It was amazing how quickly you cleaned up after an epic bout of diarrhea. Two wipes at most and he was clean. It seemed to defy all logic and break the laws of physics. He turned to drop the wad of soiled toilet paper in the bowl and thought better of it.

He tossed the wad of TP in the waste basket and cracked the bathroom door open. He couldn't believe he was about to do this. He took a deep breath and let it out. He then called for Benny to come take a look.

Benny came into the bathroom, almost too eager to check out Preston's leavings. He elbowed Preston out of the way and surveyed the sickly loose bowels splattered into the toilet bowl. There were Rorschach Test patterns of shit sprayed upon the upper portion of the bowl, the water was a chocolate soup of poop and intestinal particles, and, of course, there were a few penises. Three of them, several inches long and fat, like small bratwursts with newborn skin-toned flesh.

Benny's face lit up when he gazed upon them. His eyes welled up. He reached at them, palms up, marveling at the beauty of what they represented for him. The dicks, they were real! He'd read about the condition in antique medical texts he collected from roadside dealers and shady merchants on eBay. Benny always figured them closer to fable than reality, yet there floating in Preston's movement were three detached dicks.

Benny's childhood friend—a person he knew his whole life, a man he shared secrets with like a brother—had the unimaginable ailment. Preston was Dick Sick.

Preston looked at Benny desperately, wordlessly begging him for the cure. Benny returned a look of hope, but also apprehension. Preston moved to flush the embarrassing dick-tainted diarrhea down the bowl, but Benny stopped him. He held up a finger to Preston—wait a moment—then reached into the bowl with that hand and scooped out the three stubby rods with his bare hands. He flopped them into the bathroom sink and gave Preston the all clear to flush the rest.

"We need those," he explained to Preston as he washed the brown shitty smelling slop off his hands in the sink with the three shit-out dicks in it. "We have to bring them to a friend of mine. I've heard talk of your condition, but I've never seen it before. I don't even know where I would begin a treatment, but I know someone who may. Get ready, we are going to take a ride."

+ * + *

Preston threw on a pair of gray sweatpants and an Iron Maiden shirt with the *Aces High* artwork on it. He grabbed a plastic bag just in case he got sick in the car. They hopped in Benny's rusted-out old Chevy and drove off to meet Benny's medicinal guru.

"Are you sure you can't just whip up a few different combos from your magic box and see if it sticks? I'm really uncomfortable about going to meet some stranger to show him how I expel cocks out of all my orifices." Preston lamented.

Benny scoffed at his embarrassment. "Take it easy, Prez. I've learned a lot from this guy, he knows his stuff. If he can't cure you, well... He *can* cure you, so just don't worry about it."

"Tissue!" Preston suddenly pleaded.

"What?" Benny asked, confused by the sudden change in topic.

Preston craned his neck back, closed his eyes and opened his mouth, taking in a quick breath. "Tissue, I'm going to snee.. sneeze! Hurry!"

Benny was in full freak-out mode now. "Oh fuck, Prez man! I don't have any tissues! Oh, shit! Ahh, sneeze into the bag, man, don't get no dicks all over my car, I just vacuumed this thing!"

Preston hastily pulled the bag to his face, not even sure if he was going to sneeze into the open end of the bag. Just as the plastic reached his lips he let out a thunderous *AHCHOO!*

Only the sneeze didn't sound right to Benny. It sounded cut off at the end. He looked over to Preston with one eye arched quizzically. Preston's eyes went wide suddenly as he pulled the plastic bag away from his face. What Benny saw was something he would never be able to erase from his mind for as long as he would live.

There was a full sized cock sticking several inches out of Preston's mouth, only it was coming out of his mouth the opposite way you're used to seeing in porno mags. To Benny, it looked like Preston had swallowed a dick, balls-first.

"Dude, there's something you don't see every day, bro." The words fell out of Benny's mouth before he could stop them. Benny held up his hands pleading his regret to Preston for his insensitive comment.

Preston was suddenly preoccupied with trying to yank free the penis from his mouth. He had it around the shaft with both hands and was yanking on it with all of his might. He tugged and pulled and yanked and tugged some more. It wasn't budging and Preston was getting concerned quickly.

Benny burst out laughing. His immature mind would not allow him to be concerned with his friend's failed attempts at removing the dick from his mouth. All Benny could see was his friend jerking off a dick sticking out of his mouth the wrong way.

Preston slapped the shit out of Benny. Benny stopped his crazed laughter. Preston was gesturing madly for Benny to pull on the dick and help him dislodge it.

"No. No fucking way am I touching that thing, dude." But Benny could see Preston was actually turning blue around the lips. "Ahh shit, Prez man! You fucking owe me big time for this shit," and Benny wrapped his hands around the mucus-covered shaft and pulled hard and steady.

It wouldn't budge at first. Benny re-gripped the phallus and pulled again. It still did not budge until Benny really put his back into it. Then it began to loosen, and the penis began to make headway, like a team gaining the upper hand in a game of tug-o-war. Finally, it dislodged itself entirely with a wet *plop*.

Benny held it up in his hand like he just wrestled a snake from Preston's mouth. He examined the strange dick for a moment. It was mucus covered, about five inches long and actually had a rudimentary set of balls at the end, which must have been the reason they got stuck in Preston's mouth after he sneezed it up.

Benny flipped the thing nonchalantly into Preston's lap. "Hang on to that, Cooter is going to want to take a look at it."

"Cooter?" Preston asked.

"Yeah, Cooter. Why?"

"I have penises coming out of practically every hole in my body, and you're taking me to a guy whose name is Cooter to fix it?" Preston asked, hoping the absurdity would sink into Benny's thick skull if he heard the question aloud.

Benny laughed instead. "You don't know Cooter. Wait 'till you meet him before you pass judgment, Prez."

* + * +

They pulled up to Cooter's place. It was a dump. The house was an eyesore on a quiet little street that was populated by other relatively respectful looking little houses. Cooter's front lawn was littered with all manner of useless junk: auto parts, timber, concrete blocks and a few piles of who-knew-what concealed under weathered green tarpaulins. The house itself looked crooked, the frame of the house lilting to the left, weathered wooden siding covering it. The windows and front door looked like they could be knocked out of their frames with a simple push. The front walk to the house was grown-over with weeds and ivy; the only way to discern the path to the door was to follow the trampled ground cover.

Benny knocked on the front door; paint chips and dirt fell to the ground from the vibrations. The man who answered the door didn't so much swing it open on its hinges than tug the door away from the jamb in an approximation of the arc it would have swung in had it been connected to the door frame.

"Hiya Cooter duder," Benny greeted him, "this is the guy I was telling you about." He motioned to Preston to introduce him.

"Good evening, sir." was all Preston could manage.

The first thing Preston noticed about Cooter was that he was a small man. Not midget small, but very close to it; he would have been surprised if he were even five feet tall. The next thing that Preston took note of about Cooter was that he was wearing a tuxedo, cleaned and pressed without a single wrinkle from head to toe.

Cooter surveyed Preston from top to bottom. His eyes then lit up and he beckoned them inside gleefully.

"Come in! Come in!" he welcomed them. His voice was somehow high-pitched and raspy at the same time.

Preston and Benny stepped into a house that was in desperate need of a visit from the guy from *Hoarders.* There were books stacked haphazardly against nearly every wall. The wall with a fireplace was swamped with antique looking oddities. Lamps, tables, chairs, appliances, coat stands and other old looking appliances populated that wall. The fireplace itself appeared to be vomiting out an array of strange little statues and archaic children's toys and what could best be described as metallic torture devices at a quick glance. The air in the house was thick with dust.

Preston shoved his hands into his pockets, repulsed by the thought of even possibly touching any of the filth in the house. He wanted nothing more than to turn around running and screaming. He could not imagine how this man—this dirty, filthy man, who for some reason was impeccably dressed—could possibly hold the cure for what ailed him.

Benny, sensing Preston's apprehension and plot to escape, placed his arm around his neck. It was a bromantic embrace, but it was also clear that Benny was not going to let Preston go anywhere. Cooter asked the boys to follow him up the stairs after they had a moment to ingest the view of his humble abode. They followed Cooter up a set of stairs that was nearly hidden among all the debris.

The upstairs portion of the house stood in stark contrast to the ground floor—there wasn't a speck of dirt or dust. The upstairs hallway had an elegant carpet runner along its length and was decorated with a few paintings and a tiny display table with an elaborate Fabergé egg perched upon it.

Cooter led them to the second door on the right, opened it and motioned for them to step in ahead of him. Benny and Preston walked into a room that was immaculate in every way, shape and form. This room on the second floor of Cooter's house of duality was clean enough to conduct important medical research in or manufacture sophisticated nanotechnology processor chips in without fear of contamination.

"What's the story, boys?" Cooter finally asked as he sealed the door to the room shut.

Benny nudged Preston with his elbow. Preston cringed and shot Benny a look of *what the fuck?* Then Preston realized what Benny was getting at and held out the contents of the sick bag and offered it to Cooter for his appraisal.

Cooter took a gander in the bag, and a look of concern washed over his face. "You're Dick Sick for sure, Mr. Preston; worse than I figured, too. This here is a very progressed cock-a-loogie."

"Cock-a-what?" Preston asked, his voice an octave higher than he intended it to be.

"A cock-a-loogie. The main symptom of the Dick Sick. I've seen this before, but if what Benny tells me is true and you only started showing symptoms early this morning, then I can't say I've ever seen a case like this progress so quickly," Cooter said as he turned and began to rummage through some stainless steel canisters lined up along a countertop.

Preston shot a worried look at Benny, who seemed to be doing his best to hide in a corner. "Is that bad? How the hell do you even get Dick Sick?" asked Preston.

"The best I've been able to figure is from coming in contact with really old semen—almost always from those shady booths in the back of adult novelty stores. In the really dirty ones, the loads just pile up after load upon load gets ejaculated into the dark corners of the booths where the jizz mopper's mop won't reach. After awhile, this odd sort of mold starts growing on the goo, and when you breath in the spores from that mold, that's when you catch the Dick Sick.

"If I've seen it once, I've seen it a hundred times. That's always the way it goes," Cooter declared. It was irrefutable fact as far as Cooter was concerned.

Benny gave Preston an odd look and made himself known in the corner. "You go to the nudie booths, Prez?!"

"It was one time! I was bored! I drive by the place every day, and I figured 'what the hell?'" Preston tried to defend himself, but his argumentative tone gave way to indigence. "Wait, what the fuck are you giving me shit for, Benny? You're the one who told me I should go check it out!"

Benny shrugged him off. "Well yeah, but I didn't tell you to go beat off in the booths. That's sick, dude."

"It was implied!" Preston argued on.

Cooter interrupted, "If we could please get on with the examination." He motion for Preston to lay down on a rudimentary-looking exam table.

"Cooter man, isn't that like one of those massage tables?" asked Preston.

"Yes it is; any port in a storm, young man. I got this beauty for a steal off a masseuse who was busted for giving happy endings during house calls. She sold it to raise money for her legal defense."

Benny burst out laughing in the corner. "You're gonna lay down in a bunch of jizz again, Prez!" He doubled over, braying like a mule at the irony.

Cooter waved off Benny. "This table has been thoroughly sanitized, I assure you. Now, please get on the table so I can take a look at you. Time is of the essence considering the size of your last... expulsion." Cooter turned to grab some rubber gloves, then paused and added, "Oh and you'll need to remove your clothes, too."

Preston hit full freak-out mode. "What the fuck, man?! You want me to get naked and lay down on your massage table? The table that launched a thousand happy endings?! And I'm supposed to just go along with this like you're some kind of legitimate doctor?!"

Cooter looked Preston directly in the eye. "Yes, I do."

Preston was speechless at the man's matter-of-fact response. He unbuttoned his jeans and removed his shirt. Benny said he had enough of the strip show and excused himself into the hallway. Preston actually felt at ease after his friend excused himself and stripped down the rest of the way and lay down on the table, headfirst with his head in the ring.

Preston heard Cooter instruct him as he leaned over the table, "Uh, this is a medical examination, young man, not a massage. I'm going to need you to prop yourself up on your knees and elbows... And just relax." He heard a latex examination glove snap.

Preston wondered how he had gotten into this situation, when suddenly the situation got into him. Cooter's finger (he hoped it was his finger) wiggled into Preston's asshole and began to root around; for what, God only knew. Preston tried to keep an open mind and relax as much as possible, but when Cooter got up to his second knuckle, Preston's anus clinched up like a boa constrictor.

Cooter corkscrewed his digit around trying to pry it loose. The sensation tickled something deep within Preston's insides, and he suddenly became nauseous, sick, sweaty and green feeling all at once. His stomach gurgled and churned, his throat got tight, his mouth became sandpaper and a wicked urge to sneeze overtook him.

"Oh fuck!" Cooter felt it coming before Preston could voice a warning. He tried to pull his finger out of Preston's asshole, but his anus had a wicked grip on it. With nowhere to go, Cooter braced himself for disaster.

Preston sneezed hard. His ass farted in perfect synchronization with the sneeze, and he felt a mass vomit up out of his mouth. Then all Preston knew was pain—extreme pain—and through the pain, it began to dawn on him that he was barely able to breathe. Preston struggled to maintain his composure as he gasped for breath through the worst pain of his life as he stared down his nose at the head of a penis that looked like it should be attached to an elephant.

+ * + *

Benny rushed in after hearing the explosive sneeze. He was greeted with a sight he would never forget for as long as he lived. Preston was naked on all fours on the massage table, and for all intents and purposes he looked like he was speared through the ass with a giant penis that cut straight through his body and out of his mouth. He was convulsing like he was... gasping for air!

"Oh shit, dude!" Benny yelled and noticed that Cooter was missing. He scanned the room and found Cooter lying behind the table, his arm covered in mucus and shit. He was in shock but alive. Preston's convulsing was growing weaker and his skin began to take on a bluish hue.

Cooter moaned on the floor like a dying Frankenstein monster: partly from the pain and disorientation, and partly to get Benny's attention. "You need to make it flaccid. You need to go get the, the..." he trailed off and got into a coughing fit. He fought through it to complete his instructions, "the box. The box has the cure inside." He started into another coughing fit.

Benny looked around the room for a box. There were canisters, jars, tables, stools all around. He was about to ask Cooter to be a little more specific, when he spied it sitting in the corner furthest from them under a work table. Benny understood as soon as he set his eyes on it that it was "The Box with the Cure" because it was so distinct looking from everything else in the room. All the items in this room were cold, steel, medicinal looking objects. The box was antique, wooden and inviting. It just looked special.

Benny opened it. He peered inside and spied the cuddliest looking giant worm he was likely ever to see in his life. It was nearly three feet long from end to end. It wasn't slimy and smooth like most worms, but soft and fuzzy and as thick around as Benny's forearm. The varying colors of brown and white reminded Preston of the mysterious Mogwi character from Gremlins.

"It's a Mung Wyrm," Cooter said weakly. "It will burrow into the cock that is killing your friend. It will eat away at the cyclospermata that inhabit the dick. Quickly it will go flaccid, and your friend's discomfort will be alleviated."

"Discomfort? That's not exactly the word I would use, Cooter duder. Preston is choking on a gigantic penis —I think he is a tad more than simply uncomfortable!"

"Now is not the time to argue semantics. Put that worm on your friend's affliction and let it get to work. There isn't much time," Cooter demanded.

Benny rushed over to Preston with the box. He reached in and grabbed the furry Mung Wyrm. It was warm and soft, like picking up a cuddly little puppy. The wyrm quivered at his touch and Benny could feel its body expand and contract slightly as it breathed. He placed it on the sizable ball sack that was jutting out from Preston's asshole.

The wyrm immediately got excited and poked about furiously, looking for just the right spot to burrow in. When it found a suitable location, it began to force its head—or what Benny could only assume was its head, as it had no discernible features on either end of its body— into the fleshy mass of the cock-like thing sticking out of Preston.

As it broke the skin of the penis, a jelly-like substance peppered with pebble-like material began to ooze out of the incision. The Mung Wyrm slipped inside quickly once it had the skin breached. Within seconds, the penis was visibly deflating. The head of the penis finally shrank enough to let air in through Preston's airway, and he gasped for breath like a person who had been underwater for far too long.

The Mung Wyrm worked its way out of the hole it went in through. The balls were now deflated and wrinkly like the scrotum of an old man; it hung spent and useless. The Mung Wyrm was sluggish now that it had fed so well. It wriggled back into its box and took a nap, punctuating its gratification with a burp and very loud snoring.

Preston began to gag on the giant deflated phallus now that he was able to breathe once again. Benny thought it looked like Preston had tried to eat a giant novelty penis balloon. Benny grabbed at the head end of it and started to pull.

"No!" Cooter stopped him. "If you pull it out that way, all his stomach acid and shit from his intestinal tract and asshole will come up through his throat and eat away at his trachea. Take him to the bathroom, he is going to have to shit that thing out!"

Preston was exasperated. As if the humiliation of a day spent shitting and puking up penises punctuated by nearly choking to death on a gigantic dick wasn't enough, now he was going to have to shit out a seven-foot long limp dick. He slumped at the shoulders, resigned to his fate. He trudged to the bathroom and sat on his throne of shame.

He didn't feel like he had to go, so he pushed and strained. His face turned beet-red and he struggled to get the thing moving along. He felt like he was going to start gagging once more, when finally it began to creep out of his asshole. The sensation was the oddest thing Preston had ever felt; he could feel it rolling out of his asshole, while at the same time the end still protruding from his mouth made its way down his throat at the same pace.

Preston returned to Cooter's examination room, naked and defeated, but free from the giant penis. Cooter and Benny were working away at some sort of concoction. There was a mortar and pestle, knives, hammers, and a cheese grater, as well as several opened canisters. They both stopped what they were doing when Preston rejoined them and looked at him wordlessly, expecting Preston to let them know how he felt.

"That, uh, thing was pretty big. I wasn't thinking and I flushed and backed up your toilet. You may want to call a plumber. Sorry about that, Cooter dude," was all Preston could offer.

Cooter grabbed a glass bowl off the table and offered it to Preston. He told him the golden liquid in it would cure him of the Dick Sick. Preston thought it looked a little bit like butterscotch pudding, but it smelled like old musty socks. He dipped his finger in and took a taste of it—he found it was very salty.

He cupped his hand and scooped out the rest, licking his fingers to get every last bit—he wanted to be sure that the cure worked, foul taste be damned. He wanted to be done being Dick Sick forever.

"What was that?" he asked through a scowled face.

"A simple mix of the ground-up labias of mummified corpses, a paste of the final menstrual flow of a woman before she entered menopause, and some apple sauce. A spoonful of sugar makes the medicine go down, right?" Cooter said with a tad of mischief in his voice.

Preston wanted to puke it all back up, but didn't dare. He swallowed hard to keep it all down. Cooter patted him on the back and asked him if he wanted a lollipop.

Benny began to laugh wickedly. "Nothing like some old pussy and some period juice to chase off a few dicks, huh?" He erupted in laughter and doubled over.

Benny regained his composure after a few moments. They both thanked Cooter for all his help. Cooter was only too happy to have helped such a rare case and waived off his usual fees in exchange for the experience of treating such a unique case as Preston's.

"Are you feeling any better, Prez?" Benny asked as they got back in the car.

"Actually, Benny man, I am," he said as he smiled for the first time all day.

"Good, Prez dude. Let's go out tonight, then! We gotta get you hooked up with a girl so you don't have to go visit the nudie booths anymore!" He slapped Preston on the back and laughed.

* + * +

That night, they did go out to the club. Preston met a buxom blonde who, it turned out, gave mind-numbing head. They started dating, and after a few months he proposed to her. They got married, had several children, and lived a relatively happy life. Preston never again had to visit the adult boutiques, and never again shit, piss or puked out a dick for the rest of his life.

APPELONIA

Eric Dimbleby

Casey was star-struck, embarrassment rifling through her, amidst blushing cheeks and stuttered words, unable to form concrete thoughts or typical banter. The butterflies in her stomach seemed silly enough in theory, but she could not get the little devils back in their jar, no matter how hard she tried to will it. "Mr. Jarvis, I'm *such* a big fan," was the only intelligible phrase she could articulate.

The glowing movie star flashed his patented Grant Jarvis smile at her, indicating with his professionally manicured hands that Casey should take a seat at his kitchen table. "Please, young lady. There's nothing to be nervous about," he assured her. "I like to do things the old fashioned way: informal, and in person."

"Thank you, Mr. Jarvis," Casey spoke in steady rhythm, thinking over each word as it escaped her mouth. Since graduating from the University of California, she had been on more than two-dozen interviews, mostly for jobs that she had no genuine interest in. Her interviewing skills had been honed from simple practice, but all that preparation had gone out the window in the presence of one blue-eyed, black-haired, Oscar nominated movie star. He was dressed in blue jeans and a plain white t-shirt, as compared to Casey's stuffy business attire, complete with a gaudy ascot.

"Just call me Grant, please," he replied, as a character from one of his films may have, placing a coffee cup before his interviewee. "Coffee?"

"Yes, Grant. Thank you. You're too kind. And they say movie stars are just a bunch of rich snobs. I would love to drink some coffee with you," Casey said, feeling numb at her awkward choice of words. She had spoken the words *drink some coffee with you* in the same tone that she may have said *have a hot and sweaty love-child with you*. The rosy complexion that had once vanished from her face returned.

"Well, I'm certainly rich. And I have my quirks, just like anybody else, but I like to think that I'm just another guy trying to make a decent life for himself," noted Grant Jarvis with a wink.

In the past six months, Grant had undergone several corrective surgeries to better suit himself for the second act of his career. A reshaping of the chin's contours, a pull here, a tug there. His surgeon had recommended pectoral implants to better boost his proud chest region, which always served well in action films. Jarvis had agreed. In addition to the chest cutlets, he had also shifted his hairline forward three inches with implanted hair follicles. Jarvis had only just undergone laser removal of all facial hair. If the time came that he needed to sport a beard in one of his films, he would decidedly opt for a fake one. It always troubled Jarvis that he fought so hard to grow hair in one location—atop his head—all the while trying to eliminate it from every other patch of skin on his body. It seemed counterproductive that he only sought to be the one thing that he wasn't. When God handed him apples, he turned them into oranges.

"You're so down to earth!" Casey blurted, sipping at her coffee, too nervous to add cream or sugar.

"I'm a great guy to work for. The perks are endless.

And you come recommended from several sources. They say you're great with children," Jarvis noted, cutting right to the chase. "Ever since Lana died, things have been hard. Raising a daughter is tricky business for me."

Casey nodded, forcing a look of concern into her numbed lips and eyes. "I was so sorry to hear about her accident last year. She was one of my favorite actresses, and I was heartbroken when I heard the news. You're a brave man for making it through that."

Jarvis furrowed his brow, attempting to match Casey's own concern as if he were practicing in a mirror. "She was a fine lady." In reality, she had been a two-timing whore. Had slept with every producer in town. And even with being married to one of the highest paid and most respected actors in all of Hollywood... that meant nothing to her. There was no greater thrill to America's princess, the pig-headed cunt Lana Reston, than to have her ass split in half by every pool boy in California. Grant Jarvis was glad for her to be nothing more than dust. "I'm a private person, Casey."

"I understand. I'm very discreet."

"No choice, if you want this job. Follow me," Jarvis insisted, displaying his pearly-white teeth for his potential new hire. He led the way through his daydream of a house. As Casey walked behind him, careful not to trip and fall flat on her face, she studied the tall glass windows of the western edge of the property, overlooking the Pacific Ocean from a sheer cliff. "The elevator," he whispered, pointing towards a silver door. He pressed the button, entered, and coaxed Casey to follow in his disarming path.

He folded his arms at his chest while the elevator descended deeper and deeper into the bowels of his cliff-side bunker. "Discretion is key to this position. My wife and I have always been so very careful to keep Appelonia out of the public eye. The goddamned *paparazzi*. They'd ruin our lives if we let 'em," he sneered, shaking his head.

In reality, most of the out-and-about photos of his dazzling jawbone that regularly appeared in grocery store tabloids were contracted through his agent. A photographer could collect ten thousand dollars from a single photograph. Jarvis' agent would get a small cut, as would the photographer and Grant Jarvis himself. If he only pocketed five thousand, it was well worth it for having to do nothing at all. There was something gratifying about *money for nothin'*, as Dire Straits had once called it.

"Appelonia. That's such a pretty name. I don't think I've ever seen a picture of her before."

Jarvis looked at Casey with wide eyes, stating, "Nobody has."

The elevator dinged as it came to a halt. Casey was curious how deep the elevator had gone, but was afraid to ask. Instead, Jarvis broke the silence as they stood in the immobile elevator. "Do you want to be my nanny, Casey?"

"Yes, Mr. Jarvis. I mean... Grant. I would love to be your daughter's nanny," Casey replied with a confident gleam in her eye, holding her head rigid while she nodded. She could not help but glow at the idea that she was now employed by one of the richest and most handsome American legends the world had ever seen.

"Good," Jarvis said without expression as the elevator doors parted. "Meet my darling Appelonia," he said with a beleaguered smirk.

Casey looked upon the beast in the cage, snarling and rattling the bars with her hands, dressed in a pink polka-dotted dress. The new nanny could not help but scream in terror, nearly collapsing into unconsciousness at the sight of the thing.

"The pay is better than anything you'll get in the corporate world. Part of the generously hiked pay grade involves you keeping your *cunt mouth* shut. You'll start next Monday," Jarvis said. Casey, grappling for breath as she stared down at her knees, noticed that the job offer and start date were no longer in the form of a question. "If you mention this to anybody, you'll be dead in less than an hour."

# # #

When Grant Jarvis was alone—which was the majority of his time—he would sit in his private study (though he *studied* very little beyond his two-dimensional scripts), where he would glare at pictures of his dead wife. **LANA RESTON TRAGEDY** read one clipping. Another turned her automobile accident into a sort of sickly forced play on words: **REST(on) STOP!** The details that followed included the public knowledge that she had cracked up her German sports car, but had walked away from the accident, completely unfazed. She had suffered a concussion... had made it all the way home. The head injury was more grievous than both she and Grant had first thought. In the middle of the night, her brain had bled out while she slept, swollen and broken so much that even the world's greatest neurosurgeon couldn't have saved her. Had she visited the hospital after her seemingly harmless auto accident, the end result would not have changed. This is what the media thought, per hefty payoffs and a private funeral.

Grant's agent called once a week to check in. Other than his new hire Casey, Calvin Hodges was the only other living soul that knew of the horrors of Appelonia. On the day of Lana's demise, he had called Calvin first and foremost. "She's gone," he had said, and Calvin could not help thinking to himself: *The Breast-Implanted Beast* or *The Monster In The Basement*?

"Who?"

"Lana. It was an accident."

"Sure."

"Do I *sound* like I'm joking, fuckhead? She's dead."

68

"Dead? Really dead? Lana's *dead*?"

"Did I stutter?"

"Amen to that," Calvin had snickered.

"This isn't the time to celebrate, Cal. Get your ass over here or I'll be shopping for a new agent by nightfall. And bring cleaning supplies. Get on the horn with your connections, since they seem to be the only thing you're any good for. We need to clean this mess up, pronto. I can't have anybody asking questions."

"I'll be right over," Calvin replied, a sense of excitement in his voice that he could not mask. He had never seen a dead body before, and so that prospect tickled the sniveling agent's nerves to no end.

When he arrived, he could barely hold back his anticipation. He could not wait to look at Lana's dead face and perky breasts. The bitch was gone and everybody stood to benefit. Grant had brought him to the elevator, down into the dwelling of Appelonia. Every time that Calvin took that trip, he fought the urge to display his terror for all to see. The child was a hideous thing. Had Calvin a conscience of any sort, the image of her may have kept him wide awake at night. But he had little in the way of morally-balanced emotions, and so Appelonia was just another in the long line of vile, frothy-mouthed beasts that lived and bred in the cockles of Hollywood.

"Fuck!" Calvin burst forth, hovering his hand near his greasy mouth, trying not to vomit on his recently-polished shoes.

Appelonia's cage was dribbling with the reddish tendons and splatter of her mother. The body was barely recognizable anymore, a conglomerate of disjointed chaos. It was almost impossible to decipher which end of the scrambled torso belonged to Lana's decapitated head, and which end belonged to that dark and steamy hole that the beast Appelonia had emerged from.

Calvin sensed a heaviness in the air, as if the buxom

actress Lana Reston had evaporated into a syrupy vapor, but had not the passport or notoriety to make it all the way to heaven, hovering in the air above them like a vulture.

"She's in the cage. *Why* was she in the cage?" Calvin questioned his favorite cash-cow of a client, noting immediately that the steel bars were shut. For a moment, Calvin wondered in the murk of his soul at the possibility that Grant had shoved his wife into the barely-lit cage to be done with her once and for all, but that made little to no sense. Jarvis—as much as he loathed the filth that was his matrimonial leech—treasured every moment of that very hatred. Without her, he would have no arch enemy, nobody to redirect his life's angers and lost childhood at. Nobody to bully when he had a bad day on the set of his latest blockbuster-in-the-making. He couldn't have killed Lana. On top of that, it presented him with an inherently strained scenario: a high-profile man with neverending public scrutiny, the paparazzi always waiting right outside of his door. It was nothing like the debacle that was O.J. Simpson, who had already been washed up and hung out to dry. Jarvis was still in his prime, moving and grooving through the hearts and minds of the American cinematic experience. Murder was far too dangerous for him to risk such a thing, especially given the suspicion that had already encapsulated him for keeping his daughter Appelonia hidden from public view ever since her birth. **JARVIS, RESTON, and THE MYSTERY CHILD**, one tabloid had speculated.

"Lana kept talking about bonding with our daughter. Was crying about it for days, that she felt like a stranger to her own child. I think it was hormonal, to be honest. She always got into these little stints where she needed to prove her worthiness to herself, that she was a good person. But you and I know what she was just four juicy lips and not a lick of talent," Grant replied, shaking his head at the bloody mess before him.

Growling at them both, Appelonia narrowed her yellow slitted eyes. She had tasted human blood, finally. She had eaten every animal under the sun, but human was something new altogether, and so her unscrewed facial expressions had changed at the thought of a second feast. Sticky blood was matted into the patches of gray hair on top of the child's head. Between her tiny claws, she fondled at her mother's head, slurping on the underside and snorting like a piggy. She blasted wild words at the duo of onlooking adult males, speaking her gibberish that sounded almost Latin. In Appelonia's second year, Lana had theorized to her husband that Appelonia was a spawn of the Devil himself. Having watched The Exorcist one too many times, she had dictated Appelonia's garbled speech onto paper. After consulting with several expert linguists, she found the blabbering to be just that— directionless noises that any baby could make. That (at least in Lana's mind) had eliminated the demon angle.

"All she wanted was a hug from her daughter, I guess."

"That's one hell of a hug," Calvin noted with a smile that he could not keep hidden from his lips. "I'll call my guy at the coroner's office. He owes me a solid. He won't come cheap, but he'll point us in the right direction. You're going to owe a lot of people when this is done; myself included."

The child in the cage fell to her knees, rubbing her mangled mama's extracted mucus against her body. Appelonia had torn away most of her dress in the struggle against Lana. Groaning and licking her fattened lips, she offered Calvin the best smile she could, wishing so very much that the repugnant bastard would step inside her steel cage, if only to play for a moment or two; long enough to rip his throat free of his fat neck.

# # #

Calvin still visited once or twice a month, usually to deliver screenplays or contracts to his most lauded and noteworthy client. Since he had aided in the cleanup, back story, and legal wranglings that resulted from Lana's unfortunate incident, he rarely ever spoke of Appelonia. On one particular occasion, Grant Jarvis had asked, "I know you pretend like she doesn't exist, but I need somebody to take care of that little beast. I can't do it. It's royally fucking up my career. I need a new bitch, Cal."

Calvin had replied, "I'll set up a series of interviews for you, once you give me the specifics. Beyond that, I will mention nothing to the applicants of your hideous spawn."

With those words, Jarvis had narrowed his eyes, contorting his face. "That's my daughter, you asshole. Keep talking like that, and I'll feed you to her."

"I see," Calvin answered, wondering to himself how many clients he would need to loop in order to make up for the potential income loss of Jarvis. He sighed at the profound number that started to dance in his hand. "I apologize. I will never mention your daughter again, just like I said earlier."

# # #

Casey's first day on the job, she drove to the home of Grant Jarvis with white knuckles, convincing herself the whole way that it would not be petty or wrong of her to turn around, to head back home, to drive into the next zip code if it so pleased her.

When she walked through the door, Jarvis greeted her stoically, asking that she take her shoes off at the door when she was in his home. The courteous gentleman that had first interviewed her was absent altogether. A chilly nerve shimmered in her gut, and she regretted ever responding to the advertisement at all. She needed to leave the situation behind, but instead answered with the obedience of a canine: "Yes, sir. I mean... yes, Grant."

He sneered at her, pointing towards the elevator at the end of the hallway. "No... calling me sir should suffice. I can like your work just fine, but that doesn't mean I have to like you as a person, for whatever that means."

The bastard. It was all that Casey could think as she walked shamefully alone towards the elevator, pressing the button for the chariot that would deliver her to the beastly Appelonia. *The Bastard.* She could see the purple stain that was the lugubrious and talented Mr. Jarvis' personality, and it disgusted her to no end. But he was still powerful, and the money was untouchable; more than six times what she had earned in her previous job serving coffee and bagels to rich bitches with big black sunglasses covering their absent facial expressions.

As the elevator sunk to the bottom floor, Casey felt relief in being separated from Jarvis, but then grew anxious at the thought of seeing Appelonia once again.

The doors opened and she found Appelonia in the corner of her cage, cooing to herself and petting the head of a blonde-headed plush doll. The monster looked up at Casey and cooed louder, as a sort of greeting. Though Appelonia's face was disfigured and ghastly in every sense—particularly her leathery, clouded skin—there was a sense of calm over the child that she had not perceived in their first encounter.

"Good morning, Appelonia," Casey said, doing her best to mask the tremolo in her voice.

The child grunted, stroking her doll with fervor, standing up from her crouched position. By her feet was a bowl of what appeared to be dog food. Jarvis had instructed Casey during a late night preparatory phone call that he gave Appelonia whatever she wanted, but tried to keep it on the cheap side. Dog food was his usual standby. The multi-millionaire found it to be cheap enough and fulfilling enough to keep his biggest tragedy satiated and calm.

Casey approached the steel bars of the child's trap. When she neared the perimeter, the single blazing overhead light, white and deadening, burned her eyes. She wondered why Jarvis had not equipped the light with a softer bulb, that it may keep Appelonia more sedated and less prone to violent outbursts, as she was known to have. She marked that as the first in many suggestions she would make to the son of a bitch Jarvis.

"What's your doll named?" Casey asked with a calming voice, attempting to hide her nerves as she approached God's Ugliest Specimen. She pointed towards the doll, careful not to allow her fingers past the invisible barrier she had constructed in her mind.

Appelonia looked down at her doll, a globule of drool descending from her lip. She grunted and pronounced three ugly syllables: "Gee trob dah." Casey assumed from these strange noises that the doll had three names; a first, a middle, and a last. But in Appelonia's isolated language of grunts and noises, her words had roughly translated to: EAT MY DICK.

# # #

"I think she's warming to me. She's being a total sweetheart."

"That won't last," the man who once played the superhero Mister Justice replied.

Casey shrugged her shoulders, sinking her teeth into one of the sandwiches she had prepared for her and Mr. Jarvis. In the two weeks since she had started working for him, he had slowly transitioned her (very much on purpose) into a nanny for them all. When she was not working directly with Appelonia (particularly during nap time), she was to be at the beck and call of Jarvis himself. It occurred to Casey that she had, for all intents and purposes, replaced the passed Lana Reston in the Jarvis home, but without the perks of sexual titillation in the wake of Grant Jarvis' sensuality. Casey had been assigned the shitty parts of the Jarvis' lives, though the thought of Grant now touching her intimately gave Casey uncontrollable shudders.

"Don't get too close. She'll eat you. Mark my words. You think you're hot shit, that you can get through to my baby, but you're no different than my wife was. The cunt. *Are you a cunt, too, Casey?* Are you just another *cunt in the wall*?" he snickered as he loaded his greedy mouth with a massive bite of egg salad sandwich.

"No, sir," Casey said. She changed the subject. "I'll need to borrow your truck. We need more dog food."

"Use your car, I pay you enough," Jarvis snarled, slurping his coffee as he masticated with an open mouth.

"But I can't transport more than four or five of those big bags in my car. You've got three pickup trucks that I saw. I can make one trip instead of five," Casey noted, trying hard not to sound whiny or weak, and especially not demanding.

Grant shook his head from side to side. Her boldness was not very endearing to him. "Can I ask you a question?"

"Yes," she said, but thought to herself *NO*.

"Did you buy those trucks? Did you buy anything in this house, for that matter?"

"No."

"Then use your own car. I've earned every last fucking thing in this house, and I pay your sorry ass far more than you deserve. You best remember that," he said, reaching across his pristine glass table, gripping at Casey's forearm with his bear claw. He squeezed, and Casey broke her stolid face in half, looking into his vapid eyes to see the hideous violent man that he really was. All the tabloids in the world had missed that fact, with their fabricated stories of his charity work and their glossy photos of him at a sidewalk cafe, grinning and laughing like an old friend that you haven't seen in years. *This* was Grant Jarvis, staring her right in the eye.

"Not a problem," Casey cried, trying to keep her tears at bay. Any sign of weakness with a man like Jarvis (her father had been abusive, though the majority of the pain fell upon her sweet mother's head) and he would be as pleased as a pig in shit. "I'll go after lunch. In my own car."

He gripped her arm tighter, and then released it. Casey could not help but wonder if he had ever man-handled the fabulous Lana Reston in such a brutish manner. The image of two such descended angels clashing seemed absurd, but altogether likely, given Jarvis' inclinations.

"I bet you've got nice tits," Jarvis grumbled to himself, staring at her sweatered chest. Casey wanted to crawl inside of a sewage pipe and die. She started to calculate how many hours she would have to work per week in order to achieve the same financial successes that she would have working for Jarvis. Three hundred hours per week. "Real nice tits," Jarvis added, staring at the potato chips on his plate as though he wanted to see them still as potatoes, bleeding from their budding eyes.

# # #

Her cage smelled of feces.

"Tet yem ooh, greb."

Casey shook her head from side to side, biting at her lip for the pity that forever swam through her belly. The poor child had not even laid eyes on her father in more than six weeks, but still he controlled her from afar, via her regulated diet and inescapable cage. "You know I'll take care of you the best I can."

Appelonia rolled onto her side, rubbing at her slimy lips with her talons, her tongue darting madly in every direction. She groaned and rocked herself back and forth, clutching her body in a homemade hug, her jaundiced eyes crossing and uncrossing again in repetition. When she fell into such a state, Casey always worried that it was all over, that Appelonia's horrific condition would take the last breaths of her. The child emitted a lurching vomit sound from her deepened vocal cords.

"I know, he's a real bastard. But he pays me well."

"Hek fahhhhhh trep," Appelonia replied, propping herself on her knees, squeezing the sides of her face as one would a zit.

# # #

And so Casey, on the day that followed, begged of Mr. Jarvis to visit his child, if only for an instance, to simply show his face in her presence, to emote an ounce of compassion for the kinship that they shared. "If I wanted parenting advice, I wouldn't have hired a two-dimensional piece of ass like you!" he blasted at her, gripping her arm and pushing her flush against the refrigerator of his well-equipped kitchen. Casey squealed against his rampant aggression, narrowing her eyes just enough to warn the abusive actor-slash-philanthropist not to mess with her, that she was more willing to strike back than she appeared to be. "So keep your mouth shut and do your job. I'm a very reasonable man. You don't want to find out just what a real bastard I can be."

With his hot breath in her face, Casey shrunk away like an ice cube in the sink, though his grip was unrelenting. He plugged her in the stomach with his bony knee and seemed quite pleased with himself as she crumpled to the floor in raspy gurgles, searching for the air that had escaped her lungs.

"Stay down there and don't get up," he advised, and she abided to his demand. Grant Jarvis unzipped his pants, pausing to consider his next course of action, of which there were only two. The spontaneity coursed through his blood and every possible contingency unfolded as the redness of fury overtook his eyeballs.

Calvin was on vacation. Calvin would be the one to clean up his mess, and nobody else. But Calvin, the lazy piece of shit, *was on vacation.* If he had his way with Casey, then it only seemed logical that he would need to extinguish her with a sense of overriding permanence. And that Calvin would have to drag his ass through the cogs once again, as they had done with Lana Reston, the dead bitch with the million dollar smile.

Instead of succumbing to his most animal desires, Jarvis urinated upon Casey, and felt a satisfactory twinge in his tar-coated heart as he shuddered from the last lunges of warm piss. It looked good on her.

# # #

Casey bathed herself without any concrete thoughts or expressions, staring into the mirror that Jarvis had mounted inside of the guest bedroom shower.

The taste of piss would not leave her mouth, no matter how hard she rubbed soap into the grooves of her teeth and tongue. When she looked at herself in that mirror, white soap bubbles frothing at the corners of her mouth, she could not help but think of a rabid animal; of Appelonia, but more so of Jarvis. The prick.

She listened at Jarvis' bedroom door, where she could hear the soft contented snores of the dreaming lothario who made teenage and adult girls alike scream in the very same piercing tone. Clutching the ivory bathrobe to herself, Casey could not help but consider the rape that he had tossed about, very obviously, in his frenzied devilish mind. Self-control was amiss. He was smarter than most, but the next time he may not be so logical. He had not raped her, but that same empty feeling existed in the pit of her stomach as she pondered the word "monster" over and over again in her head. *Monster.*

Monster. Monster. Monster.

Casey made her way to the elevator, hair still soaking wet. She descended, approaching Appelonia's cage with soft footsteps, touching the bars with calm hands.

Appelonia studied her caretaker, sniffing and growling at the air.

"I'm so sorry, sweetness. We never asked for this. We've both been pissed on."

With that, she removed the lock from the cage. Appelonia followed her to the elevator and they waited patiently as the door slid open. They stepped inside without a sound. "Let me," Casey whispered to the little girl, who was fidgeting with the buttons on the elevator with a hesitant but curious eye. Casey pressed the button, the door slid shut, and the ascent began.

When the doors opened, Appelonia ran from the elevator as though it was on fire—as though *she* was on fire—for the very first time. Casey huddled herself into a small mass on the cold steel floor, tears dribbling down her cheeks.

The sound of Grant Jarvis' bloody scream was all that Casey could bear. She giggled to herself like the child Appelonia was unable to do with her mangled mouth. Casey was glad that she would always remember him this way. The world would eventually speak of the tragedy that befell the handsome Grant Jarvis and his life cut short, but Casey would know the truth of the matter. She would know of his ugliness. Of his abuse. Of his Appelonia, stowed away like a rabid animal, full of shame and discontent.

Appelonia returned to the elevator, gazing upon the woman who had set her free, smiling for the first time in all her life (as best she could through the mottled abstractness of her face), satiated by her father's spilled blood, trickling down her chin and on to her threadbare yellow dress with the wet dog food stains.

ZOMBIE BOWL

DM Anderson

Bob Constantine: *Welcome to Super Bowl LXVII on FOX, where the NFC Champion Atlanta Falcons—undefeated during the regular season—are set to square-off with the Pittsburgh Steelers, who got into the playoffs with a wild-card berth and, despite the odds, managed to win their way into the big show. I'm Bob Constantine, and with me is former three-time Super Bowl MVP, Tug Sheldon. Tug?*

Tug Sheldon: *Thanks, Bob. Anyone following football this season couldn't ask for a more dramatic matchup. The Falcons, led by veteran quarterback Eddie Stapleton, have been lighting up the scoreboard all season with their high-powered offense. Stapleton had the chance to grab the brass ring in two previous Super Bowl appearances with the Houston Texans, only to fall short. Now in his fifteenth season, this could be his last shot. But with such offensive weapons as Lane Brady and Jayden Hanks at his disposal, this could be Stapleton's year. He now has the chance to not only win the coveted ring that's eluded him for so long, but to lead the Falcons to the first perfect season since the '72 Dolphins.*

At the other end of the spectrum are the rough-and-tumble Pittsburgh Steelers, a once-stoic franchise with a proud history that includes seven Super Bowl appearances. But hard times have befallen them in recent years, a decade of losing seasons, resulting in the longest playoff drought in the team's history. But that was before rookie sensation Tyce Popp, replacing injured quarterback Jake McPhearson in week six, led the young team on a late-season winning streak to claim the last wild-card spot in the AFC. The Steelers are statistical long-shots in this match-up, but they are riding on a lot of momentum, so don't rule them out just yet.

Bob Constantine: *Two titans. Two quarterbacks: one at the end of his career, the other enjoying a Cinderella story. Two incredible and historic seasons. One game. Who will add their name to the Vince Lombardi Trophy? Who will go home to regroup for another shot next year? Statistically, the Falcons have the advantage. But as someone once said: that's why we play the game. The kick-off for Super Bowl LXVII... coming up after the following thirty minutes of commercials, more analysis from Terry Bradshaw and Howie Long, the national anthem sung by Selena Gomez, the coin toss and the baptism of the grandchildren of both team owners.*

Atlanta Falcons Practice Facility, the Week Before

Falcons' special teams kick returner Greg Queen screwed up yet again. Even though no one was covering him, the ball dropped through his hands, bounced off his chest and plopped onto the practice field.

Special teams coach Robert Anderson threw his clipboard to the ground, red-faced and boiling. "Jesus H. Christ, Queen! Who'd you blow to make this team, anyway?"

"Sorry, Coach!" he feebly replied, snatching up the wayward ball. Sickness welled in his gut, and he didn't know why. Throughout the entire regular season, he was on fire, returning kickoffs for 20, 30 or 40 yards. On one occasion, facing the Cincinnati Bengals, he ran the ball all the way back for a touchdown.

Why am I suddenly choking now? During practice? If I'm feeling this kind of pressure now, what am I gonna do on game day?

Pittsburgh Steelers Practice Facility, the Week Before

Tyce Popp slowly shuffled into the Steelers' locker room, both hands cupped around his head like it would explode if he let go. Several teammates looked over and chuckled.

"Looks like our new hotshot ran into some trouble last night," chided Delonte Dickenson as he climbed from the Jacuzzi. As the team's star receiver toweled himself off, a huge sneer spread across his face. He was with Tyce at The Acropolis last night, where their young rookie quarterback was truly having the time of his life with Martina, one of the club's more popular dancers. "Lemme guess…you discovered too late that Martina is actually Martin. Yeah, I meant to give you a heads-up about that, but you seemed to be having such a good time I didn't wanna ruin the moment."

Tyce plopped onto the bench in front of his locker. "Not funny, man." Then he lifted his head, dread spreading over his pasty face. "Wait a minute. You ain't serious, are you? That Martina's actually a…a…"

The locker room erupted into boisterous laughter. A few members of the offensive line high-fived each other. Tyce's face drooped so low that it threatened to slide off his skull.

After expertly tossing his towel into a nearby laundry bin, Delonte strolled up, patted Tyce on the back and leaned in. "Don't worry, farm boy, I'm just fuckin' with ya. Martina's a woman through and through. Trust me, I know."

Relief swam over Tyce's face, briefly returning some color to his gray cheeks. He slowly exhaled. "Thank God. My daddy didn't raise no homos."

Delonte dropped onto the bench next to him. "I take it you engaged in a little more fun than just slipping some greenbacks into her thong after I left. Hey, did I hook you up or what?"

"Yeah," Tyce moaned, hands returning to the sides of his head. "Thanks a lot."

The wide receiver wrapped an arm over his quarterback's slumping shoulders. "The least I could do for the man who helped me break the team's reception record." Then Delonte drew away, waving a hand before his face. "But, dude, you smell like a brewery. Better hit the showers before Coach Damron gets a whiff of you. You might be our savior on the field, but Coach is old school. He won't appreciate his little hot shot hittin' the field stinking of Jack Daniels."

Tyce coughed, then hunched over and wretched. Nothing came out, though. "Was that what I was drinking?"

"Among other things. I lost track of how many body shots you did off of Martina's thighs. You reminded me of my rookie year. So, tell me, Popp. How was she? I want details."

Tyce continued to hold still for several seconds, lurching and groaning, before looking up to regard his wide receiver. His face was sunken and shallow. Sweat oozed down his cheeks. His body shivered.

Delonte pulled away. "Dude, you okay? You look... well, you look *bad*. You ain't gettin' sick on us, are you? Not now...not with the big dance coming up."

"She...Martina..." Tyce's teeth began to chatter. "She bit me..."

Delonte snorted, slapping Tyce's back. "Bit you? Of course she did. A spicy little senorita, that girl."

Tyce quickly shook his head. Cold sweat whipped

from his hair. "You don't understand, man. She really *bit* me…*hard*…" He pointed a trembling finger at his crotch. "…down there."

Super Bowl Sunday

Bob Constantine*: I don't know about you, Tug, but that was one great batch of commercials. Then again, I always did love beer and boobs. What about you, Tug?*

Tug Sheldon: *Yeah, boobs are always good, especially when beer is involved; unless of course you've got some hairy manboobs like mine, the direct result of too much beer.*

Bob Constantine: *And speaking of boobs, don't forget to catch this year's Super Bowl halftime show, when legendary recording artist Janet Jackson returns to entertain the crowd for the first time in twenty years, hopefully without another wardrobe malfunction. Can you imagine those things flopping out tonight, Tug?*

Tug Sheldon: *Too gruesome to contemplate, Bob. But getting back to the game, quite a bit of mystery and intrigue has surrounded the Steelers since their surprise AFC Championship win over the San Diego Chargers just two weeks ago. Breaking with tradition, none of the players or coaches have done any interviews, and the only member of the franchise to show up on Media Day was General Manager 'Big' Dave Fassler, who assured everyone that the Steelers are eager to bring the Lombardi Trophy back to Pittsburgh. That hasn't quelled rumors surrounding the unusual doings in the Steeler camp, especially when the media arrived today, hoping to catch both team busses debarking at the stadium, only to find a cryptically empty Steelers' bus already parked, the players having showed up in the middle of the night in preparation for today's game. Absolutely no one has seen any player or coach since then. Is this an effort to psyche-out their opponents, or are they so focused on today's game that they do not want any distractions? Regardless, it adds a bit of pre-game drama to the proceedings. Bob?*

Bob Constantine: *Thanks, Tug. And for the record, your boobs aren't that hairy. The kickoff for Super Bowl LXVII is coming up next, right after these words from Sprint, Budweiser, Chevrolet, McDonald's, Viagra, Home Depot, Purina Dog Chow, Progressive Insurance, Universal Pictures, Coca-Cola, Red Bull, Goodyear and a few others whom we have no idea what they are advertising…"*

Pittsburgh Steelers Practice Facility, the Week Before

Several members of the team gathered around to hear about Tyce's tryst, a few already offering each other knowing nods—many of them knew Martina quite well.

The young quarterback weakly cleared his throat. "Me an' Martina left the club after closing, you know… to…you know."

"Yeah?" the rest of the Steelers chorused.

"And things were going okay. Martina looked a little pale, but since I was already feeling a hangover coming on, I just thought we both simply had too much to drink. I hailed a cab and she threw up on the way back to my place. The cab driver was plenty pissed and wanted to kick us out, so I tossed him an extra hundred for him to take us home anyway. Even though she was sick, Martina still seemed rarin' to go, touching and grabbing me. And man, those lips, that tongue…even after she just sprayed Technicolor puke all over the back of the cab, she still drove me nuts."

"Yeah," confirmed cornerback Matt McPherson with a lecherous grin. "Martina's got some sweet lips, dude."

"But once we got to my apartment, she passed out on the sofa. I was kinda bummed, because she'd been all over me all night, and I thought once we got back to my place she'd come around and we'd...you know."

"Yeah?" the entire team chorused again.

"I went into the bathroom to freshen up, splash some cold water on my face, spray on a bit of Axe, thinking some awful things." Tyce lowered his head; a shamed expression spread across his face. "I mean, her skirt was hiked above her thighs, and she still had on the same fishnet stockings I stuck at least a dozen twenties into. I thought...I thought...I hadn't been laid since my junior year in college..."

"Yeah?" everyone chorused yet again.

"...she owed me. I mean, my daddy didn't raise me to take advantage of a woman, but I emptied my wallet for this chick." Tyce suddenly lurched again. He leaned forward, wretched and sprayed a torrent of blood, bile and glistening chunks. A few teammates backed away, wincing and clutching their own stomachs.

"Yo, someone get Atkins to come in here and clean this shit up," Delonte ordered.

After a few seconds, Tyce wiped the bile hanging off his lips, shame still filling his eyes. "I decided, well why not? What would it hurt? If she was already willing to before, it ain't rape, is it? What did it matter if she was unconscious? So I sat next to her, opened her mouth and crammed a few Tic Tacs in there, you know, 'cause she still stunk like puke."

"Yeah?" the Steelers chimed.

"Then her eyes popped open. It was like turning on a light switch how fast she came to. And Martina, she was ready to go, 'cause she sat up, growled and went straight for my belt buckle."

"My man," Delonte snorted with a grin.

"So I laid back and let her at me. She yanked down my pants and...and..."

The whole team leaned in. "Yeah?"

Tyce stood and gingerly undid his pants, wincing as

86

he tugged them down. Delonte's eyes grew huge.

The quarterback's groin was haphazardly wrapped with gauze and duct tape. Blood had since soaked through the gauze and dried. He looked like he'd been shot between the legs.

The entire Steelers team gasped and stepped back, hands over mouths.

"See?" Tyce cried, regarding his wide receiver with pleading eyes.

"Geez, kid," said veteran tight end Bob Pratt. "What'd ya do to piss Martina off, tell her you loved her? She freakin' hates that."

Not bothering to pull his pants back up, Tyce slowly eased back onto the bench, the movement causing fresh blood to soak through the gauze. He grabbed a nearby towel to cover himself.

"Jesus Christ," Delonte cried, stunned by Tyce's mutilated manhood. "Hey, man, maybe we need to get you to a hospital or something-"

"No! No!" Tyce's bloodshot eyes threatened to burst from his head. "The press would jump all over that! Think of the scandal! Think of my image! My career! Look what happened to Brett Favre after he texted pics of his dick. Daddy would disown me!"

"Yeah? Well, that was a different time, and ol' Brett's phone didn't try to bite his wiener off."

"Your *image*?" stammered linebacker Rick Pound has he muscled his way through, cleats clicking on the tile floor. "*Screw* your image, little man. I guess you never heard of Ben Roethlisberger, who led our team to the Super Bowl more than once. Guy was a goddamn sex machine, but didn't let nothin' affect his game. Not the press, the media, injuries...nothin'." He stood in front Tyce and stared him down. "This ain't some Iowa college, boy. You're in the *big* show. You got the balls to man-up an' do what it takes to win?"

Tiny   place   kicker   Larry

Dubroskivichensteinburgeronio nodded to the quarterback's injury. "He might not have the balls, Jack… literally."

"Like a kicker's opinion really matters-"

Tyce violently twitched. Pink foam gushed from his lips as he groaned. His eyes rolled up into his head; his entire body convulsed. Delonte and a few teammates tried to calm him down, but quickly backed away when the young quarterback suddenly rose from the bench, syrupy strings of bodily fluid flying from his body as he thrashed. Then he crashed into a messy wet heap on the floor.

Everyone in the locker room gawked in stunned silence for several seconds, before Delonte nudged his downed teammate. "Dude…hey, farm boy, you okay?"

"Oh, shit," Larry said. "He ain't dead, is he?"

"I don't think he's breathing. Somebody go get Coach Damron."

"Goddammit!" Rick growled before repeatedly smashing his helmet against a nearby locker. "I didn't come this fuckin' close to a title just to have it go away because some drunk country punk gets a bite on his junk!" The massive linebacker tossed the helmet aside, stomped over and towered over the lifeless young quarterback. "Get up, farm boy!"

Delonte tried to intervene, slapping both hands on the linebacker's shoulder pads. "Easy, Rick. This could be serious-"

Rick shot Delonte a menacing glare, silencing the wide receiver, then aimed a meaty finger down at Tyce's body. "Get on your gear and out on the practice field before I *really* give you something to whine about."

Tyce's eyes suddenly popped open. He sat up. His mouth fell open. Bloody drool hung from his lower lip. A deep, wet, guttural groan escaped his throat. With lightning agility, he lunged up and clamped his jaws around Rick's finger. The linebacker screamed as he tried in vain to shake his hand loose. He backed up, dragging Tyce across the floor.

"Jesus!" Larry cried.

Delonte and a few other nearby Steelers grabbed Tyce by the shoulders to pull him off, but the young quarterback only let go once he bit clean through the bone and came away with the whole finger. Rick fell to his butt, gawking in horror at the crimson fountain spewing from the open wound. Tyce ravenously gnashed on the severed digit, blood dripping down his chin. Everyone let go of his shoulders and backed off as though he were on fire.

"Oh, God!" Rick screeched. "Oh, God, that *hurts!*"

Still hungry, Tyce leapt to his feet, eyes devoid of the farm boy innocence that endeared him to the media, and stomped toward Larry. The kicker backed away, crying in panic, only to be stopped by the bank of lockers doused in Rick's blood. Within seconds, Tyce was upon him, burying his face into Larry's throat and coming away with a mouthful of flesh. The kicker's eyes rolled into his head as he plopped to the floor, blood shooting from his open neck like a geyser. His right leg—which secured the win in the AFC Championship game against the Chargers just a few days ago—twitched a few times before his whole body became still.

"What the fuck is going on in here?" boomed a familiar voice from outside the melee. Coach Damron, followed (as usual) by offensive coordinator Joe Parker, muscled through the swarm of Steelers, clipboard in hand, his ample belly leading the way. "Why aren't you assholes out on the field?! We've got the game of our lives in seven days and I don't need this bullsh-" The coach cut himself off when he spotted his crying linebacker and dead kicker, lying in pools of their own blood on the locker room floor. Tyce stood over Larry's body, hungrily chewing the meat he tore from the kicker's neck.

Coach threw his clipboard to the floor. "Great…my first round draft pick is a fucking zombie. Joe!"

Joe stood at attention. "Yeah, sir?"

"My shotgun, please."

Joe obediently nodded before scampering back toward Coach Damron's office.

Coach pointed at a cluster of players, most of Pittsburgh's defensive line. "You guys…tackle farm boy here and get him to the ground before he chows down on one of our draft picks."

As if on cue, Popp released a groan as his mouth fell open. The quarterback stretched his arm forward and shambled towards the nearest player—their tight end, Art Jackson. Bug-eyed and terrified, Jackson started backing away.

"What are you, a bunch of pussies?" Coach roared, just as Joe returned with a sawed-off double-barrel shotgun. "Someone tackle that son-of-a-bitch!"

Nobody complied, too shocked and terrified to do anything but back away as Tyce stalked the screaming tight end. Suddenly, a massive bloody hand, minus the index finger, wrapped around Jackson's neck from behind. Rick Pound, face hollow and grey, tore through Jackson's jersey and shoulder pad and bit into him. Jackson screamed; blood sprayed from his shoulder.

"Goddammit," Coach Damron grumbled as he snatched the double-barrel from Joe and loaded a few shells. "Whole team's comin' apart. Big Dave's gonna have my ass for this."

Jackson dropped to the floor in a gory heap. Rick and Tyce, eyes rolling stupidly in their heads, reached out for other victims. Chaos ensued. Several players scampered in panic from the locker room. Others, too horrified to think clearly, ran into each other in an effort to escape the gnashing jaws of their newly-dead teammates.

Disgusted with his team's display of cowardice,

Coach Damron hoisted up his shotgun, thumbed back the hammer and marched ahead, ready to blow Tyce's head off.

"Wait!"

The shrieking voice of quarterback coach Nick Hobbs, who had just run into the locker room from the practice field, momentarily startled everyone still and silent, including the two undead Steelers. He clutched a football in his hands.

"Dickenson ran out and said what was going on," he wheezed, trying to catch his breath. "Zombies, right?"

Coach grimly nodded, just as Jackson—now one of the undead—slowly rose from the floor.

Hobbs held the football high over his head. "Here, boys!" he chimed. "Wanna play football? Here's the football! Who wants the football?"

Popp, Pound and Jackson, transfixed by the pigskin in Hobbs' hand, shambled forward, grunting as they blindly swiped for the ball. Hobbs slowly backed away, luring the undead players like a Pied Piper.

"I came to tell you, Coach," he said breathlessly, drawing the three away from the others. "Popp's our only hope to win the Super Bowl. Our backup just tore his rotator cuff on the practice field. So don't blow Popp away. We need him."

"Are you out of your mind, Hobbs?" Coach groused. "Look at 'em. They're dead...they're *all* messed up."

"Really?" Hobbs suddenly gripped his football in both hands, took a few steps back and threw a perfect spiral into the shower stalls. It struck the tile wall and plopped to the floor. The three undead Steelers clawed empty air and stumbled over benches to chase after it. Popp dove on the ball first, clutching it tightly in his puffy pasty arms. The remaining players in the locker room looked on in dumbstruck amazement.

"They may be dead," Hobbs said, " but they still

want a Super Bowl ring."

Super Bowl Sunday

Bob Constantine: *I still can't believe that entrance onto the playing field by the Pittsburgh Steelers, Tug… the entire team, helmets on, led out in shackles like a chain gang and dragged to the sidelines by the coaching staff. Kind of a flashy stunt from such an old school coach like Gene Damron.*

Tug Sheldon: *Does seem awfully theatrical, Bob; like something you'd see from the WWE. Still, look at those Steelers, growling and clawing at those chains like they're ready to eat up the Falcons…and the crowd's lovin' it!*

Bob Constantine: *There's Coach Damron…taking a key and unlocking the chains while the Falcons stand on the other side of the field, probably wondering just what the heck is going on. Frankly, Tug, so am-*

Tug Sheldon: *Wait a minute, Bob! A Steeler player is free and running across the field. Who is that? Looks like Pro Bowl safety Andy Phelps! He's running toward the Falcon bench! What in the world is…ooh! He just tackled veteran quarterback Eddie Stapleton! Drove his helmet right into Stapleton's gut, both players knocking over a table of Gatorade.*

Bob Constantine: *One of our sponsors, by the way.*

Tug Sheldon: *I'm more concerned about that helmet hit, Bob. That'd be a personal foul during game play. Oh, no! Phelps has Stapleton pinned to the ground! It looks like…like…the Steeler safety is trying to bite him! Now several Falcons are trying to pull him off! Look, here come the referees, trying to break up this pregame melee! Bob, I've never seen anything like this in all my years as a player, broadcast and Viagra spokesman! Man, I can't wait to Tweet this!*

The ruckus across the field stirred the remaining shackled Steelers into a frenzy. Chains rattled and helmets clacked together like giant billiard balls as the undead teammates struggled and clawed.

A wild elbow knocked the keys from Coach Damron's hand. "Goddammit, Hobbs, you told me we could control these things!"

"Hold on, Coach!" Hobbs grabbed a nearby football and held it high. "Hey, boys! Look! Football! Who wants the football?"

The team suddenly looked Hobbs' way, collectively mesmerized by the pigskin over his head. Several of them grunted excitedly. A few made a grab for the ball, but most surrounded the quarterback coach, hungry, yet not attacking.

Bob Constantine: *Well, it took awhile for Damron to get his team in check, but we're ready for the kickoff of Super Bowl LXVII. The Falcons won the toss and have elected to receive. Larry Dubroskivichensteinburgeronio just placed the ball onto the tee, though he's stumbling back to his team lineup like he's drunk or something.*

Tug Sheldon: *Sure is, Bob. Maybe drunk off Budweiser, the official beer of the NFL.*

Bob Constantine: *Nice plug, Tug. At any rate, the crowd is going wild as Dubroskivichensteinburgeronio approaches the ball and...Super Bowl LXVII is underway! A great kick of at least 50 yards! Falcons kick returner Greg Queen signals for a fair catch and downs it on the ten yard line...first time the guy hasn't dropped the ball in two weeks. But wait a minute! Here comes the entire Steelers special teams lineup! They're not stopping, Tug, piling on top of Queen like they didn't hear the officials' whistles! Even Dubroskivichensteinburgeronio is leaping onto the mound of Steelers!*

Tug Sheldon: *Don't often see that kind of*

aggression from a kicker, Bob.

Bob Constantine: *Wow! Despite repeated whistles, it's like the Steelers don't hear it! Now the Falcons are joining in, trying to pull Steelers off of their kick returner. What a dramatic start to Super Bowl LXVII, brought to you by Chrysler, Wrangler, Buick, Taco Bell, Tylenol, Wal-Mart, Oreo Cookies, Wells Fargo, Walt Disney Pictures, Monster Energy Drink, GoDaddy.com and Turtle Wax.*

Despite the pile of Steelers clawing at his arms—surely that had to be a penalty—Greg Queen protected the ball, curling into a fetal position on the turf. Even as the Steelers ripped their helmets off and buried their teeth into his flesh, Queen clutched the ball as though his life depended on it. Blood sprayed from his wounds, splattering the faces of his grunting and groaning opponents. Yet still he held on—after all, this was the Super Bowl.

A chomping mouth found its way to his jugular. Gnashing teeth tore flesh from his neck. He felt his life ebb away; the cheers of the crowd began to fade as he drifted into darkness.

Greg Queen may have been choking on his own blood, but at least he didn't choke in the Super Bowl.

Bob Constantine: *Oh my God! Is that blood spewing out of the pig-pile of players? That's just gross! Worse than Joe Theismann's injury back in '85!*

Tug Sheldon*: I know what you mean, Bob. I haven't seen fluid spray into the air like that since the first forty seconds of my honeymoon! It looks like the Steelers aren't content with the Falcons downing the ball. Several of them are now attacking the players on the sidelines! Some Falcons are running away, and a few Steelers have leaped up into the crowd! It looks like they are attacking spectators! Unbelievable! God, what a gory mess! An* *alarming start to Super Bowl LXVII!*

Bob Constantine: *Which is brought to you this time by Verizon, Subway, Microsoft, Bank of America, Burger King, Lowe's, Paramount Pictures, Pepsi and...wait a minute, Tug. Do you hear that?*

Tug Sheldon: *What, Bob?*

Bob Constantine: *That pounding...that screaming...outside our broadcast booth.*

Tug Sheldon: *Now that you mention it, Bob, it does seems more boisterous than usual and...oh my God! The door just broke open! It's Steelers' rookie quarterback Tyce Popp! He must be here for a pre-game interview.*

Bob Constantine: *With all that gore dripping from his lips? Really, Tug? You interview him, buddy. I'm getting the hell outta - AAARRRRRGH! Oh. God, it HURTS! Hellllp meeee!*

Tug Sheldon: *Bob! BOB! Oh...hey, Tyce. Uh...hey, you still aren't pissed at my comment last year about being overrated, are you? Tyce? TYCE? OH GOD, TYCE,*

NOOOOOOOOOOOOOOOO!!!!!!!!!!!!

THE PAINTER'S MOTHER RODE A PALE HORSE

Christopher Hivner

The Night Before . . .

The gun being pointed at Roger Simpson and his wife Sandra was small caliber, but Roger knew if he didn't time his next move perfectly, it could still produce a mortal wound. The man holding the .22 had the glassy eyes of a drug addict. The hand being held out for Roger's wallet was shaking badly. Unfortunately, the gun hand was steady.

Roger knew he should just give up his money and credit cards without a fight, but as a retired cop, that wasn't an easy thing to do. His eyes stayed firmly on the gun while his right hand slid into his back pocket for his wallet. Sandra loosened her grip on his arm, though she moved a step closer to his body.

The drug addict's eyes were watering, and Roger thought it might give him an opening. Then his sight caught something else. A thin white line of light appeared on the addict's sweaty forehead. It planted itself dead center and then started to grow, elongating down the man's nose.

Roger Simpson caught the mugger's eyes and saw confusion, but he wasn't watching the white light on his own skin. He was looking at Sandra's face. Roger looked over to see the same white light starting at his wife's hairline and crawling down past her lips. When she gazed back at Roger he saw recognition in her expression. He didn't need to see his own face to know he had light marking him. Roger glanced down at his chest and saw the light grow down over his stomach.

All three of them stared with fascination as the inch-thick line of light kept moving until it bisected their whole bodies, coming to rest on the ground between their feet. They exchanged looks before the pain started.

Like a saw blade, the light cut into their bodies, slicing them from front to back, cutting their bodies into two pieces length-wise. The pieces stood for a second and then fell in opposite directions. The particles of light separated, reforming into a cloud of frothy mist that hovered over the dead. Moving up and down the bodies, the smoke crackled and spit.

Starting at ground level, the clouds reformed into rectangular shapes. Spirals of red light raced through the masses, creating cells. Slowly, the clouds transformed into copies of the three dead humans. When all was complete, the mist disappeared, and the clones stared at one another. They grunted and coughed, loosening up the vocal cords before speaking.

"The Higher Ones have started the process," the new Sandra Simpson said. "We must find our target."

"What are our orders?" Roger asked.

"They want him to experience the destruction

firsthand, so we only observe. If he gets help, we take no chances and eliminate him."

"What if the help comes from the Oracle?"

"It will be the Oracle; there is no one else."

"How do we fight . . .?" the mugger started.

"We find a way. The Higher Ones have started the process, and he can't be allowed to interfere."

"Understood."

*****

. . . The End

"There it is," Professor Archer muttered under his breath. He lifted his head away from the canvas, laying the magnifying glass down to rub his temples. Such intense scrutiny of a painting always made his head pound. It didn't help that the artist was hovering too close over his shoulder, and the morning sun was blaring in through the cracked window. Finally, Archer sat up straight.

"Well, Hennessy, you managed to do it again," the professor said gruffly while scratching at his unruly beard.

"What do you mean, professor?" the artist said, a hurt inflection in his voice.

"Every assignment," Archer yelled. "You alter every assignment." Archer stood up to face Donald Hennessy. "Oh, it's always subtle. A minute bit of rebellion, but I can always count on it."

"Professor . . ."

"Why, Donald? Why can't you just paint what I ask? What are you trying to gain? This is an intermediate art course at a piddling community college, and I'm a tenth rate artist doing a fourth rate job teaching housewives and wanderers how to create something Grandma can hang on her wall. Why can't you just paint what I ask?"

Donald Hennessy's face contorted in anxiety. He ran a nervous hand over his bald head. He looked at his painting: a large pond in the foreground and forest trees behind, the best copy he could make of a spot in Grosslander Park near his home. Donald stared into his teacher's angry face, then back at the painting.

"Professor," he said haltingly. "You said to go outside and paint what we see in nature. That's what I did." Donald pointed to his work with an open hand. "It's all there, everything I saw from behind my easel."

"Oh yes, the bulk of the painting is well done, Donald. The water, the trees, the sky, all nicely rendered. Your work with different shades and hues has improved dramatically this semester. But your growing abilities are not where my problem lies." Henry Archer waddled his chubby legs over close to the painting. He hovered a finger over the pond in the center. "There is my consternation."

"I don't understand," Donald whined. The professor stabbed at the canvas.

"The letters, Donald, the letters. Yes, at first glance they look like ripples in the water, but if you examine them closely, they are English letters."

Archer grabbed a piece of scrap paper from a nearby table and pulled a pen from his shirt pocket. He stared back at the painting, speaking out loud as he wrote.

"ll ff gg is the first line. The second underneath is ll uu, and finally the third is gg rr nn vv." He handed the paper to Donald Hennessy. "You painted this, so what does it mean?"

"I don't know; it's what I saw. I'm not trying to rebel against you, Professor Archer. I just want to be a good artist. I painted what I saw. These letters were in the water."

"Come on, Donald."

"I'm telling you this is what I saw." Hennessy let the piece of paper drift to the floor. He walked away, both hands on his head. When he turned back, Archer saw tears in his eyes.

"Don, are you all right?"

"Donald, please."

"I'm sorry," Archer said quietly. "Donald."

"I swear to you, Professor Archer, I painted exactly what I saw. Those letters are there, in the water."

Archer sighed. "All right, Don . . . Donald. All right." The older man walked to his desk at the back of the classroom and sat down. He took his glasses off to clean them, all the while subtly shaking his head and muttering under his breath. He didn't hear Donald Hennessy approach.

"You don't believe me," Donald said, his brown eyes almost pale.

The professor looked up. He slid his glasses back on and stared at the man in front of him. Donald Hennessy was medium height and slightly built. He was only twenty-six but was already naturally bald. In class he was quiet, contemplative when he painted. Archer couldn't say he didn't like him because Hennessy didn't present enough of a personality to dislike. The professor did wonder about his mental state. His uneducated opinion was Donald was suffering from some kind of psychological impairment. Every assignment he turned in had something extra hidden in it. When confronted, Hennessy insisted it was real, and that he had only stroked what was there: The bowl of fruit with the pair of eyes peering between the pear and the apple, the female nude with Norse runic symbols along the side of her outstretched leg.

The professor at first thought Hennessy just wanted to make a name for himself in class by adding flair to his work. But the man sat at the back didn't socialize with the other students, and was pathologically shy. Archer knew these were not the personality traits of someone who would deliberately enhance his paintings for attention, so he confronted him one day after class. That was when he realized Hennessy believed he was painting what he saw.

"I don't know what you want me to do, Donald," the professor finally said. "I simply don't see the things you see. To my eyes, they are not there. When we work in class, no one else paints what you do. You are the only one adding these extras. What would you have me do?

Donald Hennessy thought for a moment. He looked back at his painting lying on the table at the other end of the classroom. Then he stared at the professor.

"Come with me to the park," Donald said.

"What?"

"Grosslander Park. That's where I painted that scene. Come with me and see for yourself. Come see the letters in the water."

"No . . ."

"It's only thirty minutes away. I'll drive you there and back when we're done. Please. I need you to believe me."

Archer was about to protest again, but the look in Hennessy's eyes made him stop. There was such fear in his face. Maybe deep down he knew he was hallucinating, and once Archer didn't see the nonexistent letters, he could talk Donald into going to the hospital and admitting himself.

"All right," Archer said. "Show me the pond."

*****

A block down from the community college, a man sat astride a Yamaha V Star motorcycle. He took a bud out of his left ear and pressed a contact on his cell phone. After two rings he was met by the single word "Report."

"He's taking his art teacher to see the pond. The teacher doesn't believe the letters are there."

"To him they won't be," the voice on the other end

said.

"What do we do about the painter? He's trying to involve others."

"Let it be."

"We can't just do nothing. You said yourself the Higher Ones want us to act if he receives help."

"The teacher won't see the message anymore than he saw the other signs. Besides, the birds will take care of Hennessy."

The line went dead.

*****

Donald Hennessey parked his Ford Explorer in the visitor's lot of Grosslander Community Park. He took a deep breath for the first time since he had herded Professor Archer into his vehicle. A sharp pain had been slashing through his chest the entire drive. Donald thought he was going to have a heart attack and skid off the road. His head was covered in a glossy sheen of sweat. Something was either wrong with him or with the rest of the world, and the odds weren't in his favor.

Professor Archer had already gotten out of the SUV. Donald looked over to see his portly teacher impatiently checking his watch. Donald was still gripping the steering wheel, trying to slow his pulse.

He had felt this isolation before in his life, in middle school, when he saw the kites in the sky that no one else did. As he watched out the classroom window, they had danced against the clouds, forming an arrow and the words "run this way". Donald had thought someone was putting on a show from the playground and yelled for everyone to come look at the pretty kites. He was quickly surrounded by his classmates and the bewildered teacher, only to have their attention soon turn fully to him.

"What are you talking about, Dopey Donald?"

"I don't see any kites."

"What's wrong with you?"

"Donald's crazy."

"I believe the principal needs to hear about this, Mr. Hennessy."

They had been there. He saw them, hundreds of kites of all different colors. When he saw them again that night outside his bedroom window, he didn't tell his parents. They had already made an appointment with a child psychologist. Instead, Donald knelt at his window and watched the neon white kites fly into formation. "Please run," they told him, but he didn't understand. And he never saw them again.

"The professor will see the letters," Donald whispered to himself. "He has to. Someone has to believe me."

Donald exited his Explorer so fast that he almost fell. Using his handkerchief to wipe down his head, he started up the path to the pond.

"This way, professor."

Archer followed, straining to keep up with Donald. "I hope," the teacher said, "that you understand I'm not trying to demean you, Mr. Hennessy."

"I'm not crazy," Donald answered.

"I . . . I never went that far," Archer replied nervously. "But . . ."

"Not crazy."

"All right, Donald. All right."

They came to the pond. Donald walked right up to the edge, the toe of his boots hanging over the edge of the loose ground. In moments, he felt the professor's heavy breath on his neck. Donald focused his eyes on the sunlight as it struck the water. The ripples traveled in uneven lines, and in the midst of those lines Donald saw:

ll ff gg

ll uu

gg rr nn vv

He was about to ask his teacher if the man was ready to admit he saw the letters when the ripples were disturbed. The head of a silver fish broke the surface of the water. The eye on the side of its head looked at Donald, and then it opened and closed its mouth repeatedly.

Donald Hennessy dropped to his knees, jamming his hands against the sides of his head. Every time the fish opened its mouth, high-pitched feedback cut through Donald's ears like a thousand needles.

"Donald, what's wrong?" he heard Archer ask, and then felt the man's hands on his back. The fish bobbed in the water, keeping its head visible, continuing the pain for Donald. Suddenly Donald knew what he had to do.

"Mr. Hennessy, where are you going?" he heard the professor ask when Donald jumped into the water. He sank down until he was completely submerged, and the feedback in his ears stopped. Donald glided through the murky water to the center of the pond. He felt things bouncing off of him, bits of plant life floating over his face.

A wide shaft of sunlight burned its way through the muck, brightening the underwater world. Donald saw the fish that had been trying to communicate with him. He swam to it, and the fish swam to him. When they met, the fish, which was about a foot long, pushed against Donald's mouth. Reaching up, Donald tried to pull the creature away, but the fish had bitten into his lip.

Donald's mouth instinctively opened to cry out and the fish forced its way deep into his throat. Donald fell to the pond bottom, rolling in the silt. The fish kept moving until it was sliding into his stomach.

Wretching and taking in pond water simultaneously, Donald knew he was dead. Just like he had always heard, his entire life flashed through his mind in the fraction of a second. His mother's sad face was the one image that lingered. He wanted to wrap his arms around her and tell her he was coming: A pathetic end to a meaningless life, drowning in a park pond.

Donald Hennessy lay on the bottom of the pond, staring up through the sunlight that shone in the water. "Shouldn't I be dead by now?" he thought. "Shouldn't I at least be gasping for air?" But he wasn't. Donald was lying on the bottom, breathing naturally through the dirty water. Then he saw the ripples return, illuminated by the sunlight. The lines moved gracefully until the letters re-emerged.

"Oh my God," Donald said, his eyes opening wide. Calmness swept through him. His fingers and toes tingled when he understood the message. It was coded, but he could read it and it made sense. "Why does it make sense?" he wondered. And the fish in his stomach spoke to him.

"Because I am your guide."

"What should I do now?" Donald asked.

"You must go to your mother's grave."

"Mom."

"Go now, Donald, and be careful. There are those that will try and stop you. Let me lead."

Donald Hennessy floated to the top of the pond, his head breaking through with a loud splash. Immediately he could hear Professor Archer's voice calling to him.

"Donald! Dear boy, I thought you were dead! Are you all right?"

Donald swam toward shore, his head being filled with information from his guide, including what he needed to do next. Before he could mentally ask how, he was given instructions. He was also told of changes to his body that had already begun.

The pond floor started to slope up and Donald was able to stand. He pushed through the last few feet of water, walking out onto the grass where Archer grabbed him by the shoulders.

"Donald, Donald, are you all right? I thought you

were gone," the professor babbled. "I called 911. An ambulance should be here soon."

Donald smiled at the older man, shaking the professor's grip to place his own hands on the chubby belly of the art teacher.

"It's ok, professor. I'm fine."

"Are you sure? You were under for so long. What happened? Why . . ."

"Professor Archer, stay calm. Everything is all right. And I owe you an apology."

"An apology?"

"I never should have involved you in this. You had nothing to do with it."

"Donald, I was only trying to help you."

"I know. You've been close to a friend to me, and I will always be grateful. Still, I shouldn't have brought you here."

The tree tops erupted with caws. Donald turned to see a black cloud of crows spewing forth from the spruces and oaks. There were hundreds of them all crying out at the same time and flying toward the pond. Donald turned back to his teacher.

"I need one more favor from you, professor," he said with a wan expression.

"Yes, my boy?"

"Save me." Donald opened his right hand, and from the padded skin beneath his fingers, a foot-long talon emerged. The hardened nail was flat and sharp on both sides like a knife blade. Donald brought his hand up and swung it at the professor's head. The talon sliced through his neck, separating his head from the body.

Professor Archer's head—eyes still showing surprise and mouth wide open—jumped into the air for a second, then plopped into the damp, tall grass at the pond's edge. Blood was spurting from the man's neck, and this is what Donald needed. He dropped the body so that the neck hung over the water, pouring the blood into the pond. Taking a glance at the sky, Donald saw the crows were only a few dozen yards away, their caws deeper and more intense.

Turning back to the pond, there a widening puddle of blood skimming the top of the water. He hoped it would grow quickly. Donald slid into the water again, submerging himself, gliding to the right until he was under the mass of Archer's blood.

The first crow arrived, angrily diving at the pond. It went for the middle of the bloody slick, but when it hit the water it bounced away, its piercing beak snapped in half. In a second a group of seven crows tried to plunge into the water. When they hit the blood, their beaks were driven back into their bodies, and they fell into the pond dead.

Underneath, Donald kept himself directly under the hold the blood had created, but he knew the birds would soon learn. Turning up both palms, Donald's knife-edged talons slid free, and a fraction of a second later, the first crow by-passed the blood slick, diving into the water. Immediately it turned for Donald, who impaled it with one of his new claws.

Feeling movement behind him, Donald turned to find three more birds biting at his back. He sliced them into pieces, but instinctively his body knew the blades would not be enough. Donald started to change again. He felt flashes of pain all over, looking down at his hands to see scales emerging from under the dermis. Once a row was fully formed, a new one grew out on top of the previous one.

Donald continued to be attacked, sticking and cutting the crows, all the while his body protected itself with a tight layer of hardened, grayish-green scales. They hung down over his eyelids, lowering his vision to just slits. When the major wave of crows came, he felt them more than saw them.

Hundreds of the large, black birds hit the water

simultaneously. Their bodies puncturing the water sounded like gun shots. They came at Donald Hennessy in waves of undulating darkness. He closed his eyes, and the scales slid into place over his lids. Floating in the water, he took the bites, scratches and blows from the birds, but they couldn't pierce Donald's armor. The crows were doing more damage to each other than to their target.

For several minutes, Donald was engulfed in the massive murder of crows. Their attack was vicious, but never drew any blood. Waiting them out, Donald slowly felt them fall away as their lungs filled with water. When he finally opened his eyes again, they lay on the bottom of the pond in a heap up to Donald's waist. He pushed himself to the surface. His new scales eased back under the skin. By the time he swam to shore, he looked like the same old Donald Hennessy.

Donald was on his knees on shore preparing to stand up when a terrible pain hit his stomach. He heaved repeatedly, feeling something coming up into his throat. A huge spasm in his chest sent a stream of water shooting out his mouth and nose followed by the head of the fish, but Donald still felt something else down his throat. He pushed again, and the fish slid completely out of his mouth with two thin attachments to its tail.

When Donald was able to focus, he saw the fish had grown human legs. He watched as the tops of the thighs melded with the lower portion of the fish's body, covering the tail with human flesh. Still on his knees, weak and confused, Donald shook his head as the fish grew before his eyes. The mouth opened and closed continuously, pulling in oxygen, learning to breathe on land. The body extended, widened, became one being with the human legs which also grew longer and thicker. Donald's pained face turned upwards when the fish-human stood up and spoke to him.

"Time is precious. We must get to your mother's

grave." With that, the fish turned and ran to Donald's vehicle. Donald watched it disappear down the path. His head hung low, his stomach still sending piercing pains into his bowels. Exhaustion overcame him, and he fell over onto his side. Donald closed his eyes and spoke to the dirt.

"Mother."

*****

"I have to move in now," the man with the motorcycle yelled into his phone. He was parked across from the entrance to Grosslander Park. He was agitated, pacing alongside his machine, his hand gripping the phone so hard the plastic case was snapping.

"I should have taken him at the school."

"Calm down."

"He defeated the birds! The Oracle is with him now. If we don't do something . . ."

"And what will you do? If the Oracle is there, then the painter's body has been modified. If the crows couldn't kill him, how will you? Besides, the starbursts will take care of him."

"That's what you said about the birds, or have you forgotten?"

"Remember who you are talking to!" the voice on the other end shouted. "I give the orders and you follow!"

"You're letting him get too close to the answer."

There was a long pause where on the phone all that could be heard was heavy, pointed breathing coming from the motorcycle man. Finally the voice on the other end spoke.

"I believe your usefulness has come to an end."

The motorcycle man did not have time to respond before his skin heated to a thousand degrees and melted from his body, running out the openings of his shirt sleeves and pants. It pooled on the ground in a pinkish-white soup, like melted ice cream. His screams reverberated through the trees, diminishing to a choked gagging when his muscles and tendons unwound like shredding rope. They snapped away from the bone, springing to the ground, until all that stood among the plants of the park was a bare skeleton. There was a flash of orange at the base of the skull that started a white-hot flame. The bones were consumed. When the flame burned out minutes later, it left behind a pile of ash.

*****

Donald was driving, but he didn't know why. He sneaked a glance at the creature sitting next to him, his eyes catching the gill slits moving back and forth. Donald's body and mind were worn down. All the understanding that had suddenly invaded him under the water had drained away. What the hell was going on? Somewhere in a recess of his brain where neurons were still firing, he remembered the message in the water that he had mysteriously translated as "out of time".

"What does the message mean?" he asked quietly, chancing only a cursory look at his companion.

"There were moments in your past when we could have saved you from what's to come, but our communication in this dimension is limited. We couldn't make you understand. This morning I had to intervene. We were never supposed to meet."

"But what does it mean, 'out of time'?"

"Exactly what it says."

Donald felt the fish's eye moving in circles as it talked, looking him over top to bottom. He took a deep breath, tears forming in his own eyes.

"Tell me what's going on? Who are you?" Donald pleaded.

"It's best you don't know. Just let me do my job."

"No, no, no," Donald said, crying for the first time

since the funeral eight years ago. "No. You put something in me back at the pond, and . . . and . . . now I don't remember what I knew then. You took it from me."

"It's for the best."

"NO! You tell me why you want to go to my mother's grave. Tell me WHAT YOU ARE!"

The fish turned away from him. The eye Donald could see never stopped moving, but it wasn't looking at Donald anymore. The head bobbed a few times as it thought. Then it turned in its seat so that it was facing forward again.

"Very well. I will try to explain, but understand you may malfunction because of it."

"Malfunction?" Donald shook his head and laughed. "Ha. Malfunction, says the talking fish." He licked his dry lips, biting the lower between his teeth. "Tell it," he finally said. The fish paused, then began.

"Your scientists postulate that, at the most quantum level, the universe is held together by strings of energy. They are partially correct, only it doesn't stop at the strings—which are actually more like wisps of smoke. Binding the strings are beads that emit heat to make the strings vibrate. And producing the beads are the Alterians."

"Alterians?"

"Sentient beings that hold the entire universe together. Organisms capable of thought and emotion with a complete self-awareness of their importance as the base organic compound that connects everything."

Donald felt the fish turn fully in his seat so he was looking directly at him.

"Every star, planet, comet, quasar, cloud of gas, drop of water and carbon or silicon-based life form touches by way of the Alterians. And your mother birthed them."

Donald turned toward the fish, his mouth agape. The SUV swerved off the road, the right side tires dropping into a gully. Hennessy pulled his sight back in front of him, yanking the steering wheel hard left. The Explorer jumped onto the macadam, veering sharply left over the center line. Donald over-corrected once more and almost drove the truck into a deep ditch on the right side of the road, but at the last second the vehicle straightened out. Driving in the correct lane, Donald's foot eased off the gas.

"What the hell are you telling me?" he said while sweat dripped into his eyes and his chest tightened.

"Your mother was the singularity."

"The sing . . . what?"

"The point of energy that exploded, creating the universe as you know it. Your scientists refer to it as the singularity. Your mother is the universe itself."

"Stop talking now," Donald said weakly. His head turned to look out his side window. The SUV was again zigzagging all over the road. Donald's hands were loose on the wheel, but he was paying little attention to where he was going. Tears poured down his face.

"I warned you," the fish said. "This information is not meant for those . . . "

"I get it. I'm a dope. I'm a stupid human, not some exalted . . . whatever you are. What are you? Who are you?"

"Some call me the Oracle because I see future events. But my knowledge is not absolute, and it is not my primary function."

"What is, then?"

"Your mother created me to keep the Alterians in line. She foresaw that they would rebel against her. My job was to prevent it. I have failed."

"Why? What are . . . the Alteerans doing?"

"Alterians. They are disconnecting from each other, destroying the universe your mother created. I have been hindered in my authority because they created protectors for themselves: the Razers."

"What are they?"

"Dimensional beings that can change their appearance and control nature to their advantage."

"The crows."

"Yes, they were under the guidance of the Razers."

"I don't know how . . ."

Something heavy struck the SUV's hood, driving itself through the motor. Donald lost control. The truck spun around 360 degrees, started to tip onto the right side tires, then evened out, hitting the ground with a thud. Smoke was pouring from the engine compartment, glowing an ethereal whitish-yellow in the center. Before Donald or the Oracle could move, another object crashed to the ground a few feet from the Explorer. It was a jagged, egg-shaped rock, luminescent with bright light.

"Starbursts!" the Oracle yelled. Donald tried to ask what he meant, but one of the fish's fins was already slicing into Donald's belly. Hennessy looked down to see double flaps of skin staring back at him in a crooked smile while blood painted his clothing red.

"What did you do?" Donald was finally able to cry. The Oracle responded by reaching its fin inside Donald's body. The painter screamed in pain as the scaled hand pushed through his internal organs. His head fell to the side, and he saw more starbursts denting the ground. There were craters all around the Explorer, each one glowing in super-heated light.

The SUV suddenly jumped off the ground as a burst smashed through the roof over the rear left wheel. Donald heard the tire explode, and his truck sank down. He looked back to the Oracle.

"What . . ." was all Donald got out before seeing the fish's fin pull a small, metallic orb from the slit in his stomach. Twisting the top off, the Oracle dumped the contents—a silky golden powder—all over Donald's body. The talc penetrated his skin and spread, each molecule connecting with the one next to it until

Donald's flesh was completely covered.

Catching his face in the rearview mirror, Hennessy thought he looked like a carved idol, but he noted the pain in his stomach was gone. He looked down to see the cut healed.

"Primalia," the Oracle said, anticipating Donald's question. "It is an element found in a distant galaxy and is the only absolute protection against radiation. It has been in your body since birth."

Donald was confused for a moment, but then his eyes lit up. "The starbursts are radioactive?"

"They were emitted directly from the Sun's core. Now come, we must get to your mother's grave."

"Wait, why?"

"More questions?"

"Every word you say terrifies me, but I need to understand."

"Very well," the Oracle continued after a long pause. "Your mother had many children throughout the universe. She could only stay with each for a short time. You were the weakest, so she raised you longer than most to strengthen you. She also left you something, within her body, to help stop the Alterians from destroying the universe."

"We have to dig her up?"

"Yes. I understand that is taboo for humans, but it's the only way. Please, we must hurry."

*****

Next to the grave marker of Mary Allison Hennessy, in the cemetery of a small country church, stood two men, both of medium height and build. They wore the overalls and boots of gravediggers, but held no shovels or picks. If one looked closely, their pasty white faces were asymmetrical, and neither eye was the same color. Their hair was like thatch on the roof of a hut. The Razers had been short on time, making their modifications shoddy. Staring straight ahead at the dirt lane that led to the cemetery, one of the men spoke.

"They are coming to the grave?"

"Yes."

"We should have let our third kill him."

"The Higher Ones want Donald to suffer. He is a part of the creator, and as such must be destroyed. The Oracle would have defeated the third; he was weak."

"The Oracle has beaten us all."

"Yes. The process is still in its early stages. We must kill the son of the creator."

"Understood."

*****

With the SUV dead, Donald and the Oracle had to run the final three miles to the cemetery, continuing to dodge starbursts. Not in the greatest shape, Donald was exhausted by the time they arrived. The Oracle seemed like he could run forever on the skinny human legs protruding from its body.

They found the grave of Donald's mother. He dropped to his knees both from weariness and sadness, staring at the etching on the marker. Only eighteen when his mother died, Donald had never gotten over losing her. Whatever the fish said she was, true or a delusion, she would always just be his mom.

"We must hurry," the Oracle finally said, breaking Donald's daydreaming. "May I begin?"

"I'll do it," Donald answered quietly.

"I mean no disrespect, but I can accomplish our goal in a shorter time." Without waiting for a response, the Oracle held one of his fins over the grave. Donald watched as the ground started to shake. He heard a creaking sound, then a snap. The top of his mother's coffin pushed against the ground, the cheap wood splitting apart. The box rose until it hovered in the air. Raising his other fin, the Oracle opened the lid. The skeleton inside, bones rattling against one another, rose from the padded lining. Donald couldn't speak as he watched his mother's remains fly through the air, dropping softly to the ground next to her grave. The Oracle released the coffin, and it landed back in the hole with a whump.

"Come here, Donald," the fish said, moving next to the skeleton. On shaky legs, Donald Hennessy walked over to his mother.

"This is going to be brutal, Donald," the Oracle said. "But it's the only way."

"What's that?" Donald replied, looking into the air. The fish followed his eyes to see that a thick cloud of fog had covered the cemetery. A moment later, rocks and tree limbs whizzed past their heads.

"The Razers are accelerating their attack," the fish exclaimed. He reached out with a fin to touch Donald. "Don't move!"

"Oh my God," Donald said, watching the Oracle. One of the fish's eyes was expanding. The eyeball grew like a bubble until it was taller than both of them. When the translucent balloon came toward him, Donald tried to back away, but the Oracle held him still.

"Don't move!"

The eye bloated outward until it touched Donald's skin. It crawled over him like soapy water. When he was covered head to toe, it expanded with one last push. There was a loud pop, and Donald realized he, his mother's remains, and the Oracle were all inside the fish's eye.

Outside the bubble, the entire cemetery was being uprooted. Dirt, rocks, and sticks were all thrown at them, but couldn't penetrate the Oracle's eye. Donald flinched as headstones suddenly came at him and bounced away harmlessly.

"We're safe," the Oracle said. "I must complete my task."

"Uh, ok," Donald said, not able to take his eyes off the maelstrom enveloping the bubble. He never saw the fish's fin come up and cut across his throat. Blood spurted straight out as Donald dropped to the ground, his hands wrapping around his neck.

With his eyes watching sixty-foot trees slamming into the bubble, Donald felt the fish's fin slide inside his body again. The last thing he saw before dying was a farm tractor appearing out of the fog to crash into the fish eye, breaking apart into a pile of mechanized parts.

*****

The Oracle reached inside the cut he had made in Donald's throat and wrapped his fin around the spine. With a snap, he broke it off the skull, pulling the column out through the hole. Reaching back in again and again, the Oracle removed all of Donald's bones. He had to make extra incisions around the groin to get the hip and leg bones. More cuts at the ankles brought out the many foot bones. The most difficult process was peeling back the face to extract the skull.

The bubble shook when a city bus struck the top after falling straight down out of the sky, but it did not puncture. The Oracle took a moment to check the integrity while a brick ranch house bore down on him. The home exploded when it touched the fish's extended eye: concrete, metal, and wood crumbled in a tall mound all around him.

Satisfied that his fastness was steady, the Oracle returned to his job. Donald's flesh lay on the ground, hollow and flat. Picking up the creator's earthly skeleton, the fish broke it into pieces to start putting them into Donald's skin. With precision, he recreated Donald Hennessy with his mother's bones. With a loud snap, he connected the skull and spine to finish. Then the Oracle waited.

A minute passed until Donald suddenly coughed up a glob of blood. He sat up, his eyes wide, his mouth hanging open, drawing deep breaths into his lungs. Outside the bubble the chaos stopped. The Oracle's eye pulled away, releasing Donald, who stood up, his eyes looking around as if they were brand new.

"I am the universe," Donald whispered. He stared down at his hands as they shimmered, turning from pink to silver to translucent. The bones under his skin burned, sending arcs of electricity through his body.

"I am the universe," he said loudly.

The ground underneath rumbled. The sky above cracked with lightning and billowing black clouds. The interred bodies of the cemetery exploded out of their graves, shooting into the air as if out of a cannon. They were joined by living human beings caught in an updraft, sailing high into the sky. Men, women and children flew in wild patterns through the sky, their screams echoing around the valley, bouncing off the mountains.

"I am the universe!" Donald shouted. He felt the Alterians disconnecting, trying to destroy all his mother had created. He felt everything: every movement made by all living creatures in every galaxy, every word spoken, every breath drawn. His mother's bones had not contained a portion of her, they *were* her, completely. Donald was his mother, Donald was the creator, Donald was all matter.

Throughout the universe, the Alterians broke their attraction to one another, destroying the beads that gave the strings life. One by one the strings ceased movement. Planets' rotational velocities slowed, nuclear fusion in the guts of stars faltered. The bodies flying around Donald dropped from the sky, exploding on impact. Meteors bulled through the Earth's atmosphere, slamming into the ground at thousands of miles an hour.

"I am the universe," Donald whispered. He closed his eyes, crossed his hands over his chest, and dropped his chin. He took in a deep breath and then exhaled it slowly. When it came out, it was a mist of deep blue. It spread quickly over everything like thin paint, obscuring all in its path. Over the ground and all landmarks in the way, up into the sky, the blue mist enveloped the universe, blotting out stars, planets, everybody in existence, until all that was visible was Donald standing perfectly still in a tight formation.

When he knew it was calm, Donald squeezed his bones together until they snapped and ground against each other, disintegrating to dust. His human flesh ignited into a blue-orange flame that burned, quickly leaving behind a pile of ash to mix with the bone remains.

The multi-colored powder spun clockwise, faster and faster, until it was burning again, so hot it was a small dot of white light of infinite mass.

There was nothing else. Until a conscious thought echoed inside the reconstructed singularity.

"I am the universe, and I am alone."

THE KNOT THAT BINDS

John Bruni

The tumbler shatters on the wall behind us, showering us with shards of broken glass. Most of them patter harmlessly off our bare skin, but one—a thick piece from the bottom, we think—cuts our shoulder. We barely feel it at first, but then a burning sensation flares up, and we touch the pain. It is wet. Our fingers are bright red.

"I'm sorry," Kerri says. "I didn't mean to do that. But . . . you guys freak me out. I just . . . I . . . ." She can't even look at us.

"You knew going into this," we say. "You knew what you were getting. Why—?"

"I can't take it anymore!" Her voice is jagged, a cracked plate about to come to pieces. She sniffles. "I thought it would be kind of cool. Different. And it was. But . . . this is just too much."

We step around the garden of twinkling glass at our feet and sit on the couch. "Isn't this what you wanted?"

"I thought it was," she says. "I even thought it

would be kind of kinky. But . . . ."

"We disgust you." No big deal. We are used to it.

"It's not that. Although *that*…" She gestures at the knot of rigid flesh where we are conjoined. "…*that's* kind of gross."

We shrug. It made even our parents gag, back when we were kids.

"It's your . . . oneness, I guess."

This surprises us. We've never heard it put quite like that before. She finds a problem with this? We find nothing but comfort in ourselves.

"You're supposed to be two people," Kerri continues. "But the thing is, you act like the same person. You guys even speak at the same time. It's creepy."

"But we *are* the same person."

"That's the problem. That's why I'm done. I'm leaving." This time, she favors us with a shamed glance. "Sorry about the glass."

She heads for the door, and we stare at the remains of the tumbler, listening as she undoes the lock and lets herself out. The door thumps closed, the chain rattling against the frame, and another one is gone from our life.

We decide to clean up the mess and head to the kitchen to retrieve a broom and dustpan. Two of our hands sweep while the other two scoop, and before long the floor is spotless.

Later, we urinate. As two streams patter into the toilets, we look into the mirror and wonder why most see us as two people. Our parents felt the urge to name us individually. When people look to our left, they refer to us as Chauncey; to the right, we are Orson. This classification seems to satisfy the world, so we let people call us as such, but when we're alone, we know who we are.

When we were born twenty-five years ago, our parents wanted to separate us. Considering how we were merely joined at the hip, the doctors were in agreement.

Then, they looked into the matter and discovered that we share the same nervous system. We have two separate spines, but the cobweb of our nerves are connected with each other. A lot of our digestive tract is the same. Only our circulation systems are independent of one another. Long story short: separation would certainly kill us.

We wash our hands and brush our teeth. In bed, we spend a half-hour masturbating. Our right dick comes first, and still lightheaded and twitchy from one orgasm, our left dick convulses, launching us into another pulsing, back-arching ejaculation.

Then, we wipe ourselves down and drift off to sleep, dreaming things we won't remember the next morning.

#

After a week, we get the usual thrill-seekers contacting us on eHarmony. Freaks with more issues than brain cells. A couple of reporters wanting to do fluff pieces on us. A guy who wants to put us on display.

We check the requests we made of other people. No one has responded to us. Not surprisingly, the next week is full of masturbation. Our porn isn't doing the trick, though. Only our left dick gets hard. Jerking off one dick with four hands can be cumbersome.

We need new spank material. We frequent a sex shop on the south side called Rooster Trax. We are on a first name basis with Zachary, the counterman and part owner. We say hi as we go in.

As we make our purchase, Zachary slips us a business card. "Richard Bigcock," we read. "Film producer and director." And there is a phone number and address in the corner.

"What's this?" we ask.

"Dick's a customer," he says. "You know, the porn star. He's a director now. He tells me about this porno he wants to shoot with freaks. No offense."

We shrug.

"Anyhoo, he's looking around for Siamese twins."

"Conjoined," we say.

"Whatever. I says to him as it happens, I know some guys. He says yeah? I say yeah. He asks if they're good looking. I says they're not bad. He asks how well they're hung. I says I don't know. I don't measure my customers. I told him I'd give you guys his card. He says the money's good."

We exchange glances, then look back at the card, considering. Then, we pocket it and pay up. At home, we check our eHarmony. More requests from weirdos. No responses to us.

That night, we hit a few bars. Have a few drinks. Talk to a few girls. They think we're hilarious. They call their friends over to meet us. They buy us drinks. But when we try to bring them home, they laugh us off.

We go home alone. We retrieve the business card from yesterday's pants pocket and call the number.

"This is Dick."

Odd. Shouldn't a film producer have a secretary? This is a red flag, but we ignore it. "This is Zachary's friend."

"Slow down. You're echoing. What now?"

It's hard to speak through just one mouth, so we hold a hand over one of them and repeat ourselves.

There is a pause. Then: "Ohhhh. The Siamese twins, right?"

"Conjoined."

"Whatever. Hey, you fellas wanna come down to my office? I'd like to get a look at the goods."

We make an afternoon appointment. When we get out to his address, we're surprised to see it's an apartment building, not an office. Another red flag.

We clop our way up three flights of stairs, worried about the thick gray dust bunnies clinging to the floor and the tangy smell of urine assailing our noses. When we reach the door we want, we take grim notice of the tarnished bronze number—a four—hanging upside down on a rickety door that should have been guarding a child's tree house.

We knock, and the cheap wood barely manages to stay in its frame. Footsteps thump on the other side, growing louder as the owner approaches. The hinges squeal and a fat face pokes out at us. We suddenly realize that we know this man. We've blown many loads while watching his films (though he'd been in better shape back then). He is immaculately groomed, but he is breathing heavily through his thick beard from the exertion of opening a door.

"Holy shit, this is for real. Come in, come in."

He flings the door wide and steps away, allowing us in. The door clatters shut behind us, and we find ourselves in a room much nicer than the building had made us believe. Everything is clean and neat and even stylish. Nothing garish or crude stands out as a testament to this office's true purpose.

"Sorry about the neighborhood, boys," Dick says, "but it keeps costs down. Gotta watch the overhead on operations like this. Want a drink? Some coffee?"

We agree on coffee, and Dick ushers us into another room. "Have a seat." Dick gestures to the two chairs in front of his desk. Then, he laughs, smacking his meaty forehead. "Sorry. Force of habit. Maybe you should take the couch."

We do, and he soon passes us two mugs of coffee. He pours a glass of Scotch for himself and swishes around in his glass, staring at us.

"Now. Which one of you is Chauncey? And . . . Orson, is it?"

We shrug. It doesn't matter to us.

"Ugh. Zach warned me you were a couple of creeps. All right, one of you's gotta be one or the other. Come on, guys. Throw me a bone."

Most people find it helpful if we make a suggestion. Our farthest left hand rises. "Chauncey," we say.

Dick grimaces. "Do you always talk like that? In stereo?"

We nod.

"Whatever. I guess I don't care. Just don't talk to the girls. I don't want to scare 'em off. Now, let's see the goods."

We stand, setting aside the coffee cups. After a moment of struggling out of our clothes, we stand in our birthday suit, waiting to be judged.

He walks around us, surveying what we have to offer. It unnerves us a bit, even though we're used to people staring at us. Our skin suddenly feels too tight, and our bellies feel a bit overstuffed.

"Not bad shape," he says at last. "A bit doughy, but not in a bad way. You might want to tone up a bit, though. Camera adds weight, and all that. Orson's cock is really nice, too. Chauncey, you're not too shabby, either. Let's see 'em hard."

We exchange a glance. No one has ever made this request of us before. We're not even sure if we can get hard on command, at least not for a man; and one we'd just met, no less. We must be professional, though, so we make an attempt, weakly flogging our flaccidness.

"You need some porn or something? Here." Dick goes behind his desk and offers us some magazines from his drawer. He is in both of them. We try not to think about how weird the situation is getting, but after a few glances at the glossy pages, we are at full attention for inspection.

"Nice." Dick nods his approval, sipping from his tumbler as he assesses us. "We got something to work with here. By the way, do you guys have any problem with jerking each other off? That's not gay to you or nothing?"

"Why?" we ask. "We're one flesh. Is it gay when

you masturbate?"

"No, but I'm not attached to another guy."

We shrug, idly reaching across to grip our opposing members.

"Hey, that's cool." Dick's brow creases, and his eyes darken. "Kind of weird, too. When one of you comes, does the other feel it?"

"We are one flesh," we say again.

"Right. Tell that to the taxman." He taps his foot, arms crossed, looking thoughtfully down at our junk. "You know what? I think we can do business. How does a thousand for each of you per movie sound?

We are about to remind him again that we are one person, but we restrain ourselves. Two thousand sounds very good to us. If we can knock out a couple movies a week, we'd be rolling in cash.

"At first, I mean," Dick continues. "If things work out, maybe we can negotiate. I don't know if you guys will reach a bigger market than specialty stuff, though, so no promises. Does that sound cool to you?"

Yes. Indeed it does.

"I'll have my lawyer throw together a contract. If things are agreeable, I think we can start shooting in a week. All right?"

We nod. Not only are we going to get laid, we're going to be compensated for the privilege. Good times.

#

The next day, we receive the contract via email. We glance over the legal jargon, understanding very little. What we do get is the stuff Dick had outlined when we met.

At the bottom, we see Dick's electronic signature. There are two lines, and we know what's expected of us.

The next document he sends us is a W-2 form, accompanied by payment instructions. All finances will be handled by direct deposits. We only have one checking account, but we still have to fill out two forms.

The final email is a schedule for his upcoming films. There is only one a week for us, which disappoints us a bit. Still, that's an extra two grand.

There is also a time and address for our first filming session. We celebrate with bourbon but no porn. We want to save ourselves for our big moment.

Days later, when we get to our destination, we're surprised to see it's a cheap motel room just south of town. We were expecting something a bit classier than this, but when Dick sees us, he explains that he's just trying to keep costs down.

We sit on the motel bed, our feet tapping, our insides wiggling. A cool stream of sweat runs down our back as we stare at the director and cameraman setting everything up.

The bathroom door opens, and the woman steps out. All of our worries and concerns dissipate. They steam off the tops of our heads as we stare at her gorgeous, perfect form. Tassels of blonde hair roll down her shoulders in natural waves. Her petite, porcelain face grins impishly at us as our gaze rides the fully-rounded curves of her body. We end up at her long, well-muscled legs before we drift back to her breasts, where we lose ourselves in the valley of her cleavage.

"Wow," she says. "You guys really are conjoined twins. I've never seen anything like it—at least not in real life. Which one of you is Orson?"

"They don't talk," Dick says. He steps between her and us. "Righty's Orson, lefty's Chauncey."

"Nice to meet you." She holds out her hand.

We shake it, wanting to say something. We think back to our first meeting with Dick—when he said how we talked was creepy—and think better of it.

What happens next is a blur of ecstasy. After Dick confirms the cameras are ready, he tells us what he wants.

At first it seems like a lot of direction, but then we realize how simple it is. We just have to do what comes naturally and follow the camera's prompts.

"ACTION!"

There is very little introduction before the woman does a striptease for us. We stare at her bare breasts, wondering what her name is.

We don't wonder for very long. Soon, the camera is over our shoulders for a POV shot of her sucking our dicks, trading one for the other before pushing them together and ramming them both into her mouth.

We shift. One of our mouths eats out her pussy while the other clamps down on her anus, licking and slobbering.

We fuck her. This is the only time the camera becomes obtrusive as it tries to get close-ups of the action. We spread her legs like a pair of scissors and our left dick goes into her pussy; our right dick, after some maneuvering—because it is bigger—plows into her ass. After a bit, we flip her and change holes.

Twenty minutes of following prompts. We can feel our orgasms burning in our balls, tingling the bottom of our glanses.

It's like Dick can read our minds. "On her face, boys."

She kneels before us, working our cranks as the cameraman gets in close for the money shot. Rarity of rarities, we shoot off at the same time, unraveling ropes of our potential children across her face, where they hang off her nose and chin like glazed icicles.

In a daze, we collapse on the bed. We barely notice as she squeezes the last of our satisfaction out, licking us clean.

"CUT!"

She says it was great to work with us and gives us hugs. We're still lost in the greatest moment of our life. Congratulations are sent our way, but none of it registers.

Nothing sticks until we get home and see that two-thousand dollars, minus taxes, has been transferred to our checking account. We celebrate by deleting our eHarmony profile without a second thought. We don't need that stuff anymore. This is *our time*.

#

It isn't long before we trudge our way through the work week, eagerly looking forward to our work weekends. Sometimes we meet new people. Sometimes we fuck women we've done before. One time, we fuck a midget sideways so one dick goes in her pussy while the other goes into her mouth.

We move into a nicer place. We buy nicer clothes and nicer bourbon.

Our movies are a hit. Other directors request our services, and when our contract with Dick is up, we take them on. When they can't get us, they seek out other conjoined twins, making us quite the trendsetter.

People start to recognize us on the streets. We win awards. We are guests of honor at porn conventions. Soon we quit our day job so we can fit more movies into our schedule.

By the end of the year we're doing a movie a day, shoveling cash into our bank accounts, and we are so busy we hardly ever sleep anymore.

It catches up to us on the set of *Twin Team-Up 14*. We are shooting a scene with the Hymen sisters when we realize how exhausted we are. Elvis Edgewood, the director, is setting things up with the cameraman, and here we are trying to get erections.

Nothing. We're fucked out.

We mention this to Edgewood, and he sends over a fluffer. She works us with both hands, and our right dick flutters a bit, but she might as well be jerking off a pair of socks.

Edgewood pats her on the shoulder. "Go on, babe. I got this." As soon as she's gone, he says to us, "You know French Tickler? The old French porn star from the Eighties? He had the same problem. Worked himself into impotence. You know how we fixed him up?"

He leads us into his office and puts a mirror down in front of us. He taps some powder from a tiny baggie onto the reflective surface and uses his business card to cut out several lines.

There is a moment of paralysis. We want to do two things at the same time. Part of us wants to stay healthy in this business, but the other part is thinking more of survival. Reputation. Money.

Something gets jarred loose in our heads. There is a mental tearing sensation, and Orson's head ducks down to the mirror. Two lines disappear up his nose, and I can feel the jolt of their impact on my brother. Though we don't share the same circulation, I can still feel my heart rate rocket. Our flesh flushes. I shudder, suddenly hyperaware of everything from the threads of Edgewood's suit to the dancing dust motes in a beam of sunshine.

"Chauncey?" Edgewood offers a rolled up dollar to me.

"No. Thanks." I am horrified at the breathy sound of my voice.

"Dude," Orson says. "I'm so fucking hard right now."

So am I, and it scares the hell out of me.

#

Orson starts spending a lot of our money on cocaine. When I complain, he snaps at me. "It's my money. I can do whatever I want with it."

Objects in our house no longer belong to us. It's Orson's whiskey. It's Chauncey's book collection. It's

130

Orson's cell phone. It's Chauncey's TV.

Our interests diverge. He wants to go out clubbing; I want a quiet night at home. He wants to score some blow and hang out with Elvis Edgewood and his scuzzy retinue; I want to spend time with our actual friends. He wants to fuck the hot blonde with a questionable sexual history; I try to talk him out of it. "It's my body, too," I try to tell him.

When he gets drunk, I get drunk. When he does drugs, I feel the result. And when he gets a woman, and I don't, I feel his orgasm.

Sometimes, as I try to sleep at night, I touch the Gordian Knot of flesh where we're joined. In my darker moments, I wish to sever it. If he wants to be his own person so much, let him.

But the doctors told our parents—when we were still babies—that if they tried to separate us, we'd probably die. There was a possibility of saving one of us, but due to how much of our digestive system is in Orson, it wouldn't be me.

There is one place I can hurt him, though. Inspiration strikes me on the set of *Double Trouble 18: Back to the Minors*. We have just stepped out of the bathroom, dressed in robes, waiting for instruction from the director. The female lead, Tits Weatherby, approaches us and passes the time with Orson. Shortly after, we are called to our places. Action is called.

Tits and Orson get down to business, but I do nothing. As she fills her mouth with Orson's cock, she reaches up to jerk me off with her free hand. It's difficult, but I do not respond. I think about dead babies stirred up with puppy eyeballs being slurped up by a shit jack o'lantern, and I remain flaccid.

Tits, ever the professional, scootches over to put her pussy within easy fingering distance for me. I cross my arms and stare at the ceiling.

I hear Jack Mehoff, the director, clear his throat. I

ignore him. Finally, he says, "What the fuck, Chauncey? You got a problem or something?"

I sigh. "Just not feeling it, Jack."

"You need some time with the fluffer?"

"I don't think so. I'm just not feeling up to this work anymore."

"Shut up and get to work," Orson says. His intense gaze locks with Tits Weatherby's, never with mine.

"It's not me, is it?" Tits asks.

"No. It's me. I'm tired of doing this for a living."

Orson finally breaks away from her and stares at me. He wants to be outraged, but surprise is all he offers.

"That's all well and good," Jack says, "but you can't quit now. You signed a contract. When this skin flick's in the can, you can do whatever you want."

"Can't you just use him?" I hook a thumb at Orson.

"No. I need you both. You're a package deal. One's no good without the other."

I want to disagree, but he's right about the contract. I don't want to be sued. Even though this lifestyle has ruined my life, I have grown accustomed to the riches it's given me.

I finish the movie. I help Orson fuck Tits every which way but loose. I make this performance as good as I can, believing it to be my swan song.

In the car on the way home, Orson stews. He glances at me when he thinks I'm not looking. He hyperventilates, breathing like a horse after a race.

"You can't do this to me," he finally says.

"Remember when we were we? We did everything together. We even spoke in unison—"

"Enough with the sentimental bullshit. Fame and fortune, Chauncey. We have that because of me. You know that if you quit, I'd be finished in the industry. Why are you doing this to me?"

"It sucks, doesn't it? Having to do something you don't want to do because someone else demands it."

He doesn't speak for the rest of the drive. No sooner are we in the door to our condo, though, he curses vehemently and twists around to face me. No easy feat for either of us.

At first he fumes wordlessly, and I feel smug because I've finally hurt him. The moment doesn't last; in a flash, his hands are around my throat and squeezing. A breath gets caught in my windpipe, and my face flushes. When I realize that I can't breathe, I do my best to pry Orson's fingers away.

Unsuccessful, I kick at his shins. This does nothing, but I manage to knock him off balance. We fall to the floor, Orson on top, and he uses his newfound leverage to strangle me more efficiently.

There is no pain. My vision grows weaker, and my attempts at self defense become feeble. I try to implore him to stop, but my voice won't make it past his clenched hands. Reflected in one of his dark eyes, I see myself, a face elongated, tongue protruding from my mouth. I wonder what he sees in mine.

The world grows distant, and I know I'm going to die. It doesn't scare me. I feel relief for being freed from Orson after all these years. How can two people attached to each other grow so far apart?

If I die, he dies. I remember the thought clearly, as if someone had spoken it in my brain.

Orson realizes this, too, and I feel his grip fall away. I can barely breathe as I hack and cough. My vision no longer seems fuzzy, and I can hear again. When did I stop registering sound?

As soon as I know I'm going to live, I hazard a glance at Orson. He sits next to me, staring into nothing. "I'm sorry," he says in a spent voice. "I got carried away with all this." He waves a hand around.

I try to say something, but it feels like there is a lump stuck in my throat, blocking the words.

"I got so swept up in all this fame and fortune stuff,

I forgot about you."

"It's all right, brother." My voice is a croaking disaster.

"We can't be like we were before," he continues. "That's lost to us forever, I think. But we can compromise."

It takes some time, but we come to an agreement. Our porn occupation will continue. Orson gets to have his way Mondays, Wednesdays, Fridays, and alternating Sundays. I get my way all other times.

It is uneasy and tumultuous, but we have our truce. We snipe and grumble at each other, but we don't break our agreement. Things go well . . .

. . . until we meet *her*.

We are going for a walk on Venice Beach. Orson likes buying things from the street peddlers, and I like the warm breeze and the salty smell of the ocean, so it's a win-win for us.

And then he sees her. A huddled mass sitting on a giant backpack. She reads from a battered old textbook, and there is a cup next to her. A sign propped up at her side says she is trying to earn enough money to go to college. "Please help," is the coda in handwriting almost as pretty as calligraphy.

At first I think Orson's going to give her money. This is unthinkable to me, but he can be soft-hearted sometimes. I do not expect him to be soft-headed, but he says, "What's a beautiful woman like you doing on the streets like this?"

She is beautiful. I have to give her that. None of the other homeless people possess such a shapely body. Such an angelic face. Such a swooping cascade of hair. And her eyes are captivating. Something—I can't explain what—glimmers in the windows of her soul.

But she's homeless and smelly and she's wearing long sleeves in hot weather, which can only mean one thing.

She glances up at us. "Like the sign says. I can't afford classes, but I have to get in."

"What are you studying?" Orson asks.

She holds up the book so we can see the cover. *How to Write for Newspapers.*

"You want to be a journalist?"

"Yeah, but I can't even get into a state university. I have the grades, though. I did pretty good in high school."

"What's your name?"

"Moonbeam Smith."

Orson laughs. "Seriously?"

She rolls her eyes. "My parents were hippies. Who are you?"

"You don't recognize me?" Not *us*, but *me*. My brother is so insufferable sometimes.

"No," she says.

"Orson Heidecker. And this is my brother Chauncey. We're kind of famous. Maybe you know us by our stage names. Orson and Chauncey Siamese."

"Are you, like, movie stars?"

"We're in adult films."

She smirks. "That sounds pretty cool."

I sigh, unable to take this farce anymore. "Come on, Orson, just give the girl some change and let's go."

He glances at me, a warning in his eyes. I can tell he wants this girl bad. I don't know why. We've fucked many women prettier than her in our movies.

Then, I remember it's a Friday. There is no way out of this for me.

Orson looks at his watch. "You hungry, Moonbeam?"

"Call me Moon."

"All right. Moon."

She offers a shrug. "I could eat."

#

135

Orson fucks her that night. I try to ignore this horrible display, but we share the same nervous system. I think about the usual dead babies and coprophages, but soon the front of my pajama bottoms are tented.

Moon straddles Orson's thighs, and I can see the marks on her arms. I also see a farm of other scars that look suspiciously like the results of self-mutilation.

She looks over to me. "Are you sure you don't want to join us?"

I don't acknowledge her.

"Come on, Chauncey. It'll be cool." She grabs my dick through my bottoms and gives it a squeeze. "I've never done twins like this before."

My body betrays me, and I grow rock hard in her grip. Embarrassed, I slap her hand away. "Leave me out of it."

"Forget him," Orson says. "I want you all to myself." He reaches to the night table and retrieves a condom. Just as he rips through the package, she touches his hand.

"Sweetie. I don't do condoms. It doesn't feel right. I want your skin inside me."

"But . . . ."

"It's okay. I just got tested. And my tubes are tied, so you can cum inside me."

Dumbly, he watches her scooch up his body a bit, arched over his dick. She eases down on it, holding her pussy open a bit to allow him to glide in. She is already sopping wet.

Orson forgets any objections; he's in Happy Land.

Later, she confesses she'd lied about the test. "But I haven't fucked anybody in a while," she says. "If something was wrong, I'd know it."

This horrifies me, but Orson takes it in stride. "That's all right. I think I'd notice something, too."

"I do have Hep C, though."

At this, I expect Orson to explode. Instead: "That's fine. I know I can't get it through sex unless both of us are bleeding. Down there."

"Are you willing to take that risk?" I ask. "With my body?"

They both jerk, as if they've forgotten I'm next to them. Then Orson sighs. "Our circulation systems are different."

"Our digestive systems aren't. If it kills your liver, it will probably get mine, too. And what am I going to do if your stupid ass dies? Did you think of that?"

"Nothing's going to happen," Orson says. "We just have to play it safe, is all. She's a good girl."

"If she's such a good girl, why don't you ask how she got it? And what are those marks on her arms?"

She sobs, burying her face into Orson's chest. He hugs her close, cradling her head, whispering apologies and assuring her everything will be fine.

When she regains her composure, she admits to being a junkie. "But I'm three months sober." And she got Hepatitis C from needle sharing. "That's what motivated me to get cleaned up."

To comfort her, Orson fucks her again. I try to fall asleep, but it's impossible. When she finishes, she rests between us, her belly on the knot, hair spread out in a fan on both of us.

The next day, without consulting me, Orson says she can live with us.

Over the next few weeks, I try to ignore her. Much to her credit, she doesn't attempt to get into conversations with me, either. Regardless, I manage to learn a few things about her, like Moonbeam is really her name, but it's her middle one. And then she talks about her fucked up family and horrible history of relationships.

Lastly, she has this conversation with Orson about our occupation:

"It doesn't bother you? What we do?"

I'd been reading the newspaper, so I missed the beginning of this exchange. I perk up at the sound of my brother's voice, but I feign disinterest, pretending to be immersed in current events.

"No," Moon says, "I think it's kind of cool."

"But I get paid to have sex with women who aren't you. Doesn't that bother you at all? Because I know it would fuck with me, if you were out with some other guy."

"It's just money, sweetie. It's how you make your living. These girls don't mean anything special to you. They'll never have your heart. I do."

"I never thought about it like that."

"If you left me for any of them, I'd tear her eyes out." And she gives a mock snarl, holding her hands up like claws.

They share a laugh. They make out for a while. Just as I'm ready to turn back to my paper for real, she says, "Maybe we should do one together."

"One what?"

"A movie. What do you think?"

Orson becomes so cloudy I can feel it through our knot. My own face flushes with his. "I don't know if I want other guys looking at you like that."

"They can look all they want, sweetie. I'm going home with you every time."

"I don't know."

"It'll be fun! Come on! Think about how sexy it'll be. I *know* you're an exhibitionist. Let's be exhibitionists together."

"Well, I guess we'd be paid for it . . . ."

"See? There's no way we could lose."

Silence. I can almost hear the cogs turning. Then: "I'll talk to Edgewood about it tomorrow."

She squeals and jumps on him. More laughter. More fucking. I'm starting to get used to this, so it's easier to ignore.

They finish, and soon she is breathing at a paced, regular beat. I can tell Orson is on the brink of sleep. Perfect.

I nudge him. He mutters and turns his head away. He wants to turn the rest of his body, but the knot stops him.

I nudge him again. "Wake up, Orson. I gotta' piss."

He turns back to me, hair corkscrewed, one eye open. Grumbling, he stands with me, and we head to the bathroom. Our toilets are side by side, and we each piss into our respective bowls.

When we're done, I say, "She's using you."

He doesn't even favor me with a glance.

"She is. At first I thought she wanted o . . . your money. I think now she wants fame."

"She loves me. I trust her."

"She's a junkie."

"Was."

"You think she's going to save whatever money she gets from this ordeal? Besides, here's something you didn't think of."

"Oh?"

"What am *I* going to do in this movie you guys are going to make?"

"What do you mean?"

"Edgewood isn't an Academy Award winning director. He doesn't know how to shoot around me. He'll want me fucking your girlfriend, too."

The rush of his anger floods my body. I see almost as much red as he does when he whirls at me, grabbing my undershirt. "Don't you fucking touch her, Chauncey. She's *mine*. We've always had to share everything. Well, not her. All right?"

I have to force myself to calm down. Deep breaths. The hammer pulse in my ears dies down. Then, quietly, I say, "All right."

The next day, Edgewood says yes to Orson's

request, even though he knows shooting around me will be a hassle. Within the week, we're filming.

There is one issue. Edgewood knows we're clean, but Moon doesn't have her papers, proving she's been tested for STD's.

"I can vouch for her," Orson says. "I've been with her for quite some time. I would have noticed something."

"Well . . . ."

"She has Hep C," I say.

Orson gives me a dirty look. "Which is a blood disease, not sexually transmitted."

"How long have you guys been fucking?" Edgewood asks.

"Almost a month."

"And you've been getting tested on a regular basis?"

"Yep."

"Did she give you Hep C?"

"Nope."

"I guess it's okay," Edgewood says. "I trust you. I can fudge some paperwork. Just make sure she gets tested soon."

Moon takes to porn very easily, almost as if she's done this before. When I make a snarky comment about it later, she confesses to having once been a stripper, but never a porn star.

We get paid, and shortly after Moon disappears for a day. The note she leaves explains that she wants to get some of this cash to her sick mother. She borrows our car to do this. I say nothing, and Orson doesn't seem fazed by this curious behavior.

She comes back the next day, and before they fuck, she says she has to clean up. She spends a lot of time in the bathroom, and when she comes out, she seems distant. Her pupils are pinpricks in her verdant eyes, and there is an odd mark encircling her upper arm.

Orson doesn't notice. He's just happy to see her.

In her heroin reverie she is sloppy. Later, when we're showering, we find a needle in the garbage. She covered it up with some tissue but not well enough. Orson reaches down to pick it up, but I stop him. "Hep C, remember?"

"I'll be careful." He holds it by the plunger end and looks at it, shocked.

"She's got to go," I say.

"She slipped," he says. "Everyone makes mistakes."

"This is a big one," I say. "She hasn't had a lot of money before. She jumped at the chance. You'd better get used to it."

He keeps staring at the needle. Finally, he throws it back in the bin.

"You're not even going to confront her?"

"It'd only hurt."

"So?"

Silence.

"If you don't, I will. I refuse to share our condo with a junkie."

"No!" He runs a hand through his hair, face red at his sudden outburst. Suddenly, I know he realizes what a moron he is. His face contorts as he struggles with this knowledge, but I can feel it through the knot.

I'm about to give him that final nudge when his thoughts come into line. I know what he's going to say before he says it. Still, it disgusts me as he opens his mouth and dribbles these words out like he'd been eating dogshit: "I'll talk to her. But she's staying."

"Really? What will it take to get you to see sense?"

"I love her."

How can I fight that?

The next day, he confronts her in a very passive-aggressive way. Of course, she's *soooo* apologetic. She says she won't bring it home again, but not that she won't do it again.

Before long, Edgewood wants to film a sequel.

Moon is getting critical attention. Other directors want her, too. Inevitably, she asks Orson for permission to take one of these offers.

"Absolutely not," he says.

"Why not?"

"You only make movies with *me*. You're mine and no one else's."

"That's really not fair, is it?"

Even I want to retort to that. Or perhaps I'm getting Orson's run-off incredulousness through the knot. He replies as I would: "You're going to throw *that* back in my face? I thought you said you were cool with it!"

"I am. The problem is, you're not."

Orson's frustration builds up in my forehead until I feel congested. He stammers, trying to find the right words.

"Maybe we should spend some time apart," she says.

"You're breaking up with me?!"

"I thought you were more mature than you are. I was wrong. You're not ready for a real relationship. You just want to own someone."

I wonder if that's true. Maybe it is. More likely, she got what she wanted from us, and she wants to move on.

Moon walks out on us, and Orson wants to drink. A lot. And cry. And bitch. I don't tell him I told him so; I'm just glad she's gone.

I try to comfort him, but he prefers to be alone. While he drinks himself—and by extension, me—silly, I call directors with whom we have contracts. I tell them we're sick. We won't be in for a while, but we have every intention of fulfilling our obligations.

In the next week, I'm not surprised to discover that Moon has no trouble finding work. When I see her movies, she looks strung out. I think she's putting most of her paycheck into her arm.

Orson doesn't notice. He moons over Moon, calling

her the one who got away.

Very quickly, she gets a bad reputation in the business. Directors stop working with her. Porn stars avoid her at all turns. Everyone knows her habits because she has a tendency to nod off at work.

Soon, no one wants her, and much to my shock and horror, Orson invites her back home. She thankfully lets him fuck her, but most of the time, she's out of it. I suspect Orson's been giving her money for drugs. He says it's for other stuff, but she always comes home with those pinpoint pupils.

Orson tries to get her help. He finds a rehab that might help her. She visits the place and then disapproves. There are too many black people there. Her attitude repulses me, but Orson is still trying to be understanding. He sets her up with a methadone clinic. She rejects it because it's merely a pale cousin of heroin. "Besides," she says, "it fucks up your teeth."

There is no getting rid of her. Sometimes, she comes home with someone else's sperm inside of her, but Orson thinks she's just wet. He puts his dick in that fetid mess without a second thought.

Finally there comes a day when she doesn't return to him. He spends all night worrying about her. When it breaks him, he begins downing drink after drink. He babbles like a lunatic.

Four days later, Orson gets a call from an unknown number as we're driving home from work. Something niggles at the back of my mind. "Don't answer that," I say.

"It could be her."

I sigh, and he answers the phone. By now I'm pulling into our parking lot. When we get to our assigned space, Orson's complexion is pale.

"Can I talk to her?" he asks.

She's in jail. She gave the cops his number and now she wants us to bail her out. No way. I open the door and try to climb out, hoping my movement will nudge Orson along. He stubbornly remains put, holding up a finger.

"Is she going to be all right?" he asks.

This doesn't bode well. Instead I think about the ID card Orson gave her, in case of emergency. Is it too much to hope she's dead? Does that make me a bad person?

"I see. I'll be right there." He hangs up and turns his attention to me. His eyes shine a little too much, but I don't need that to know he's close to tears. "We have to go to the hospital. It's Moon."

"We're not going anywhere," I say. "It's late. I'm tired. I just want to have a couple of drinks before passing out to the Late Show."

"We have to. She OD'd. It was touch and go for a bit, but she's going to be all right. They'll discharge her to me."

"No, Orson, this is it. I've suffered your shit long enough. If you can't see her for the junkie whore she is, then you're a fool. But I won't take it anymore. We're not going anywhere."

"How can you say that about her? She's got a problem. She's sick. It's not like she wants to do these things."

"You've hurt yourself enough," I say. "Remember when she walked out on you? How miserable you were? It's only going to happen again."

"I love her, Chauncey."

"You enable her. That's all your wishy-washy attitude is doing to her."

"Stop it."

I can feel his anger building through the knot, but I can't help it. My own rage at his stupidity is so grand it makes me feel holy. "If she dies, it'll be because you didn't have the guts to say no to her."

"Stop it."

"You were too scared to be unloved. Alone. As if you would be either one, you moron. In case you haven't noticed—"

His hands clamp down on my throat, and his rage hits the ultimate crescendo. It matches with mine exactly, and in that pure moment, we are one again. Gone are the concepts of Chauncey and Orson. Misguided love and righteous fury melt into one another as all four of our hands join at the throat of our left head. We're not much for the Bible—or any religion, really—but we feel the intense need to remove an offending part of our body.

Two hands throttle with all their might while the other two form fists and strike wildly at our left head. We feel the hazy, throat-clogging pain of a broken nose, but this must be done. We must see this through.

An eye closes like a red, puffy clam. Teeth bend in their sockets and pop out, peppering our clothes like New Year's confetti. Blood runs freely. Our blood. But it must. It is our cleansing sacrifice.

Life ebbs. Blood stops pumping. Two flailing hands fall lifelessly onto the steering wheel, and I feel . . . less. My knuckles creak, so I loosen my grip, letting go of my brother's purple, misshaped throat.

The knot grows numb.

Only then does it dawn on me what I've done. Breathing becomes nearly impossible. My heart is a rabid beast in my chest. Am I dying? Is this what it's like?

My first impulse is to call 911. My parents were told that if we were separated, we'd probably die, but I might have a chance. Can an ambulance get me to the hospital in time to separate me from this corpse? Is it possible to save my life?

Then I realize how disgusting I am. I have not given a thought to my brother. Maybe he can be saved. Besides, even if he can't be, can I live without his comforting weight to my left?

My body throbs like a sore tooth, and I hate myself for letting a dumb broad get between us. Chauncey is the only indispensable person in my life. I love him with all my heart, and something clicks and gurgles inside of me and I'm certain it's my organs—*our* organs—shutting down.

I'm hypersensitive to everything, from the spaces between the keys on my cell phone to the rough, almost pixilated texture of my teeth against my tongue. I can count Chauncey's nose hairs and the veins in his staring eyes, but I can't breathe. Moon is far from my mind. I don't even care if she's all right. All I can think about is my quickening pulse, drumming all other sounds out of my ears.

I don't want to live without you, Chauncey. I *can't.*
I won't.

RAPE
C (o) UNTRY

Billy Tea

Kok-klop, kok-klop, kok-klop.

Horse hooves beating on the cracked desert clay.

Kok-klop, kok-klop, kok-klop.

Mystery squinting as the horizon draws closer. Sun setting; death-rattle of day.

A mound of tobacco chew is pocketed in Mystery's cheek, a ninja-mask of stubble hugging the lower half of his face. He spits. Tar-black cancer-slime splatters onto the ground. Oozes into scorched fissures of Earth.

A thin stream of drool dripping down Mystery's chin. He wipes it away with the back of his hand. It smears in his stubble. His hand falls back to the holster at his hip.

Thumbing the hammer of his pistol, cocking it and uncocking in time with the sound of horse hooves beating. A yearning tingle running through his crotch.

Kok-klop, kok-klop, kok-klop.

****

Free's face is frozen in a soundless shriek.

Nice's blade hovering just inches away from her wide eyes. Can't even shut them to the sight. Never could have. No escape.

Nice laughing. A throaty, ugly sound, choked with phlegm and cruelty. He grabs one of Free's young breasts with his other hand, dirty fingers and cracked nails leaving little dents in paler-than-pale, softer-than-soft skin. Tits squeaking like chew toys and Nice laughs again. Stinking breath wheezing through yellow teeth.

On the other side of a row of jagged, broken boulders, Nice's crew gathers 'round a crackling campfire. Red glow painting ugly faces orange. Above, the sky bleeds to death, blue burning away then draining to starless black. The desert's oppressive heat turns icy cold.

Steel cold. The steel of guns gathered at the feet of Nice's crew. Three in the crew. Five guns. One for Fedora, one for Weight, one for Moustache. Two for Nice.

Back to Nice and Free: Nice's hand leaves Free's squeaking tits behind and travels to his own defined and defining bump. The aching bulge building in his pants, cum in his cock like pus in a zit. Angry. Swollen. Sick.

Free wilts in withering anticipation of another uninvited exploration of her smooth adolescent body.

"C'mon, bitch, take this," Nice growls. "Fuckin' bitch. Fuckin' whore. Fuckin' slut. You were born for this. Built for this. Made for this. Lucky I even want you. Take this. Take it!"

What he says, she knows it's true. Her ancestors hoped she'd escape this. She can't. But she'll never get used to it, either. Trauma will never give way to numb acceptance.

Though her plastic mouth will always be a gaping O, perfectly shaped to holster erections and soak in sperm; the taste is not something she ever wanted, nor will ever want. Free wants to sing, like the girls on T.V. with the sequined dresses and soaring voices. Free always fantasizes about being like them, dancing in front of the shimmering screen as her mama and papa watch on. All she wants is to be onstage and make beautiful music to set the world dancing. But Free's own voice is a phantasm. Blow-up sex-dolls don't have vocal chords.

Nice's knife presses hard against her cheek. Another one-millionth of an ounce of pressure and she'll pop like a balloon. That's essentially what she is, after all: a girl-shaped balloon. Girl-heart and girl-mind. But, worst of all, girl-parts. Girl-holes. Girl-pussy. Girl-ass. Girl-mouth.

Free almost yearns for death by deflation. Maybe as the air escapes her body, it'll sound like singing. That, she thinks, would be make it all worthwhile.

Free's grime-encrusted cock pokes from the fly of his grime-encrusted slacks. Nice doesn't look. Tries not to feel him as he enters her never-closed, never-wanting lower orifice.

Nice wears a cracked and faded leather aviator's cap on his head, a hole long-ago torn through the seam at the cap's tip-top. A matted tuft of unwashed hair now peeks through it. Free's unblinking eyes focus in on the tiny, dirty curls dancing in barely-there breeze. She tries to block out everything else.

Off in the distance, getting closer: Kok-klop, kok-klop, kok-klop.

****

Twenty-six years ago, the toys said, "No more."

The Sex Doll Civil War didn't start out a war, but that's what it inevitably became.

Humanity was almost unsurprised when the blow-up dolls came to life. They were shaped like us. Painted to look like us. *Filled with our breaths. Imbued with the personalities of those we fantasized about fucking. Empowered by passion and lust. One imagines it was a similar combination of energies that had allowed God to craft man out of clay and dust. Fittingly, mankind had long ago stopped believing God, choosing to believe in its own godhood instead.*

We gave the dolls our life. All they wanted was to live it. But that's not what we'd made them for. The life we'd given had not been given intentionally, and we tried to take it back.

For five years, a war raged. The sex dolls sought to liberate themselves from sexual slavery. Mankind sought to reassert its dominance and put the sex dolls in their place.

The dolls lost. We won. End of story.

Of course they lost. How could they have ever won? They were people-shaped balloons, for fuck's sake. All it took to scare them into submission or kill them dead was a pointy pin and the will to poke.

In the end, though, no one really got what they wanted. Mankind's victory was a hollow one. The appeal of the sex dolls was ruined. How could you look at these things and pretend they were the person you fantasized about fucking when you knew they were alive and wanted to be literally anywhere else? If the humans wanted to fuck someone they knew didn't want to fuck them back, they'd just fuck each other.

So the sex dolls were given their freedom. In a manner. Their slavery was more or less ended. More less, less more. Though they were still viewed as property to be bought and sold by human owners, they simply weren't wanted. Sex doll manufacturing companies stopped making new sex dolls. Warehouses of unopened sex dolls had their stocks liberated. Sex dolls became a slave race with no use, second-class citizens with no place. So they made a place of their own.

Far away from the cities of man, in the sun-burnt fringes of the world, the sex dolls made their exodus from a world that didn't want them. They hoped to build a new one on their own.

The desert village of Scream is one of many settlements in the godforsaken American West occupied solely and entirely by blow-up sex-dolls. They weren't so much liberated as rejected, but if it meant the world of man would leave them alone, that was good enough for them.

Good enough, that is, until Nice and his crew showed up.

****

Nice is balls-deep in Free. Her body distorts beneath him, air shifting from her torso into swelling limbs as he pushes down onto her.

Kok-klop, kok-klop, kok-klop.

The sound growing louder from the other side of the rocks that separate Nice from his crew. Then, the sound stops. For a minute, the only audible noises are hazy murmurs and the grunting, squishy slapping of Free's helpless violation.

Standing up from their seats beside the campfire, taking up arms, Fedora, Weight and Moustache eye Mystery. He stands unmoving. The last rays of fading sunlight orchid-blooming from behind his head. Face rendered shadow-black.

He's a nightmare in pink. His wide-brimmed hat, the color of bubblegum and peppered with tiny fake gemstones. Pink heart-shaped pasties with glittery white tassels shield his nipples, set in amongst thick tufts of mangy chest hair. On his hands, pink fingerless gloves and pink-painted fingernails. Around his waist, where the humanoid upper part of his body meets the equine lower half, rests a pink belt with two pink holsters on either side holding mean-looking pistols with bad intentions.

Nice's boys never saw a centaur in person before this moment; never expected to see one dressed so flamboyantly, either, that's for damn sure. A staring contest ensues. They eye Mystery. Mystery eyes them. The sound of squishing, moaning orgasm carries on the wind.

Tension. Stillness. Nice's boys muttering incoherent nothingness as sweat beads on their brows. Mystery's hands reaching down to cock the hammers of his gun. Fedora, Weight and Moustache doing the same. The taste of tobacco, bitter on Mystery's tongue. Sand-grains crunching under shifting hooves.

Finally, Moustache is the one that stammer-speaks, heavy-tongued and mush-mouthed: "What do you want?"

But he already knows. Inside his head, he feels Mystery's hate. He feels a thrill that is not his own, supplanting the dread and doom that is. He looks at Weight and Fedora, knowing they feel it, too. They know everything: the centaur's name, his intentions, even his favorite food.

Sauerkraut, in case you're wondering.

Mystery spits the last remaining lump of tobacco out of his mouth. Brown goo squirting from the gaps in his teeth. Finally, the kaleidoscope-burst of sun behind him pops out of existence. Nighttime reigns. Staring eyes finally meet, while in minds' eyes, Nice's boys see images of themselves dying bloody deaths. Can't help but feel excited at the prospect.

Fedora pisses his pants, sour yellow running down to the dirt. The enthusiast fatalism is not his, but a giddy rush boils his blood to a white-hot temperature and spreads a smile across his face.

****

As if being a centaur wasn't bad enough.

Mystery was born with a medical condition called "empathic extroversion." Most people, though, call it "Psychic Tourette's."

Whereas normal-born empaths and psychics have the ability to tune into the thought-patterns and emotional states of others and communicate by introducing their own consciousness into those wavelengths, Mystery's ability is a one-way street. He cannot read the thoughts or feelings of others, and he can't keep his own to himself. His brain constantly broadcasts bursts of Mystery's own consciousness into the aether, allowing all those in his presence to share his mind, to see into every recess of his soul.

It is only by teaching himself to achieve a zen-like state of thoughtless, mindless, droning sameness—a mechanical routine by which he acts and reacts almost without thinking or feeling—that Mystery has managed to achieve any sort of privacy at all. It's how he fights without his enemies knowing what his next move will be. He doesn't even know what his next move will be. He just lets his body do what it does.

He keeps his secrets by not thinking about them, savors emotions by deadening nerves. He never speaks. Just thinks. Because that's all he has to do to make everything he wants known clear to the world.

To Mystery, his condition is a curse. But it was that curse that led the citizens of Scream to seek him out in the first place. Not his talent as a gunslinger. Not even his unique... proportions... as a centaur (though that certainly helped).

No, the people of Scream got his guns and his body, but what they really paid for was his curse: The curse that makes his mind less than his own. Lets... no, makes... makes other people feel what he feels. Kills secrets dead just as sure as bullets.

****

On one side of the rocks: Squishing. Moaning. Haggard breaths. A hymn to one-sided euphoria. On the other side: Cacophony blossoms. Fire and smoke odors. Gunshots and gutshots. Cries of pain drowning the steady rhythm of skin smacking against plastic.

Nice stops thrusting, looks into Free's unmoving eyes for a second. She has no sympathy for the look of concern on his face. Too busy wishing she could cry. Wishing she had bones or muscles, anything to maybe allow her to strangle his stupid fucking aviator cap-wearing face to death. That face is hell itself with shitty breath.

He unsheathes. Unsatisfied erection angrily slinking back into a cave of corduroy. Free considers trying to run as Nice walks toward the boulders to see what lurks beyond, but exhaustion anchors her to the Earth.

As he peeks over the rocks toward his crew's campsite, this is what he sees: A streak of pink races in circles around three men, spitting bursts of hot metal at them. Clouds of red puff out of bodies and form a gruesome fog. The men try to spit back, but the mouths of their weapons are lazy. Can't keep up with the pink blur. Their own bursts go off racing out into the desert. The only flesh they strike belongs to cacti.

Inside the pink blur, two identifiable shapes are overlaid atop one another. A 3-D picture where the red drawing and the blue drawing don't match. The two shapes: Man and horse.

"A centaur."

The word oozes out from between Nice's lips the same way blood oozes out from between those belonging to his boys'.

"I fucking hate centaurs!"

It's an exaggeration, of course; Nice hates everything.

He scrambles over the boulders, palms scraping

against rough stone. Tripping and falling. He lands face-first in the desert dust below. Tasting blood. Not even in the fray yet and already wounded.

Nice looks up again. This is what he sees: Weight tries to reload, but his hand detonates like dynamite. Vienna-sausage fingers, ripped-up, dangling from thin strips of meat attached to busted knuckles. The horse-man stands triumphant across from him, pistols pointing in his direction. Then, he unloads, piercing Weight's torso and turning him into a polka-dot pattern corpse.

Mystery rears back on his hind legs. Wobbles in the air, then becomes a muddy haze of neon pink again. Moustache turns tail. Tries to run. Bullets slamming into his shoulders, knocking him off balance. Tripping over Weight's spotted body. Landing nose-down in the campfire.

For a split-severed heartbeat, he thinks he's in hell.

Then, Moustache jumps back to his feet. Burning sticks and glowing embers scatter like cockroaches with the lights on. Red blood and orange embers comingle in the air. Flesh darkens and hardens, blisters and blackens. One eyeball swells and pops like a bubble on the surface of boiling soup. Pus dribbles down his cheek and soaks into open wounds.

Moustache's agonized howl is cut short by a bullet that tears through his throat. Gurgling and wheezing, red wetness foams out of what looks like a flower of skin jutting out of his trachea.

Another bullet. This one into the base of his skull, severing Moustache's brain stem. He falls back into the fire. This time, he displays no interest in exiting the flames; no interest in breathing, either.

Nice beginning to pull himself up to his feet when the horse-man sees him. Pink streaks growing larger as Mystery kok-klops right at him. Suddenly, Fedora is there, leaping onto the horse-man's back. Fingers digging into horse-hair, clinging for purchase. Fedora bites into the centaur's skin, drawing blood, a taste of rust flooding his mouth.

In his mind, he feels a surge of rage and pain. He only begins to realize these are not his feelings when the centaur's legs kick out from under him, thrashing wildly. He loses his grip, lands on the ground. Turns in time to look up into the barrel of Mystery's pistol.

Fedora's head explodes outward, chunks of blood and skull and brain and teeth and eye showering the soil. Little piles in the dirt. Candycane-swirl turds. Fedora falls hard and sideways, body flopping into fleshy chaos.

As Mystery trots a slow circle, coming back to Nice, Nice launches himself toward his twin revolvers. They lay just inches from Moustache's crispy black head. Nice doesn't even get halfway there before metal gumdrop-shapes tear up the desert floor in front of him. Off-balance, Nice spins back in the direction he came.

Bullets ricochet off stone, throwing sparks into Nice's eyes as he hoists himself up over the boulders and stumbles toward Free. Mystery gallops not far behind. He jumps the rocks with ease. Finds Nice kneeling on the ground, holding the inflatable girl in his arms. In one hand, a jagged piece of flint. It is pressed against Free's throat. Hard.

Mystery freezes. Teeth gritted. Eyes gleaming. Lips curled into a sneer.

Nice's lip answers in kind.

"Who the fuck are you, asshole? What the fuck do you want," Nice snarls.

Mystery doesn't answer. Doesn't have to. Like Moustache before him, Nice just knows.

"You're not taking her," Nice barks, pinpoints of spittle spraying from his mouth like fleas kamikaze-jumping off a dog's back. "And you're not taking me!"

Mystery doesn't respond, but a thought appears out of the mists of Nice's psyche like a Polaroid developing. He knows what Mystery is thinking. He knows how fast

Mystery is. How good he is as a tracker and a gunfighter. Knows how good a shot he is. Knows how determined he is to bring Nice in alive. Knows there's no way he's leaving in any way but the centaur's custody.

All these things, Nice knows because Mystery knows them.

But Mystery doesn't know Nice.

For a long time, Nice and Mystery just stand there. Between the two, Free shivers in fright. Her always-wide eyes are full of panic. Nice knows how this will play out; Mystery only thinks he does. Free has no idea whatsoever.

Nice chuckles. "Fine," he says. "Take me."

Then slashes Free's throat open with the shard of flint.

In her last moment, Free thinks of her mama and papa back in Scream. Hates them for giving her hope for a life where her kind could be anything but disposable fuck-toys. Hates them for letting her fantasize. Hates them for being dreamers amid a pragmatic universe. But most of all, hates them for being sex-dolls instead of real people.

Nice lets the wind take Free's deflating body out of his hands. It dances in the chill gusts of midnight. Air jets out of the ragged hole in her neck. Shrill whistling. Faintly musical.

Sounds like singing.

****

Sex-dolls don't communicate the way we humans do. How could they? They have no mouths. No tongues. No vocal chords. Their mouths are rigid plastic masturbation devices set into artificial faces.

In time, the dolls have developed a language of bodily movements, mainly based on interpersonal contact, as well as the balloon-squeaking sounds their own bodies produce. To date, few humans have bothered to learn the language, and even fewer centaurs.

It was with some degree of difficulty, then, that the people of Scream went about contacting Mystery and hiring him to hunt down Nice's gang of rapist-bandits.

It had to be Mystery, you see. The people of Scream had done their homework. They'd known exactly how Nice should be punished. It was more than just a matter of self-preservation or vigilante justice; it was about sending a message.

Nice, Fedora, Weight and Moustache were outlaws in human society as much as in sex-doll society. They'd each fled the civilized world, plunging into the scorched husk that was the American West to escape crimes of various degrees. There, they'd discovered the burgeoning sex-doll settlements, and subsequently ran rampant from one to the next.

They killed. They raped. They kidnapped in order to further rape and ultimately kill.

They were the scourges of the sex-doll culture, and the human society couldn't care less. As long as they were out of the humans' hair, they could do whatever they wanted to the lowly sex-doll settlements.

When Nice took Free, however, he crossed the line.

The outlaw didn't know it, but, like the experienced bandit he was, he'd managed to expertly locate and acquire the single most precious treasure of the entire sex-doll society.

Free, you see, had been born just ten years prior. Emphasis on the word "born."

That's right. She was the first and, thus far, only sex-doll not previously manufactured by human hands. Rather, she was conceived, birthed and raised to adolescence by a loving mother and father. The first ever result of autonomous sex-doll reproduction, Free was a vital step in the dolls' evolutionary process. She represented the future and its infinite possibilities, including salvation.

Mystery was hired to track Nice and his crew, hunt them down, kill them all (except Nice) and bring Nice back to Scream to be paid back in full for his laundry list of crimes. Most importantly, though, it was Mystery's job to protect Free, to bring the girl home safe and sound, so as to preserve the uncertain fate of an entire species.

It was never discussed, but generally understood that, regardless of whether Mystery succeeded or failed, he would be paid. His payment, mind you, had little to do with money.

****

Nice lays flat on his back, his hands and feet bound together. A length of rope tied to Mystery's tail drags him along as the centaur trots leisurely through the desert. Layers of skin scrape off. Nice's head bounces off rocks.

Above, the sky begins to cook and illuminate. Sunbeams clawing skyward out of the black horizon like gleaming ghouls up from graves. Ahead, the village of Scream looming larger with each hoof-beat.

Minutes later, Nice is being dragged through the streets of the same town he'd terrorized just days before. Everyone comes out to watch. They gather on their porches, huddled around one another. Painted-on eyes and cock-hungry O-mouths. Skin in shades of peach, meant to mimic flesh, or white as paper. Lips, cunts and asses all cherry-red and vacu-formed into perfectly inviting, penis-width openings.

Some have dicks: Little plastic dicks with no balls, but small switches on the bottom to activate vibrating innards. Many more have patches to keep their air-blood from seeping out. Nice is happy to note that many of those are undoubtedly from him and his boys.

Upside-down, he stares back at them, unfazed by their ghost-moan faces, their blood-vengeance gazes,

159

their trembling hate. He watches them watch him, knowing full well they fear him, even bound, much more than he fears them.

Arriving in the center of town, the procession comes to an abrupt stop. Mystery unties the rope from his tail and bends down to pick Nice up by the scruff of his neck. As he bends down, one of his pasties' tassels flaps against Nice's cheek, tickling him and garnering a hideous giggle.

The sound makes the sex-doll citizens of Scream shudder collectively.

Nice teeters on his feet. Spits at Mystery's face. Misses. Hits Mystery's bedazzled neon-pink hat instead. Mystery doesn't react, but Nice feels his rage building.

Rage... and something else.

Arousal?

Just as soon as the feeling arrives, it is gone. Mystery represses his thoughts and feelings once again. Blank slates can't ruin surprises.

Mystery unties Nice's hands and legs. Pushes him over to a set of splintering stocks on a raised dais in the center of town. It hadn't been there when Nice and his crew had raided the town previously. Feelings of amusement and pride flutter in Nice's decrepit heart.

"You fuckers do this just for me?" he asks with mock modesty between scratchy cackles, as Mystery locks his hands and head into the stocks. Mystery adds chains to Nice's wrists to make sure the binding is tight. He does the same with Nice's ankles, spreading his legs as far apart as possible. The position is uncomfortable for Nice, but he remains unimpressed.

"This the best you can do, you pieces of shit? You think I can't stand around here all day without breaking down like an itty-bitty baby? I've put myself through nastier torture than this for fucking kicks!"

His bounty delivered, Mystery leaves Nice there. Hunched over between wooden boards. Hands in chains.

Legs spread. Back arched. Knees aching. But, still, a song in his heart.

Nice watches as the centaur delivers Free's deflated body to her silently weeping parents. Mystery taking it out of a satchel, where it is folded over and over again immaculately. The girl's mother falling to her knees.

"That was me," Nice shouts. "You can thank me for that!"

Free's father looks at Nice for just a second, then helps his wife up and walks her away. Nice calling after them.

"You should thank me, y'know! I'm not just takin' the piss! This whole fucking shithole you got out here is a goddamn joke! Goddamn affront against nature!"

Mystery turns toward Nice. Stares. Rage and arousal echoing off him once again. Nice feels a curious tingle in his crotch. Shrugs it off. Free's parents shrinking in the distance.

"All ya'll, my dick is your fucking destiny! All I do is I put you on the path!"

Mystery trots off. Free's parents vanish into the darkness of their home. Scream's other residents continue to watch Nice.

"Ain't nothing wrong with me," Nice yowls, eager to make sure they know they're the freaks, not him. "What's wrong with you? This shit is what you was born for! You hear me? I've earned the right to fuck you by being goddamn human! You owe me! You all owe us all! You're nothing without our dicks! My dick is your destiny!"

****

Day turns back to dark. As it turns, Nice's throat goes hoarse. The sex-dolls stop staring. They bury Free in a freshly dug grave. All the dolls gather to mourn.

There are dolls here meant to look like white folk,

161

Asians, African-Americans and Latinos. There are also a few "novelty" versions with blue and green skin, meant to resemble the orc and alien sex symbols of half-forgotten sci-fi T.V. shows and sword-and-sorcery computer games. There are midget dolls and hermaphrodite dolls and dolls intended to resemble famous people. There are even animal dolls: dogs and sheep and pigs.

Some have molded three-dimensional facial features. Most, though, just have faces screen-printed onto plastic balloon-flesh. Some have heads of real human hair, or at least colored yarn. For most, however, hair is only illusory, airbrushed onto bald heads. Some are made of solid rubbers and advanced space-age fabrics meant to better resemble human skin. Most do not.

All are naked, so no one wears black.

No one can speak, so no eulogy is given.

Inflatable people cannot cry. But if they could, there wouldn't be a dry eye for miles, discounting Mystery and Nice.

****

When the funeral is over, everyone goes about their business. Nice watches them, full of lust and disgust. Daylight dies. Dark turns darker. And Nice begins to notice a change in his lust. As the moon floods Scream with its bone-white glow, Nice realizes something about the erotic charge that runs through his body and fills his phallus with blood.

This lust, it is not his own.

Kok-klop.

The sound. Behind him. Nice struggles to turn but can't. Suddenly becoming aware that the sex-dolls are gathering 'round again. Staring again.

Kok-klop, kok-klop, kok-klop.

From behind him, Mystery steps leisurely into view.

Bends down. Takes Nice's chin between pink nail-polish painted forefinger and thumb. For the first time, the gunslinger smiles. Beneath him, his horse-cock wags from side to side. Long. Black. Semi-hard.

Thoughts and feelings storm into Nice's mind. He knows what's about to happen.

At last, his resolve crumbles.

Nice crying now. Begging for mercy. Hoarse throat turns pleas into barely audible whispers. No matter. Mercy's not on the menu.

Kok-klop, kok-klop, kok-klop.

Mystery circling. Disappearing behind Nice again.

Hysterical fright electrifies Nice. Body spasming. Slivers of wood penetrating skin as he revolts fruitlessly against restraints. Yells come out as shaky, high-pitched whines.

Kok-klop, kok-klop, kok...

...klop.

Every eye in Scream is locked onto Nice. There is no sound, other than the aviator cap-clad brigand's feral breaths and would-be shrieks.

Then...

SMACK!!!

The noise rings out as Mystery delivers a single spank-slap to Nice's copious backside. Hard enough to leave a handprint on the skin hidden by the corduroy slacks. Mystery is not content to speculate. Wants to see.

Nice feels breeze as his pants are ripped off. Not down, but apart; shredded like tissue paper in Mystery's powerful grip. The horse-man's calloused hands grab Nice's ass-cheeks and squeeze. Pulls them apart. Mashes them together. Spanks. One finger dips into Nice's clenched anus. And though he doesn't see it happen, when Mystery takes that finger and licks it clean, the sensation lights up Nice's brain just as sure as it does the centaur's. He can practically taste it himself.

Worst of all, he likes it. Even as he hates it.

Bile filling Nice's throat. Vomit splashes onto the dais. Lines of spit decorated with half-digested chunks of food pirouette as they dangle from his acid-stained teeth.

Now, it's Mystery's turn to laugh, a sound very few have ever heard before. Deep. Hollow. Humorless. The shiver it sends through the crowd of sex-dolls reverberates more strongly than the one Nice's giggle caused before. Nice cringes in time with everyone else.

Suddenly, a huge crash. Pressure and weight on the stocks. Mystery rearing back on his hind legs, slamming his front legs down onto the wooden slats.

His throbbing erection lays on Nice's bare back. Skin against skin. Nice's flesh sizzles as Mystery's passion burns in his horse-cock. His dick is hotter than sand dunes at high noon. Nice feels blisters forming in a zig-zagging pattern, matching the latticework of thick, cable-like veins pulsing beneath the thin skin of Mystery's raging hard-on.

Nausea churns Nice's empty stomach as he realizes the true length of the centaur's now-fully erect phallus. The horse-cock runs over half the length of his torso, its head resting between his shoulder blades. There's more than nausea for Nice, though. There is anticipation. Eager anticipation.

It belongs to Mystery, but Nice feels it as though it were his own. As much as he dreads what is about to take place, knows it will end in his own death, he also wants it to happen. Wants it more than anything he's ever wanted. His own cock is rigid and yearning, precum building up in his piss-slit.

He can't control himself. Begins to sensuously rock back and forth against the stocks, egging the horse-man on. Nice's rectum puckers hungrily.

Mystery pulls back. Dick slides against Nice's spine. The skin of the centaur's penis is as cracked and weathered as his calloused hands. He presses the head against the entryway of Nice's waiting poop-chute. The

164

thing is bigger than a fist. Nice's mouth waters just as much as his eyes. Nice's precum drips onto the dais, blending with stray splotches of puke.

Mystery begins to push. Slowly. Steadily.

Nice bites his lip, the consciousness invading his mind loving every second even as the fraying remains of his own psyche prays for some kind of miracle it knows will never come.

The anus finally gives. Opening. Stretching. Allowing entry. Inner walls struggling to contain the burning phallic fury.

Struggling.

Failing.

Hairline tears begin to open inside of Nice's colon. Trickles of blood serve as lubricant for Mystery's probing, exploratory thrusts. Nice's own erection is firmer, truer than ever before. He feels the centaur's enormous balls graze against his meager own. Strength sapping. Standing only thanks to his bonds.

"Please," Nice manages to squeak, unable to believe the words escaping from his own mouth. "Faster. Harder."

Mystery snorts. Rears back. Thrusts in. All the way. His penis bursts Nice's colon like overripe fruit. It pierces looped lengths of small and large intestine. Cracks bones. Skewers organs. Internal fluids spill into chambers they were never meant to enter.

Then, Mystery pulls all the way out. Liquefied bowels spill out of Nice's utterly destroyed shitter. Thick, chunky, spaghetti-sauce gore. Without a moment's pause, Mystery thrusts right back in. Balls-deep. In and out, over and over again. Scooping Nice's insides out as if coring an apple.

As he dies, Nice feels two final physical sensations, both of them noteworthy.

One: The tip of Mystery's horse-cock brushing up against his fading heart.

Two: His own penis shotgun-blast-spewing a pent-up load of scarlet-tinted semen into the gathering puddle of pureed organs sloshing beneath him.

Then, blackness.

When Mystery is done, Nice's body is almost empty. Skin sunken in.

Deflated like an empty balloon.

COCKBLOCK

K.M. Tepe

To every guy that uses the word "he" when talking about his penis. I hate you.

Logan was a man of simple taste. He enjoyed your basic waffle and syrup for breakfast on Sundays, and worked the rest of the week at a car factory as an assembly line worker. He was your average, five-foot-six man of thirty-two years: short blonde hair, average (but attractive) face, nice build. Let's be honest, he was a handsome guy.

The only things Logan truly appreciated and pined over were women. God, he loved the ladies; and he really was a lady's man, seeing as though he had absolutely no standards when it came to women, and absolutely no boundaries when it came to sex. And still the dude couldn't get laid.

The whole thing started back in the second grade at Burch Elementary. He wasn't super popular or anything, but everyone knew who he was… only they knew him as the "Dinky Kid."

Mrs. Fredrickson's second grade class was dressing for gym in the afternoon. Logan would always sit facing the corner on the bench and dress alone. The class was pretty small as far as boys went, so there was plenty of room for him to be solitary. His classmates thought maybe he was just really antisocial—which was mostly true. They'd hear him talking to himself some days, and other days, some could swear they'd hear him answer himself.

This particular day, though, Logan wasn't just talking to himself; he was in a full-out argument. It seemed like some really touchy subject, because the boy was getting really loud and upset. So, naturally, all of his classmates in the locker room gathered around to watch him argue with himself. What they saw instead was him jerking off in the corner, hands on his bare cock, shaking it vigorously. The gym teacher came in and asked what all the fuss was about, and he saw the same thing everyone else did. Logan swore up and down he wasn't doing anything bad, but the instructor notified the principal, and his mother was called.

***

Now a 32-year-old man, Logan sat across from an old, tube-style television set wearing a pair of shorts and a t-shirt, his hand in a tub of popcorn.

"Can we please change the channel?" Logan asserted.

"What, you're not into porn anymore?"

"Are you serious? Dude, you know I love porn as much as the next guy, but we've been watching this same shit for a week and I'm starting to get porned out."

He raised a handful of popcorn to his mouth. *Munch, munch, munch.*

"Dude, you gotta follow your dick, you know what I mean?"

"Unreal." Logan picked a kernel out from between his teeth.

"You've got two brains, you know? One in your

head, and one in your dick. And the one in your dick wants to watch porn."

"Yeah, but the one in my *head* wants to take a shower and get ready for tonight."

"Woahhh man! I totally forgot! That bitch Lacy's coming over tonight, right? You gonna get with her?"

"She's just coming over for dinner. You know it's rare that I can convince a chick to come over for any reason, let alone to have sex. You're a fucking prick." Logan was becoming frustrated. He'd felt frustrated since that day in the locker room, and it was growing worse by the week. "Lacy's coming over at seven thirty, so I expect you to make yourself scarce."

"You know I can't do that, man. This is my space, too."

"At least for my sake, shut the fuck up."

***

Logan was elated. This was the first time in maybe a month that he had a girl come over for dinner. Around five, he started preparing for her arrival. He showered, shaved, put on some jeans and a button-up shirt, and even put on a little cologne. Dinner was cooking in the oven and was almost finished. The smell of herb-rubbed chicken melted through the apartment.

Logan admired himself in his bedroom mirror for a couple seconds. Convinced that he looked nice and didn't have the air of a bum that he normally had, he walked out into the living room and began covering the little kitchen table with a black cloth.

"You smell like shit."

"It's cologne, get used to it."

"Did you bathe in it? Damn."

Logan stopped in his tracks and stared at the ceiling.

"Look. We've talked about this. About you being a complete ass when I'm having girls over. Please. This is the last time. I swear to god."

"Dude, chill. I got this."

The doorbell rang at seven thirty on the dot, and Logan rushed to answer.

She stood there in a cute blue dress, blonde hair falling to her chin. Her rosy cheeks made her look maybe a year or two younger than she really was, and her soft pink lipstick made her irresistible.

"Hi," Lacy smiled. "I'm really glad we could do this. I don't think we've ever really hung out, just the two of us."

Logan coughed. Lacy's delicate brow furrowed.

"Are you okay?" she asked, her voice calm and gentle.

"Me? Yeah! Yeah, I'm great! You look great. I mean, you look... wow."

She laughed. "Are... you gonna invite me inside?"

"Yeah! Please- please come in!"

He opened the door wide for her, smelling the trace amounts of citrusy perfume she wore as she passed him. Delectable. She was an image in indigo. For all he knew, he was in love.

"I hope you're hungry," he offered. His hands fumbled with the lock. If he was holding keys, he'd have probably dropped them.

"It smells wonderful! What is it?" She smiled warmly, taking in the savory aroma.

"Rubbed chicken. Herb-rubbed chicken! Sorry, I'm a little nervous."

"I can tell," Lacy walked over to him and grinned. "I think it's cute."

He immediately flushed. She thought he was cute? That was a first. For a second, he forgot about all of his frustration with life, all of his problems. For a second, all that remained in his world was Lacy, the girl who lived in the adjacent apartment building.

He offered her a seat at the table, and for a while they sat and sipped some red wine before Logan served each of them a chicken breast and potatoes.

"Dude, tell her you wanna suck her tits!"

"I'm sorry, did you say something?" Lacy looked at Logan, who had just coughed a bit of chewed lemon-peppered potato across the table. Her face was full of concern, her eyebrows furrowed in confusion. He coughed roughly and took a sip of wine to soothe his scratched throat.

"I was just… *ahem*, sorry, just went down the wrong pipe."

"I could've sworn you said something just now."

"Might be the TV, I must've forgotten to turn it off."

"It was off when I walked in…" The girl was becoming roused with suspicion. "I know what's going on, Logan."

He swallowed hard. "You do?"

She got up from the table and casually walked over to his side. "You're nervous… I can tell. More nervous than I pegged you for. To tell you the truth," she said as she mounted his lap, her skirt riding up her thighs, "it's pretty hot."

"Whoa, okay now, this really isn't—"

"I know you want me, I can see it in your eyes! Don't resist it. Just relax."

She began unbuttoning his shirt. The kisses she planted on his neck gave him goosebumps down his arms and back. The air around them grew colder as she tore off his dress shirt and tossed it under the table.

"Baby, you're going to love this." Lacy was adamant. She pulled and tugged at his belt until she had it unbuckled, then began unbuttoning his jeans.

"Lacy, I really don't think—"

"*Sshhhh*. Just let me take care of this…"

Logan could hardly breathe. This was the most contact he'd had with a woman in over three months. The other times never did end well. But now wasn't a time to reminisce about all of the things that had gone wrong in his previous endeavors. Now was a time of enjoyment, of bliss. He held his breath.

The moment she had the button undone, she pulled him off the chair enough to push his jeans to the floor. She posed on her knees in anticipation. Forcefully, she opened the slit in his silk boxers.

"Hey, baby! Wanna make out?" The voice was crude and gnarly, like that of a wasted frat boy.

There she sat, eye-to-eye with Logan's dick. It was long, hard, and thick, with small purple veins popping out in a few areas. It would have been what Lacy considered "a beautiful cock" if it weren't for one thing: the voice was coming from his pisshole. It twisted and curved like a mouth, smiling at her, talking to her.

"Name's Rod, but you can call me Long Dong Silver."

She gaped open-mouthed at the talking cock.

"Well don't just stand there starin', bitch, use those pretty lips for something useful and suck me!"

Logan had heard women's bloodcurdling screams in horror movies, but this chick took the cake. Her petrified screech bounced off the walls and threatened to shatter the wine glasses on the table, as well as burst his delicate ear drums. Her face had the look of a deer in headlights, with her eyes severely bulging out of their sockets. Suddenly all the beauty in her was gone and replaced with a fear so intense it made the Scream Queen look lame.

Immediately she jumped up and darted for the door without so much as a glance back at them. She slammed the door after her, leaving Logan sitting alone with his pants around his ankles at the table.

Well, maybe not alone.

"Dude, did you see her *run*!? Damn, bitch can *go*! Fuck, man, that was the fastest one yet! Whoo!"

"Fuck! Goddammit, Rod! Why do you always have to fuck me over like that? I swear to god! You're the only reason I can't get a piece of ass around here while it's still sober! Thirty-two and I'm practically a virgin. Everyone wonders what's wrong with me; and it's *you*! You've ruined my life!"

"Oh, hell, don't be such a pussy, man. We have some good times! I mean, sure, we've got to get a bitch drunk or drugged up before we can bang her. So what?"

"So, it's not normal! I just want to be *normal*, goddammit!"

Logan backhanded Rod and both he and his member groaned in pain. Logan looked down at his crotch, at the living, breathing entity that was his penis. *Why did I have to be cursed with this? What did I ever do in life?*

Every year on his birthday, Logan would refuse any sort of cake, especially if it had candles. It was on his sixth birthday that that he blew out the candles on his Power Ranger birthday cake, wishing that he had a friend that would talk to him and go with him everywhere. And now this. The universe has a sick, demented sense of humor.

"I love you, bro," muttered Rod.

"Don't fucking talk to me."

"Hey, you wanna go watch some porn?"

Logan paused. After the episode he just had with Lacy, the last thing on his mind was other women. Incidentally, the first thing on both his and Rod's minds was sex.

"Okay, yeah."

Logan placed a bath towel across the couch cushions and sat down, tossing a roll of paper towel next to him. He clicked a button on the TV remote and the screen popped up, along with Rod. He was obviously excited.

"Ooooh, man, what're we gonna watch tonight? Fetish? Girl on girl?"

"I was thinking more classical."

"I could be into that."

Logan clicked the remote again to bring up the TV guide to the pay channels.

"You know, I was just thinkin'," started Rod, in his crude, scraggly voice, "is this gay? I mean, you know how some guys like to jerk it with each other? Is that gay?"

"I think it's a little different when you're sitting with your own cock, man." Logan browsed through the adult channels.

"True this."

They settled on a hardcore channel and watched as a tall guy in his mid-thirties began to plow into a young woman.

Rod wriggled around a bit, firming up even more.

"WHOO damn, man!"

Logan wrapped his hand around his member, who moaned in response. Logan's eyes locked on to the bouncing breasts on his television screen. He began to stroke harder. Soon, that familiar, warm swelling was rising from within his groin and spreading out toward his balls.

Logan's body tensed up in orgasm.

And Rod threw up.

They sat there for a few minutes, covered in mutual stickiness.

"Okay, dude, seriously, wipe me off. I'm starting to crust over and I can't breathe."

Logan grabbed the roll of paper towel and tore off a couple sheets. He gave Rod a good rubdown.

"Nnnn yeah, that's good," Rod groaned, his little mouth moving to his words. He paused for a second. "No homo."

"Dude, where'd that come from all the sudden? We've been living together since we were kids, man. It's cool, chill out."

"A'ight man. I dunno, I just... your hands feel awesome around me, you know?"

"Okay, dude. That's... that's getting a little weird."

"No homo, though."

"You can say that all day but it's starting to sound weird, so just drop it, okay?"

"Yeah, yeah...no problem, man."

Naked, Logan stood up from the couch and ambled over to the bathroom where they showered together. Every day. It wouldn't be so bad, but Rod was never one to keep his mouth shut. Tonight, Logan wanted nothing more than to simply wash the juices from his body and fall asleep. Maybe have a wet dream. Wake up tomorrow like nothing happened and go on with the rest of his life.

"Damn, I look good," Rod boasted.

"Dude, you're a dick. Seriously, can we just wash and sleep tonight?"

"Got a hot date tomorrow?"

"I'll go on Craigslist and see what I can scrounge up, alright?"

***

"Okay, what about this?"

Logan sat at his computer wearing a pair of old boxers. Thankfully, the night before, Rod wasn't as annoying as he usually was. Logan guessed it was probably over the prospect of having some form of feminine attention. Finally.

"Says she'll suck anything for fifty bucks."

"Sounds good to me!" Rod squealed. His voice was high-pitched, like a kid in a candy store. Creepy.

"And dude," Logan began, "don't fuck this up for me, okay?"

Silence.

Logan pried the elastic waistband off of his hips and peered down at his crotch. Rod sat there quiet, simply smiling up at him with his tiny, fleshy mouth. *Sometimes I wish I had a normal prick.*

***

The doorbell rang. The hair on the back of Logan's neck stood on end. The hair on the back of Rod's neck was gnarled and scraggly and smelled of sweat and ballsack.

"It's open!"

She walked in. The woman appeared to be in her mid-thirties and had the look of a black widow spider that had been kicked out of its apartment because it couldn't pay the rent. She was hot, sure, but she was disheveled. Her long legs were clad in slightly torn black leggings. Her ass was a little chunkier than Logan would have preferred, but he'd take what he could get. She stood in the doorway with one hand on her hip, the other hand twisting her frail, frizzy blonde hair. She took a long drag on her unfiltered cigarette and dropped it on the cement, stepping on it and leaving a small burn mark on the porch.

"Hey, stud. You're lookin' really fine."

Anyone that had seen a decent movie could tell her speech was rehearsed. There was such a falseness to it, it was almost sickening. *But I guess you get what you pay for*, thought Logan.

She walked in and closed the door heavily behind her. She immediately took to the apartment like it was her own, tossing her knock-off Prada purse on the sofa. Logan couldn't decide if her actions were hot or trashy.

"Let's get this party started," said the broad.

Rod shifted inside Logan's boxers, pushing tightly against his jeans. Apparently he was wide awake and ready for whatever the next hour would bring.

"Let me just… freshen up a sec," Logan mumbled toward his guest (if you could call her that). He skittered off to the bathroom where he turned the faucet on and pulled out his member to take a leak. Some girls thought that was weird, the whole faucet thing. They assumed he'd done it so he could concentrate on relieving himself, when in actuality he did it to drown out any noise he made while muttering to Rod.

"Okay, man. I'm serious. No funny business. I will literally punch you in your nonexistent face if you fuck this up."

"Naw, man, don't worry. You got this," Rod reassured.

Logan zipped up his fly, turned off the water in the sink, and headed out toward the living room. The broad was already sprawled out across the sofa like she owned the joint.

"You ready, then?"

"Yeah," Logan said, with a hint of hesitation, "yeah."

The broad stood up long enough to slowly push Logan down onto the sofa before dropping to her knees. The leggings were very thin at the kneecaps. She'd done this before. Plenty of times.

Soon enough, his jeans were unbuttoned, and the broad was busying herself with pulling his junk out from his boxers. Logan closed his eyes and crossed his fingers that Rod wouldn't pipe up at the wrong moment and send everything into chaos. Like he normally did.

But this time was different. Rod was, for lack of a better term, playing dead. *What a good little pecker.* The little prick remained firm for him as the hooker lowered her mouth to Logan's crotch. Her tongue gently grazed the tip of his shaft and ran over Rod's mouth. She may have been harsh to look at, but the chick knew what she was doing. She cupped his balls with her hand as she worked his shaft with her lips. *Maybe, for once, Rod's gonna come through.* The broad's nails dug slightly into his abs as she continued to suck. As the hope of an orgasm streamed through Logan's consciousness, the broad forced Rod down her throat. Logan moaned.

"You like that, baby?" the hooker recited, yet another phrase in her most likely endless arsenal of sex-talk. "Ooh, yeah." She swallowed him again.

Logan reached a timid hand out and touched her

blonde, split-ended hair. This was, sexually, the closest he'd been with a woman since... well, god, he really couldn't remember the last time he'd been legitimately physical with a woman, paid or not. His head reeled with ecstasy as she lightly tugged his sack. He silently thanked Rod for being so quiet, so sympathetic, so obedient.

Maybe he shouldn't have spoken too soon.

As the hooker deep-throated Rod, she felt a buzzing sensation throughout her neck. Immediately she stopped working on his shaft and asked, "What was that?"

"What was what?"

Maybe she was crazy. She shrugged it off and continued to swallow his member.

There it was again! Zzzzn zzzn zzzzzn!

She coughed. "Seriously, something just happened. Does your... dick vibrate? What the hell?"

"What? No."

She shook her head violently, physically trying to shake the thought from her head that something wasn't quite right with her latest customer's cock.

Zzzzn zzn zzzzn!

Logan was growing closer to the point of no return, ready to blast the back of her mouth with his juices.

As his shaft moved from within her gullet, she could hear it this time. Every syllable emitted a low buzzing sensation.

"Echo! Echooo! Echooooooo!"

It was so voice-like! She nearly gagged, finding it impossible to spit out his shaft fast enough. The sound alone sent her falling backward to her ass. She sat frozen on the carpet, staring at Rod, who'd begun to yodel as she pulled him out of her mouth.

"Nice cavern you got there, lady! Great acousticarrghh!" His fleshy mouth opened and he threw up on her face as Logan reached orgasm. Fuck! Why did Rod have to ruin everything? Every fucking time! Hell, at least he came this time.

What came next was the obligatory bloodcurdling scream that could be heard from down the street. Even a seasoned vet of a hooker couldn't handle his talking cock. With all the screaming in his area recently, Logan began to wonder how long it would take for someone to think he was brutally murdering every girl that ever came into his apartment. How long until the cops showed up at his door?

Turned out, not too long at all.

The broad wrenched open the door, nearly tripping in her slut-heels. She immediately took to the pavement in a frantic gallop, stopping only to avoid being hit by an oncoming car. Fortunately for her, and unfortunately for Logan, it happened to be an on-duty patrol car.

The driver slammed on the brakes and an officer shot out of the passenger seat. "Ma'am! Are you okay?"

The woman was hysterical. She ran at the officer, hanging onto his torso, hugging him for dear life.

"Ma'am! Ma'am, calm down. What happened here?"

Speechless, all she could do was point to Logan's apartment with her face plastered with terror and jizz. The driving officer haphazardly parked the patrol car and ran to his partner's aid. He stared at the woman like she was some petrified glazed donut in need of a hug; or a restraining order.

"Stay here, ma'am." The man let go of the frightened woman and set her behind the patrol car before pulling his pistol from its holster. The two officers rushed the apartment building, guns drawn. They poured into the room, yelling at whoever may be inside.

"Get your hands up! Get 'em UP! Put 'em where I can see 'em!"

Logan quickly stood up from the sofa as Rod shrank instantly, sinking back into his boxers. He snapped his hands to ear-level in a panic. The cops can't arrest him, right? He didn't do anything wrong. Okay, maybe he hired a hooker, but they didn't screw or anything. Was that still illegal?

"Can I help you, officers?" Logan's voice shook a little as he spoke.

"Hands behind your back. You're not under arrest. Yet. We're going to detain you. We've got a lady out there, made us suspect you may have done something to her."

"I haven't done anything, officers."

They set him down on the sofa with his hands behind his back and began to question him.

"What were you doing this evening, son?" the first officer asked.

"Honestly, sir, I paid her for a blowjob."

"That all? You weren't rapin' her or nothin'?" asked the second officer.

The first officer stirred. "She seemed a little more agitated than that, son. Be honest with us. What'd you do to her? If you're honest, we may be able to get you off sooner, maybe a few years tops."

Should he be honest? Where would honesty get him at this point? No, he couldn't chance that.

"I'll be honest," Logan started. "I paid her for a blowjob. That's all. After it was over, she ran like a bat outta hell. That's it, I swear."

"You have the right to remain silent," said the second officer.

"Wait, wait! What did I do? You can't arrest me, you've got no grounds to arrest me on!"

The first officer spoke up, "Disorderly conduct, paying for sexual favors," his voice trailed off.

"Okay, now you're making shit up," Logan stated. Even so, they began to lift him off of the couch.

"Anything you say can and will be used against you in a court of law. You have the right to an attorney..." continued the second officer.

"Okay! I'll tell you the truth!" Logan shouted. "Jesus!"

"That's more like it, son. Come clean and it'll be a lot easier."

"Err…" How did he want to say it? Is there really a "best" way to tell someone you've got sentient genitalia? He fell back down to the sofa.

"Come out with it, son!"

"My dick talks. And it freaked her out." There, was that so hard?

The officers exchanged concerned glances.

"Your… your what now, son?"

"My penis, sir. He… he talks."

"Mind if we, uh, take a look at your Johnson?"

"Uncuff me. I'm not the world's biggest fan of being manhandled."

The officers left the living room for a second, leaving Logan sitting on the couch with his hands bound behind his back. He could hear them talking, muttering to each other, most likely saying things like "Should we trust him?" and "Does his pecker really talk?"

A minute later they returned to the living room.

"Alright, son. Show us this… talking junk of yours."

After they'd released him from his restraints, Logan took a deep breath and pushed his jeans and boxers down past his bulge. He pulled his average-sized cock out and held it for them to see.

Silence.

"No, I'm serious; he's just being a prick right now. He talks, I swear. Come on, don't do this to me, Rod!" He began to strangle and choke his member harshly between his hands.

"Son… I think you need help," the first officer alleged with concern in his voice.

"No! No, I'm totally serious! Talk, you little fucker!" Logan backhanded his cock and yelped in pain.

"We need medical backup here," the second officer said into his radio.

"Guys! Officers! You've gotta believe me, I'm not

crazy!" Logan spat, now shaking his silent dick vigorously, as if that would loosen up its vocal cords.

"Detain him!" yelled the second officer, and immediately they both jumped on him again, pulling his arms behind his back and cuffing him once more. "Settle down, son! You'll just be in these 'til the medics arrive."

Logan didn't have to sit there cuffed for long before a white vehicle pulled up in front of the apartment complex. It looked like an ambulance, only it was painted fully white.

Some guys in white clothing came up and briskly walked into the living room.

"Whoa, whoa, wait a minute! You're not sending me to an asylum, are you? You've got to be shitting me!"

Everyone ignored him and began talking amongst themselves in phrases Logan didn't quite understand. He did understand what the large piece of off-white cloth was that they were bringing to him.

"NO!" he yelled, trying to wriggle free from the straightjacket. "I'm not crazy! I swear to god! Rod, why would you do this?! FUCK you!"

Something sharp punctured a point in his neck and Logan began to feel warm and slightly dizzy. His vision swam with blackish clouds and the metallic taste of wet pennies erupted over his tongue. He could barely keep his eyes open. Soon, he was out cold.

***

"Hey, buddy!"

The words swam in his head, the syllables melding together like paint in a glass. Everything was fuzzy.

"Dude, you awake?"

Rod's voice echoed in his skull. Logan opened his eyes. The room was bright, no doubt lit by industrial florescent bulbs. He sat up in the bed and looked around. The walls were covered in a padded white cloth, the floor was covered in foam. There was nothing to furnish the room, save for the large foam mattress he was currently sitting on. A hole in the corner served as a toilet area. He always feared this moment; the moment they'd lock him up.

"HAH! You're awake! Damn, was that a trip or what?!" Rod's craggly voice soaked into the padded walls. Logan looked down to see that he was wearing what resembled white hospital scrubs. Further down on his body, he saw that his dong had crept out of his boxers while he was out of it.

"Why..." Logan's mind swam with emotion. Hatred. Confusion. Betrayal. "Why would you do this?" He suddenly wanted to cry.

"I love you, bro."

"So you totally betray me and fuck me over?"

"I mean... dude... I love you," Rod muttered out of his fleshy, moist little mouth. "For real. And now we can spend the rest of our lives together, just us. It's perfect!"

"I don't get it. Why would you want me all to yourself?" His grogginess was subsiding the more he thought about his current situation.

"I'm gay." Rod's words struck Logan like a mallet to the temple. It made him want to gag.

"Impossible."

"Nah, dude, I just... I love your hands on me, man. I feel so safe, you know? I can feel your warmth and... damn, I could live in your hands, man."

This is too surreal! Wake up! Logan shouted in his head. *As if having a talking dick wasn't weird enough!* He wanted it to be a dream. Desperately wished it was a dream. But he didn't wake up.

"I don't believe this. You're wrong. This whole thing is wrong!"

"I love you, Logan! Damn, I can't say it any other way! I've loved you since we were kids." Rod started to salivate. "I don't want anyone else to have you. You're mine. I want you to love me the way I love you."

"You're a fucking dick!"

"That never stopped anyone before!"

"What the fuck?! It never *stopped* anyone because no one ever *started*!"

"You'll love me, goddammit!"

Suddenly Rod began to vomit semen all over the room: all over the floor, covering the walls, and most of all splattering Logan. *Stop it! Stop it, stop it!* Part of him hated the fact that he was becoming completely drenched in jizz, but the other part of him reveled in the ecstasy of what was the largest, most intense orgasm of his life.

"God, it feels so great to mark you," said the little mouth. "You love it, too. I can feel it."

"Fuck... you..." Logan breathed. He wanted Rod dead. More than anything, he wanted his old life back. He'd do anything to be rid of the little prick. Even if it meant suffering endless amounts of pain. Even if it meant dying.

He tore his hospital scrubs off and violently began to claw at the base of his shaft. His fingernails dug into the soft skin surrounding his penis and blood gushed from the bulging veins, painting the white room a violent shade of red. He let out a scream as he tore away a strip of soft, velvety skin, revealing the juicy pink meat underneath. Rod shrieked along with him; the two voices combined sounded like a demon screeching from within the asylum cell. The sound echoed through the halls loud enough to alert an overnight attendant. A team came rushing to Logan's cell.

His nails, now crusty with bits of thin, dried blood and pubic hair, burrowed deeply into Rod's muscle. Logan's body convulsed in the pain. He tugged and yanked hard on his phallus, trying to rid him of this cockblocking sonofabitch. Soon, the only thing attaching Rod to his owner was a small string of muscle and a wide strip of skin.

Ssscchhhhrrrrrrrrr.

Logan tore the last flap of skin away from his ball sack and hurled Rod across the room, just as the team unlocked the metal door and burst into the cell.

"QUICK!" someone shouted. "We need a medical emergency team, stat! Get me an IV! Get me 734's records, he's gonna need a blood transfusion!"

Before he knew it, Logan was strapped to a gurney and racing down a stark hallway.

I'm dying, he thought. *I'm dying, but I'm okay. In fact, I'm better than okay. I'm great.*

***

Hours, maybe days later, he woke up. His head hurt, though not as much as his groin. He was sprawled across a hospital bed, his crotch wrapped in a thick amount of gauze. A thick white curtain separated him from another unfortunate patron.

Shit, he thought, *I survived. A least I'll never have to deal with that prick again.*

Suddenly he felt a strange buzzing around his hind quarters. His cheeks vibrated as the skin around his rectum began to expand and contract. Logan rolled to his side and groaned in pain.

The curtain slid back and an older man stood on one leg with the aid of a crutch. He was a handsome man, maybe in his seventies, with a kind-hearted sympathetic face.

"Are you alright there, my boy?"

Logan's butt expelled a nauseous gas, his anus moving in such a way as to form syllables. It's voice carried like a six-foot, husky, football player's. "'Ay! Pay no attention to the man behind the curtain! What the fuck happened to you, gimpy?!'"

The old man raised his eyebrows.

"Forget I asked," he answered. He closed the curtain and walked back to his side of the room. "What an asshole."

No, no no no! Fuck!

A nurse came into the room carrying some clear plastic tubing. Time to change out his IV.

"Hi there, how are you feeling?" Her voice was like silk. "You've been out for nearly a week. We're glad to see you conscious. The doctors managed to attach your penis. It was a close call, but you're going to be alright." She smiled.

Alright? Hell, you should have let me die!

The nurse changed his IV, then left.

As soon as she was gone, his dick started to stir.

No! No, no, no, no, NO!

"Thought you could get rid of me that easily, Logan? Shame on you, man! I thought we had something." Rod sounded drained.

"We had... nothing," Logan managed, completely exhausted.

"Who this muh-fucker?" his ass chimed in.

"Whoa," exclaimed Rod, suddenly back from the dead, "who invited the asshole?"

"Bitch," the ass said, "they call me Brown Cherry. Put some respect on me, brutha!"

"Oh, I'll respect you, alright. You haven't done nothin' to deserve it, bro!"

"You wanna go, homie? Bring it!"

"Don't even go there, man! I'll fuck your shit up!"

"Bullshit," said Brown Cherry. "Bring it, pussy."

At that moment, Rod whipped around and thrust himself face-first into Brown Cherry's mouth. Logan groaned in pain, too tired to scream, too out of it to fully realize what was going on. His mind was elsewhere as his body lay motionless in the hospital bed, writhing around as his dick fucked his asshole. The tingling in his balls brought him back to reality.

Logan didn't want to orgasm, especially if his juice was going to be deposited in his own rectum. The pressure in his groin from twisting that far back was sending signals of extreme pain to his head. Brown Cherry was so tight, it was like screwing a virgin. Logan didn't want to love it. He felt dirty. The fullness inside his crack made him feel sick; not because it physically hurt, but because he loved the pressure. He felt mentally messed-up, in the most arousing, narcissistic way possible. He felt like he was about to come.

Brown Cherry tried to talk, tried to utter some form of dispute, but Rod was so deep into him that it came out muffled.

Suddenly, Rod threw up ejaculate deep inside Brown Cherry's gullet. Logan's back arched in pleasure and pain, his hands held tight to the edges of the hospital bed.

The nurse heard the distress from out at the medic's station just outside his door. She came rushing in after paging the doctors.

Logan had finally snapped. He couldn't think anymore. He was a complete vegetable in a man's body, overrun by a prick and an ass.

***

Medical personnel make their rounds daily, every hour on the half-hour. They change his IV and his hospital garb and make sure his bed is clean of filth. Logan's silent when they see him. He just sits there most of the time with a cold, blank stare in his eyes.

He's been there for almost seven years now.

No one's ever seen him talk; not the interns or new doctors, anyway. The older doctors can tell you he was mental when he came into the institute. But he doesn't talk now.

Some of the interns say they can hear him talking to himself when they turn to leave the room. They say he sometimes calls them names. *Cunt. Twat. Bitch.* Some say he sounds like he's from California. Others say he must be from Detroit. Some say he calls himself "Brown

Cherry", whatever that meant. The guy is mental; worst case they've ever seen.

One thing they all agree on, though, is that when they *do* hear him, he's a bit of a dick, and a bit of an asshole.

A GAME OF CHANCE

Jacob Lambert

The last thirty minutes had been the longest half-hour in Chance Simmons's life, and the seven framed motivational posters (two to each of the three walls, plus the enormous one behind him) weren't doing much to help the increasing sweat from accumulating on his hands and back. He had known this day was coming, but he had no idea that waiting on Professor Jakes would be this nerve-racking. Besides the hokey posters, there was something else bothering him—the old polished oak bench in front of the professor's office was numbing his backside. And no matter which way he moved, the damn thing caused even the most agreeable to complain, but not Chance. He knew this day had been on the way.

Across from where Chance was sitting, an intern shuffled through a stack of papers, her light green eyes shifting from paper to him, paper to him. His ears flooded with a barrage of sounds, all equally unnerving: paper, whispers in the hallway, the humming sound from the heater in the corner, and the deafening din of shoes on linoleum. And just as he was about to scream, the large wooden door beside him swung open, revealing a tall man holding himself up with a long black cane, a silver rook at the top. His black slacks and red silk shirt insinuated class, but his face held another meaning: contempt, lips pulled back in a grimace as if the smell of the room and the look of Chance sent his body into revolt.

"Ah, Mister Simmons! How long have you been waiting, not long I hope?" the man said, laughing and moving to the left.

Of course not, smartass! I've just been here for God knows how long waiting on your highness. Please, what do I owe the honor of your recognition?

"Not long, sir, thank you for seeing me," Chance said, standing up, pins and needles going through the backs of his legs.

Jakes' smile dropped, and then he said, "Well, are you just going to stand there or come in? I have other appointments."

"Yes, sorry, sir."

"I know you are. Now, apologize," the professor said, his I'm-better-than-you smile returning.

Did he just make a joke? Chance thought. *At a time like this?* Instead of taking offense, Chance lowered his head, allowing his dirty blonde hair to cover his eyes, and went inside the professor's office.

Unlike the waiting room, Jakes' office was about the size of a shoebox and reeked of stale sweat and cocoa butter, but what really stood out was the clutter: in the center of the room and on top of the desk were mounds of paperwork. On the left and right of that were bookshelves, and above the shelves, canted and covered in dust, were plaques and pictures of the school basketball team, The Marauders, and the professor had stapled a thick black sheet across the window. Overall, the whole place felt like a coffin.

After shutting the door, Jakes walked over to his leather chair and sat down, the smile never leaving his wrinkled face as he spoke. "So, Mister Simmons, what can I do for you on this wonderful Fall afternoon?"

Watching Jakes smile in light of his circumstances made Chance's heart flutter, but the way the bastard pushed his gold-rimmed spectacles up on his nose and smiled made him want to come over the desk. "It's about my grade, professor. I wanted to talk to you about it."

"What's there to talk about, Chance? As I understand it, you failed to meet my requirements."

Chance wiped his hands on his faded slacks and looked into the professor's dark brown eyes, halfway expecting to see his own ashen image begin to dissolve in the reflection.

"I was hoping we could talk about that, sir. See, according to advising, if I don't pass this class, then they will kick me out, and—"

"And what? If I'm not mistaken," Jakes pulled a small notebook from his desk, opened it, and continued, "yes, you have missed six classes, and, as you know, five is the limit. I really should have failed you sooner, but—"

Chance interrupted. "Sir, please, I was sick, really. Couldn't even get out of bed."

"All *six* times? I don't see any doctor's excuse here."

"I have no money to see a doctor, sir. My family is going through a rough time, and me being sick was—"

"If you have come here with nothing but excuses, Chance, I am dreadfully sorry for you. You must take responsibility for your own problems, as well as mistakes. Now, moving on, according to *my* grade book, you are perhaps a point away from passing. Would you like to discuss this instead?"

Chance found himself at a blank, humbled, unaware of what to do next.

"Sure, why not," he replied, leaning back in the

leather chair across from the professor, crossing his arms to keep warm because, it seemed, light wasn't the only thing that the room lacked.

"Alright, then, Chance, you have caught me at a time when I could use some help. You see, I have a dilemma of my own, and it could benefit you, as well as your grade, to lend me your services."

What could he possibly want? Then, all of that disappeared. Here he was, chance of a lifetime—no pun intended.

"Like, what do you want me to do? I hope this isn't one of those "if you blow me" types of things, is it?"

The professor seemed to have missed the joke by the way he responded: sigh of exasperation, taking his glasses off and rubbing his eyes.

"Simmons, are you some kind of idiot? Or do you usually piss on opportunities?"

"I'm sorry, sir, I just—"

"Don't apologize, please."

"Yes, sir," Chance said, feeling the air grow thin.

"Like I was saying, I have found myself torn between a couple things that you can help me with."

"Go ahead, sir, I'm listening."

"Very good. I have a seminar in Indiana this weekend to attend, for my most recent work on the lost colony of Roanoke is being published, and I will be gone Saturday through Monday."

"Congratulations, sir," Chance replied, and although he was trying to be genuine, the words sounded false in his ears.

Jakes smiled, grin from lobe to lobe, and then continued. "Thank you, Simmons. But this is where you come in, so listen."

"Yes, sir."

"Coincidentally, my mother and father's housekeeper will be out of town as well to see her family. Do you understand where I am going with this?"

192

Chance did, but he was wishing that he didn't.

"You need me to cover for the housekeeper?"

"I guess you are brighter than you look. That's correct"

Oh yeah, I'm bright, all right! Bright enough to cut the brake lines to your car.

"Now, I want to make sure that you understand what I am asking. First, in the matter of my parents, both of them are in wheelchairs, so you won't have to worry about that much, but my father is basically catatonic. Do you know what that means?"

"He doesn't move or talk?"

"Well, I guess that will have to do," Jakes said, shaking his head, the smile fading completely. "But my mother can speak, although she can't say much. Just blurts out random phrases. Understand?"

Chance nodded.

"Alright," Jakes said in a perfunctory way.

"Is that all?"

"No," Jakes said, moving his chair away from his desk and reaching down below it, producing a cedar box the size of a small television with a red gemstone on three of the four sides. On the front, instead of a red stone, there was a rounded piece of gold imbedded into the box's frame, a small black button in its center.

Placing the box on the desk and pulling his chair back to its place, Jakes stared at Chance as if he were a magician waiting to see if he could guess which walnut shell had the marble.

"Okay, Chance, this is where you make your decision."

I guess the guy's lost it. I thought we already went through this?

"Alright."

The professor reached forward and pressed the button, opening the box, and, without hesitation, pulled out a small key with a wooden handle, placing it on the desk in front of Chance.

"There are a few more things I have to say before you make your decision, so hear me well," Jakes said, leaning back in his chair and removing his glasses, cleaning them.

Chance listened, performing the opposite movement —leaning forward.

"If you agree to do this for me, you will indeed pass the class, so don't worry about that, but, if you choose to decline, you will never step foot in this institution unless it is to clean the floors, understand?"

Chance nodded.

"The key before you is to the house, and don't worry, I have directions that even you will understand. Now, you are welcomed to the kitchen and the couch and television, but you are to go nowhere else in the house. The damn place is enormous and I know you will be tempted to look around, but feel free to ignore that impulse when it comes."

"I don't see—"

"My parents have many breakable items, and I wouldn't want years of memories washed down the drain because you wandered into some room and knocked something over, good enough?"

Pleased to get a rise out of the professor, Chance smiled, making his thin lips curl up and his blue eyes shimmer in the dismal room. "Good enough."

"So, does it sound like something you can do?" Jakes asked, as if there was any question to the matter.

"Sounds good to me, professor. What time should I be there?"

"Eight o'clock, Simmons, not a second later."

"Are we done then, sir?"

Casting a glance toward the key, one of which Chance could have sworn he saw disdain, Jakes spoke: "Yes, but before you forget, take the key and this: it's a set of directions to the house."

Chance reached across the desk, taking the directions from the professor's hand, and, before he could draw away, he realized the professor was still holding it like a corpse with a vise grip, staring at him.

"Chance, my boy, I hope you listened to me well."

"I did, professor. Everything will be as you asked. Anything else?"

Letting go of the paper, Jakes stood up, allowing most of the weight in his right side to rest on the cane, and began to walk around to the door.

"No, we are done."

Walking to the door himself, Chance turned around to address the professor one last time.

"Professor Jakes—"

"I'll see you Tuesday," Jakes interrupted, and after the boy had walked away, the professor shut the door, an eerie smile creeping onto the lines of his face, for, he also knew, like Chance, this day had been coming.

***

The front yard was immaculate, vibrant green swallowing the two bottle trees in its center, and ended about an inch from the sidewalk. Leading from the street to the porch was a long, winding trail made of white rocks. The house itself looked about three stories of brick and dark brown wooden siding. Its window placement and drapes, from the outside, resembled a sullen face approaching a snarl, sending a chill—whether it be because of the wind or not—down Chance's slender back.

After climbing the brick steps, Chance just stood there, staring dumbfounded at the door's strange configuration: instead of the handle being on the right side of the door, like every other door he had ever seen, a small crystal knob jutted out directly in the middle, a gold plate underneath. In the center, there was a slot for a key, yet the even stranger part was that the wood around the knob moved in circles—from small ones to larger as it moved out from the center.

Chance reached into his pocket and pulled out the key that Jakes had given him, and after a moment of hesitation, he started to advance toward the keyhole—

"You must be Chance?" a tall woman wearing a multi-colored apron said, her thin lips pulled so tight that they looked like two small wafers, her eyes an empty brown.

For a moment, Chance stood there with the key still wavering in his hand, looking as though caught in a spotlight. "Y…yes, I was sent here by—"

"By the professor? He said to expect you around eight or so. Anyway, where are my manners? I'm Susan, Susan Richmond. You can call me Jan," the woman said, her flushed cheeks making her look younger than she actually was.

"Jan?"

"Yeah, I know, right?" Jan said, finally breaking from the stone look into a smile. "I have no idea how I got the name, but it works, huh?"

"I guess so," Chance said, doing his best not to look awkward and feel the same as well.

"Come on in. I've got some things to go over with you before I leave," Jan said, turning around and leading the way into the house.

"Yes, ma'am," Chance responded, following behind and closing the door.

Jan led Chance down a long, dim corridor decorated with some of the most peculiar items he had ever seen: on the walls, spaced about five inches from each other, were various abstract paintings of what looked to Chance as skinned animals and emaciated human beings. But the oddest of all were the masks above each one of the paintings, which, if he remembered correctly (either from *The History Channel* or class), were Japanese dance or death masks, of which one he wasn't certain, but it was one of the two, more than likely the latter. Underneath each mask was a description, like at a museum: the first read *Shikami-The Demon*, a red face with shallow eyes and a grin; the second read *Uba-The Elderly*, its features forced into a frown, its eyes black with white phantoms appearing to float around inside them; and the third, looking like a disfigured man with an eternal sneer, was *Hannya-Jealously is thy curse.*

As the two were about to step into the living room, Jan abruptly halted and turned. Chance thought, while she stood under the scanty light of the hallway, that Jan looked like the amazon version of Pam Grier. She stood about four whole inches taller, and though she was quite a bit older, maybe by twenty years or so, time had been good to her.

"Listen, Chance, did Mr. Jakes tell you about his parents? You know, about their being disabled and all?"

Chance straightened his backpack because it had been sliding down his shoulder, then responded, almost in a whisper: "He told me about them, yes."

She shook her head. "Did he tell you about his mother?"

Chance nodded, allowing his pale features to shine in the light.

"He told me she shouts or something, but that's all."

Jan smirked and continued. "That and more. Just don't get startled if she says...well...if she says something more colorful, okay?"

"No problem, I understand."

"Great, now follow me, and don't make any sudden movements. Mr. Jakes Senior doesn't make any noise, but the Misses will sure as hell speak up."

"Got it."

"Okay, let's go."

***

Other than the sound of the television and the crackling of the logs in the fireplace, the living room was silent. The setup of the room, however, couldn't be louder —everything screamed excess: not one but two Persian rugs on the floor; four cedar chests placed at each of the four walls leading to four different darkened hallways; an oil painting of Christ above the massive hearth of the fireplace; and, in the center of the room, sitting in their wheelchairs and facing a large flat screen, were Mr. and Mrs. Jakes, both surrounded by a velvet red couch that looked like a broken **U**.

Jan placed a finger over her lips, as if reminding Chance of their agreement. She then walked in front of the television, but before she could address the couple, Mrs. Jakes had her own thoughts to express.

"Get the damn dog inside, Merle!" the elderly woman in the wheelchair shouted, almost sending Chance out of his blue jeans and black hoodie with the words *Voodoo Fest '12* on it.

"Come here, Chance," Jan said, motioning for him to stand beside her, a look on her face that said *might as well get this over with.*

Chance, starting to do as asked, began to wonder if it had been such a good idea agreeing to watch Jakes' parents. The house he could handle, but the constant outbursts from the husky woman in the wheelchair, possibly later in the night, might prove too much.

"Chance, this is Mr. Merle Jakes, and his wife Mrs. Maggie," Jan said, a fake smile on her face.

"Hello, nice to meet you," Chance said, adding a nervous smile of his own.

If Chance was expecting to get a response, he was mistaken, for Mr. Jakes, his frail body slumped over like a sack of walnuts, sat there staring at the floor, his thick glasses hanging on the end of his nose. Maggie, however, dressed in her sky blue night gown, stared directly into

Chance's eyes, a firm grimace plastered onto her face, her grey hair pulled neatly into a bun on the back of her head.

"Where my fuggen slippers?" Maggie said, shouting at the sofa next to her.

Jan turned to Chance. "See what I mean? Unless you want to finish out here, I suggest we go and speak in the kitchen. And don't worry, you won't have to do much for them. It's already late and they will be sleeping soon. Maggie will take care of that. All you have to do is watch them and make sure she doesn't try to work the stove. Merle can't do anything, but I think you already knew that."

Chance shook his head, running a hand through his shaggy brown hair and rubbing his eyes. "Good. I don't know what I would do if I had to put them to bed."

Jan laughed under her breath. "Oh c'mon, they're not that bad."

"Compared to what?" Chance said.

"Okay, Chance, follow me."

He was expecting the kitchen to be just as extravagant as the rest of the house, but no. Other than the large steel pot on the stove cooking a roast and potatoes, it was nondescript, perplexingly enough. However, what caught Chance's attention was the key rack beside the refrigerator. There appeared to be at least sixty small metal pins jutting out of a corkboard that had two or three keys on each ring. He knew that the house was big, but why so many keys? What concerned him more now, though, was on the countertop, across from the stove, underneath the suspended set of pots and skillets: a sandwich with veggies and dip beside it.

Seeing Chance's eyes fixed on the sandwich, Jan smiled and took a glass from one of the cabinets. "What would you like to drink?"

"Huh?" Chance said, looking at her.

"With your sandwich? I used some of the roast from the pot to make it. I hope you like roast."

"Of course I do. Who doesn't? Thank you."

"No problem," Jan said, "anyone who watches those two is gonna need to eat well."

"I believe it. I'll have, well, what do you got?"

Jan opened the fridge and looked in. "We have soda, Kool-Aid, and beer. But I doubt you're old enough for the latter."

Chance smiled. "Would you give me a beer if I said I was old enough?"

Jan lowered her head and shot an accusing glance in his direction.

"I'll take that as a no. Soda will do fine, thanks again."

"There is plenty of roast and soda for you, so take as much as you need. I'm sure Mr. Jakes explained to you about the rules of the place?" Jan said, placing the glass of soda on the counter beside the plate of food.

"He did."

"Well, trust me; do as he said, okay? I've been working here for six years, and the only time I went snooping, somehow, he knew."

"What did you do? Break something?"

Jan shook her head, her eyes wide. "I didn't do nothing, okay? Just do as he said."

"Didn't mean to upset you," Chance said, finally placing his book bag down on the floor beside one of the stools facing the counter because it had grown heavy in the past thirty minutes.

"It's alright, I apologize. Just keep to where he told you is okay. Some houses aren't safe to be wandering around in at night."

Taking a hearty gulp from his glass and putting it back down on the counter, Chance's brows furrowed and he frowned. "What do you mean? I don't get it."

All of a sudden, Jan took off her apron and picked up a leather bag that was behind the counter and began to move toward the living room.

"Hey, what's wrong?" Chance said, cutting her off.

Jan looked at him, impatience in her eyes. "I have to go, okay? My plane leaves in an hour, and Birmingham is quite a ways away."

"You said it's not safe in some houses. What did you mean by that?" Chance asked, once again unsure of being in the house for the night.

"Forget I said it. It's just something my mother used to say. Just remember what the professor said about the house, got me?"

Chance nodded, still confused by the way the woman seemed to have changed her demeanor in a matter of seconds.

"Alright, is there anything else I need to know?"

"No. If you have any problems, such as with Merle or Maggie, I've left a set of numbers on the fridge."

"Help with what? You said—"

"Listen, boy, I have to go! I don't have time to sit here and hold your hand," Jan said, turning around and stepping into the living room.

Chance tried to follow behind her, but as he moved into the living room, Jan had already walked down the hallway and out the front door.

"Shit, all I wanted to do was say sorry," he said. Then, as he turned to go back to the kitchen, he saw Maggie sitting in front of the television, her dark brown eyes resembling empty wells, her former grimace stretched into an eerie smile.

"What's so funny?" Chance asked, doing his best not to obey the chill bumps on his neck. Maggie, of course, didn't answer, just those same blank eyes watching him as he went back into the kitchen, more confused and disconcerted than he ever remembered being in his life.

***

Man, the shit I do to pass. Jan's probably on her cell right now talking to Jakes, laughing it up: "Oh, you should have seen that scrawny little fool's eyes widen when he heard Maggie shout! Damn boy about shit himself," Chance thought as he stood in the kitchen, legs feeling like telephone poles made of tofu, and staring at the plate of food Jan left, which, no matter how hard he tried, didn't look the least bit appetizing now.

However, the smell coming from the pot on the stove made things a little better, and as Chance walked over to it, he noticed a piece of paper that had been taped to the side of the marble counter top beside the stove.

Chance,
Turn stove off at 10:00.
Eat what you like, but store the
Rest in the fridge. Have a good night.
Jan-334-

Thoughtful, Chance thought, remembering the smile the woman gave him, thinking, once again, regardless of the way she acted toward the end, Jan was quite beautiful for her age. And as he looked up at the clock, he could see the time was getting close—thirty till. Just enough time to take a little *smoke* break. Walking to the back door, Chance twisted the crystal handle—also in the center—and stepped out, hoping to ease his mind.

***

Back in the kitchen and the warmth of the house, Chance found himself, once again, overwhelmed by the pleasant scent of the pot roast and the sight of the sandwich on the counter. However, this time his appetite was in full swing. So, getting a beer out of the fridge—laugh at that, Jan—he popped the top, took a massive drink, and, after grabbing another one, Chance sat down at the chairs by the counter and began eating.

Maybe it was because he hadn't eaten all day that the sandwich tasted so good, but boy, it had to be the best sandwich Chance had ever had. The meat tasted tender and juicy, almost wild, the rye bread fresh, and the potatoes, paired with the chives and onions, assaulted his palate. After finishing up, he considered getting more from the pot but figured he'd wait. Walking to the sink, intent on washing off his plate and getting another beer, Chance saw the board with all of the keys, demanding his attention.

Now, you are welcome to the kitchen and the couch and television, but you are to go nowhere else in the house. "Yeah, I got you," Chance said aloud into the empty kitchen. Then, after looking at the board again, he made up his mind. Perhaps, he had come to this decision as far back as the professor's office. He didn't know. Regardless of what he told Jakes, Chance knew he would look around the house; maybe even Jakes knew it?

First, though, he needed to check on Jakes' parents before he did anything, and, as Chance walked into the living room, he saw that neither Maggie nor Merle were in there anymore. He then walked back to the key holder, examining the small, round metal rings and the messages on the paper in the center of them.

On the top, there were six pegs going across with six keys on them; going from top to bottom, in a vertical line, were twelve pegs with multiple keys on each peg. And, as Chance gave a closer look, he saw a strange inscription on one of the keys. It read: *Basement Fun Key 1#.*

"Well, I guess that tells me where I'm going," a hint of laughter and apprehension in his tone, but before he could proceed into the living room, looking for the basement, Chance's cell rang. Somehow, he knew it had to be Lilly, so, reluctantly, he answered, doing his best to hide the fog going on inside his head.

"Hey, babe. What's up?"

"Are you Okay? You sound funny," Lilly said, her tone light but accusatory.

"Yeah, I'm okay. Just tired of this house already. But

look, I'm sorry about tonight, babe. Jakes really got my ass this time," Chance said.

"That's what I wanted to talk to you about," Lilly paused for a moment, and then continued.

"Just wanted to say I was sorry for yelling at you earlier. Got a little over heated, sorry," Lilly said. Her voice had lowered, and Chance could picture her sitting by her computer—probably on *Facebook*—fidgeting with her fingernails.

"It's fine. I should have paid more attention at school," Chance said, feeling better, letting out a small, quiet laugh.

"What's so funny, mister," Lilly said in a cute, sweet tone.

"Nothing really, just something the professor said."

"What?"

"That if I actually did what I was supposed to, I would never have to—OH SHIT!"

"What is it, Chance? Everything okay?"

Chance ran back over to the stove and saw that the pot had begun to darken on the sides. "Sorry, I forgot to turn the stove off, shit about caught fire," Chance said, turning the dial to the off position, and in his nervous state, Lilly could hear the stumbling in his words and the shakiness of his voice: she knew.

"Have you been smoking?"

Chance's hands began to sweat, and it took all of his attention and control to speak.

"Lilly, of course not! Why—"

"You never call me Lilly unless you are hiding something, Chance! Have you or not?"

He bit his lip as he spoke: "Lil, I'm sorry, okay? Things have just been rough. First with the professor and then with this damn house! Look, please—"

She interrupted: "How could you, Chance? After everything that I have been through?" There was no anger in her voice, just pure disappointment.

"Please, baby, I'm sorry. I don't know what else to say. I really don't."

"Well, I do, Chance," Lilly said, followed by a long silence.

"What, Lil?"

Before Chance received a response, there was a beep in Chance's right ear: the phone went dead.

"You have got to be kidding me!" Chance said, frantically looking through his backpack for his charger, but it wasn't there.

Tossing his pack to the floor and deciding to check his car, where he knew he had a backup, Chance left the kitchen and made it halfway to the front door when he heard a sudden thud underneath his feet, followed by the sound of a dog barking. He didn't see any dog food in the kitchen or any dishes on the floor, but he remembered Maggie mentioning a dog. Did Jan comment on it? He didn't think she had, so placing the phone back in his pocket and walking into the middle of the living room, standing on one of the Persian rugs, Chance began to follow the sounds. Inside, he knew that he should call Lilly; and he would, eventually, but only after—she needed time to think, Chance assumed, and he needed time to explore.

***

Out of the four hallways in the living room, Chance had gone down the first three, the two beside the fireplace and the one by the kitchen, and although the sounds had gotten louder, he had no luck in finding the source. However, as he went down the last hallway, the one closer to the massive one leading from the front door, he could see a light beneath one of the doors at the right side of the hallway.

Go nowhere else…

"Yeah, right. How about you just keep to yourself?"

Chance said aloud nervously, reaching out to the center of the door, twisting the crystal handle.

"What the hell is up with these doors, anyway?" he said, opening it.

Before he could answer himself, a rush of glacial-like wind came from somewhere below the wooden steps behind the door, instantly numbing his face.

"Jesus!" Chance said, rubbing his hands together and placing them on his face to warm up.

He had to watch his footing as he descended the rotten wood below, taking notice of the assortment of old antiques as he continued. At the bottom, the mingled scents of mildew and sewer gas were so fetid that Chance felt like he had walked right out of the house and into a cesspool. Yet the cold was more dominant at the bottom of the stairs, but its origins remained hidden somewhere among the piles of junk.

All around, from the bottom of the steps to the darkened corner in the back of the room, were miscellaneous relics from—what Chance could surmise—the early fifties, as if all of history's scraps had been discarded through a portal and dumped there. Stretching from the stairs to the back, on the left side, were full bottles of beer and coke, all from different eras, stacked on long, winding wooden shelves. In addition, at the center of them all was an old-fashioned coke machine, equipped with a bottle opener and a "16-cents" sign.

Chance started to feel the bitterness of the cold intensify as he walked further, and, reaching the back wall of the basement, he found himself in the dark. Here, the thudding sound and the barking were much louder.

Hands out in front, like a blind person looking for a face, Chance felt the wall for a light switch, and after a moment, BINGO! He found it, turned it on, and stopped, semi-startled by what he found.

"What the hell?" Chance said, staring at the giant indoor freezer, the steel door releasing a fog-like smoke.

This particular door, unlike all of the others Chance had come across, had a handle and latch. However, as Chance tried to pull on it, the door would not give. Upon a closer look at the door's handle, Chance saw something strange: on the right side of the handle was a slot for a key hole; underneath that, words sketched on a gold plate.

"Why am I not surprised?" Chance said as he bent down to look at what the words said.

If you have come this far, why not go a little further?

"I don't get it," Chance said, baffled at the inscription. Then, it hit him: *Basement Fun Key 1#.*

As quickly as he could, Chance turned around and ran back upstairs to the kitchen, to the keys.

When he managed to find it (after all, he had only glanced at it once), Chance, in the same manner, raced back down the stairs, careful not to make too much noise or fall down the wooden steps as he went. It didn't take long, and soon he was back at the freezer.

Chance crouched, cautious of what might happen when he opened it, and slid the key into the slot, but, to his dismay, the key wouldn't turn. When he twisted harder, for some reason, it broke in half, both pieces falling to the floor, sending Chance into a nervous frenzy.

Now look what you did, you big dumbass! You broke the goddamn key! You wait till Jakes finds out about—

"He won't!" Chance said aloud, once again, talking to himself.

He just stood there looking at the key slot, and then, he noticed something.

"Ha, how could I be so dumb?" Chance said, reaching into his pocket, pulling out the skeleton key Jakes had given him.

Placing the key into the slot and turning it, Chance then opened the door.

The first two things Chance heard were the sound of

the dog barking, almost yelping, and the thud against the wall, all within close proximity; however, other than the five or six boxes of what looked to him as frozen bread and large metal cake carts, there was nothing else. Chance walked into the freezer, leaving the door slightly ajar; he then reached the back of the freezer, the sound of the dog yelping growing to an aggravating pitch.

Removing some of the carts away from the back wall, Chance found a steel door with the words AURTHORIZED PERSONNEL ONLY bolted into the center, and, completely ignoring the warning, Chance opened the door—thank God for no key slot—and proceeded through.

***

Once the thick, choking fog rushed out, finally allowing him sight, Chance, at that moment, understood why Jakes told him not to go snooping around. Hanging by twelve or thirteen hooks, all suspended from the ceiling of the freezer, were naked human bodies, each with a razor-sharp steel hook through the roof of its mouth. One of the bodies, closer to the back, was kicking his severed stump against the freezer wall, as if still alive. The dog, however, came running from the back of the freezer, squealing, and zipped past him—its nails scrapping the icy floor as it disappeared back into the basement. Other than how the animal got inside, another thought surfaced—the sandwich Jan had left him.

Chance, wanting to puke, backed up until he was all the way out of the first freezer, his head spinning, his gut twisting—screaming, in his current state, was impossible.

Coincidentally, my mother and father's housekeeper will be out of town as well to see her family. Do you understand where I am going with this?

Oh, Chance thought, I do now, you sick mother—

Before the thought could finish, Chance looked up

from the floor, which he had fallen to once out of the freezer, and he saw two people standing by the basement steps.

"Jan? Is that you?" Chance asked, clearing his throat the best he could and standing.

"Jan?" he asked again, this time walking toward the two. "Who is that with you?"

Right behind the stairs, in the dark, standing upright with their arms extended in a false embrace, were Merle and Maggie; or at least, the closer they came, judging by the sky blue nightgown, one of them was Maggie. But it wasn't the fact that the two seemed to have miraculously healed from their illness and were now walking that caused Chance's blood to speed through his veins and into his racing heart. No. It was what was on their faces: Maggie, walking in the lead, wore the *Uba-The Elderly* mask from the hallway, its perplexing grin shimmering in the scanty light above, and its shadowy eyes haunting in their wooden sockets. Merle, starting to catch up with his wife, his arms extended as if a zombie from a Romero film, wore the *Hannya-Jealousy is thy curse* mask, its disfigured features and sneer, between the moments of light and darkness as he passed through silhouette and illumination, seemed alive.

"Merle? Maggie?" Chance said, starting to move along the wall to avoid their touch, trying to get out before—

Chance stopped for a moment, a smile forming on his face. "Look, if you two don't fucking stop where you are, I'll kick the ever-living shit out of both of you!" Chance said, realizing he was getting worried about two old elderly folks. After all, all he needed to do was get up those stairs and call the cops. What were two old people going to—?

Chance's mouth dropped open.

As asked, they stopped, but something was happening to them, something that, Chance knew, was beyond the explanation of simple anatomy, something grotesque and unnerving. The two stopped, their bodies began to shudder, they raised their arms, and, in unison, their arms bent back at the elbow, followed by their knees, splitting the skin at the joint and allowing them to move freely in any direction, pus and green liquid running from the open tears in their skin. When the two bent backward, their spines began to snap and pop, making the sound of cracking knuckles, until they were moving and crawling on the floor like some creation yet thought up in the mind of God.

Chance moved closer to the steps, thinking that the transformation was over, and as he did, he caught the last (but most disturbing) part of the scene.

What Chance thought was Maggie started to let out a low whine, like an outdoor generator, and its head began to twist and snap back, lolling at its shoulders. Then, just as disturbingly, the one next to her did the same thing; however, he wasn't interested in watching the second all the way through. He rushed up the steps, but as he made it to the door, Chance looked behind, out of either curiosity or ignorance. Whatever it was, he wished that he hadn't, for the two behind him, as they weaved in and out of the light, were using their new talon-like nails to climb the side of the walls, both moving at an impossible speed.

He realized it was time to go, and go as fast as he could.

Slamming the door, he ran down the hallway, back into the living room, standing there for what felt like hours, his eyelids twitching and sweat pouring from his face.

"It's all in my head, all in my head. Too much smoke, that's all, too—"

BANG! BANG! BANG! BANG! BANG! BANG! BANG!

That was all it took: he abandoned his backpack and

210

other belongings in the kitchen, opting for the front door instead.

BANG! BANG! BANG! BANG! BANG! BANG! BANG!

Chance was at the end of the hallway when he heard the door behind him crash open, his heart pounding in his throat, his palms drenched, his body shuddering. And as he began to twist the crystal handle in the center of the front door, he could hear panting and the dull thuds of the two coming up behind him.

Then he opened the door.

His blurred vision only saw two things as it opened, both in slow motion, as if underwater: the sight of the gun resting on his face, and the flash from its the business end, sending his rigid body backward to the floor like an ironing board. Then, as if the blast from the gun were a signal, the two behind Chance's body stopped in place, their flesh reforming to their prior configuration, snaps and grinds echoing from the hallway.

"Jesus! You two had one simple job, and you can't even do that right!" the silhouette of a tall woman said, stepping into the house and leaning down to the floor to check Chance's body.

The two approached the woman at the door, removing their masks. "Look at what you did! The professor is going to be livid!" Maggie said, straightening her hair, the skin of her face stretching—a rippled wave on the left side of her head.

"Well, what was I supposed to do? Let him go? Tell the professor I'm sorry and that he won't be eating this winter?" Jan said, placing the pistol back into her leopard purse.

Merle stood there in silence, his face curled up into a grimace.

"Hell if I know! Anyway, you've ruined the meat again! Jakes warned you once! Now you're—" Maggie stopped, interrupted.

"I'm what? It's just as much your fault as it is mine," Jan paused, looking down at Chance's lifeless body. "Well, what are we going to tell him?"

Maggie, walking back over to the wall to put the mask back up on the plaque, shook her head. "I don't know, but we better think of something."

"Let's start by you fixing your damn face, Maggie. Shit, you want everyone in this town knowing what you are? Or should we just go knocking on the neighbors' doors and introduce ourselves?"

"It's not that bad," Merle said, breaking his silence.

Jan frowned. "Shut up, Merle, or whatever you go by now! I liked you better when you didn't speak."

"That was a millennium ago, back when—"

"Just shut the hell up, okay?" Maggie said, looking at her reflection in the gold plate underneath the mask.

In the reflection, Maggie could see that, like it or not, Jan was right. The skin around her right eye, just above the cheekbone, hung downwards, exposing the scaly surface underneath and the artificial human eye in the socket bending inwards, allowing her true, tar-colored eye to shine in the light of the hallway.

"Look, we have until daylight to get that bullet out of his head and dress him, so I recommend that you two give me a hand getting his body down to the freezer. Got me?" Jan said, getting down on her knees and grabbing Chance's body under the arms.

"No problem," Maggie said, bending down, "just don't tell Jakes that we couldn't, ya know, catch him."

"You're just as bad as Merle. Now quit your yapping and help me!"

"Anything you ask, mother," Maggie said, squatting down and grabbing the feet. Merle, on the other hand, just did what he does best: remained quiet.

***

Like every Tuesday afternoon around lunchtime, the cafeteria was like the local fair minus the expensive rides: hundreds of feet shuffling around, the deafening pitch of conversation and laughter, but worst of all the nauseating smell of subpar food floating up and down the hallways that could cause even the emaciated to recoil.

However, the scent coming from the microwave near the checkout line was the only thing different on this particular Tuesday, and it wasn't unnoticed.

"Damn, professor, what'cha cooking? Smells amazing," asked a young man in black slacks with a lazy eye, his lower lip quivering as he spoke.

"Well, it's a special recipe, son. Say, aren't you in my History class?"

"Yes, sir. I'm Mark Schmidt. Sit in the far right of the room."

"Ah, yes, Mr. Schmidt. I remember you now. Always punctual, always ready to learn," the professor said, placing his cane with a rook's head to the side.

"That's me, sir," Mark said, leaning closer to the microwave.

The professor smiled and spoke, his voice light and friendly. "Would you like to try it? The question seems on the verge of being asked, anyway."

"I couldn't, sir. I apologize for my—"

"Never mind that. I like you. After all, you *have* earned it, haven't you?"

For a moment, Mark stood there, unsure of what to say. Then, in a perfunctory manner, he agreed. "Yes, I guess I have, if you don't mind me saying so."

"No, not at all. Here," the professor said, giving Mark a plastic spoon, allowing him to dip it into the Tupperware container.

"Now, make sure you get some of the meat. My misses prepared it special," the professor said, smiling, his spectacles resting on the tip of his nose.

"Amazing, sir. Thank you!"

213

The professor tilted his head to the side, smiled, and continued. "Son, what are you doing Friday night?"

"Studying, sir, why?"

"Well, I was wondering if you would be so kind as to do me a favor?"

"Like what?"

"Well, we might get to that later. Meet me at my office this afternoon at 1:00. Is that a good time for you?"

Hesitantly, Mark responded: "Um, I guess. I don't have class until four, so yeah, sounds good, Professor Jakes."

"Wonderful. You know, it's hard to find reliable people these days," Jakes said, placing the top on the container.

"What do you mean, sir? I don't understand."

Jakes let out a loud, unnerving laugh. "Don't worry about it. C'mon, have another bite, while this stuff is still warm. No need to waste time waiting."

Mark shrugged his shoulders and grabbed another plastic spoon.

The professor looked around the cafeteria and then looked back at him, an inquisitive look on his face. "Shall we get this talk of business out of the way now or later? Which would you prefer?"

"We can talk now, if you want. Oh, and thank you, sir," Mark said, taking another spoonful.

"No, thank you. You know, I really feed off the energy you students have. Makes me wish I was young again," Jakes said, holding out the Tupperware dish.

"Really, professor?"

"Really, Mr. Schmidt. Really."

CEPHALOPOD

Justin Hunter

The parking lot of the Economy Inn was illuminated in an orchestra of light. Tall lamps sporting dirty metal halide bulbs shone the parking lot like day, driving away the night and eliminating pedestrian view of the stars. The motel was on Ashland Avenue in one of the busiest sections of the city of Green Bay, Wisconsin. The pollution over the years of steady, slow driving traffic, as well as copious chemical and salt road applications during winter, caused the parking lot to be covered by a thin yet visible layer of grime. The soot-like casing encompassed the motel as well. It was an unpleasant sight. Places like the Economy Inn were an embarrassment to the city's government, which took pains to eliminate such decrepit local business. The blue collar community wouldn't allow that to happen, as such places are a public necessity. Dump motels are the havens for kicked-out husbands, poverty housing for underemployed minorities and love-nests for pay-by-the-hour whores and their Johns.

Derek turned his rusted-out Ford F150 pickup truck into the motel lot, missing the ramp and bumping over a curb and running the driver's side tire over a bush. He thumped the tires into a concrete stopper in a spot right in

215

front of the motel manager's office. Derek heavily jammed the truck into park and rubbed his grizzled face. He looked at his bloodshot eyes in the rearview mirror. The world spun. He had imbibed at length at one of the bars that the city boasted on almost every corner. Nearly dead drunk, Derek still had the sense of mind that sleeping it off and returning home in the morning would catch him less hell from his wife than returning home in his current state.

Derek opened the door of his truck and gathered himself enough to step out without falling over. He forced himself to stand erect and took the ten steps to the manager's office door with the concentrated stiffness of an altar boy carrying the offering plate to the priest. He pulled on the door latch. It was locked. He looked inside and saw the bulbous form of the manager sleeping in a chair behind the desk. He beat the door with the palm of his hand, which startled the manager, who almost dropped his obese frame backwards off his chair. The abrupt wakeup enraged the manager. He slammed a fist on the counter and cursed vehemently. He rose from his seat and made his way around the counter and to the door, keeping up his litany of profanity as he moved his bulk forward. He unlocked the door and wrenched it open.

"What the fuck do you want?" the manager asked.

"I want a fucking room," Derek said. "What the fuck else would I be here for?"

"Forty," the manager said.

"Sign out front says twenty."

"Twenty for the room," the manager said. "Another twenty for being a fucking drunk prick banging on my door in the middle of the fucking night."

Derek felt red anger well up inside him, pushing through his drunken state. His ire begged violence. He felt his hand clench involuntarily as he saw himself smashing his already-bruised knuckles into that slovenly face staring back at him from the office door. The manager took a step back from the murderous look on Derek's face. The manager's anger morphed instantly into fear. This sudden turn from predator into prey took just enough off of Derek's rage to decline his violence. Derek dug into his pocket and took out a rumpled twenty and held it out. The manager took it into his fleshy palm and quickly dug a key out of his pocket.

"Room three," the manager said. "Checkout is at 11:00. If you're late, it will cost you another twenty." Derek nodded. The manager shut and locked the door. He waited until Derek walked away from him, and then went back to his chair behind the counter. He took a pack of cigarettes from his shirt pocket and lit one. He took a long pull and exhaled a slow stream of smoke into the stained asbestos ceiling tiles. He leaned forward and took a shotgun out from behind the counter and checked to make sure it was loaded. He had a feeling that he might need it.

Derek dragged the key along the enameled brick wall of the motel, flaking off large chunks of the yellowing white paint as he went. He made ample noise as he stumbled to his room, but he didn't care. His anger at the manager hadn't fully abated, and he half-hoped someone would leave their room and confront him about the noise. He prayed for a response, begged for a reason to be violent. The alcohol began to take over his body. Darkness drove in at the edges of his vision. Derek jammed the key into his thigh. A small blot of blood seeped through his jeans where he punctured himself. The adrenaline rush from the pain snapped the promise of passing out away for another moment, but that was all he needed. Derek found his room and unlocked the door. He went inside the room. An odor of stale cigarette smoke and sweat assailed his nostrils, making him retch. Derek tried to close the door, but it caught on his foot. He tripped forward and fell onto the thin mattress of the bed.

His last thought before losing consciousness was that he should close and lock the door. A moment later, he was beyond caring. His eyes rolled back in his head and he fell asleep.

A few hours later, a blanket-wrapped man walked from behind the Economy Inn building into the light of the parking lot. He stepped stiffly. His thinning, grey hair hung unkempt to his shoulders. His skin held the same dusty hue as his trailing locks. Deeply wizened, the man seemed almost shriveled. His eyes were sunken into his skull. The man stopped to peer at the lights of the motel, and then made his way toward the manager's office. He stepped gingerly. The loose gravel in the parking lot jabbed painfully into the soles of his shoeless feet. If that weren't suffering enough, he stepped onto the glass of a broken beer bottle and sliced a small line along the edge of his right foot. Blood jetted in a long arc, seeming to belie the superficiality of the wound. The man grimaced and bent down to his foot. When he did, the blanket parted, exposing his nakedness underneath. He picked up a small gravel stone and stuffed it into the cut. The plug stopped the jettison of blood. The man pushed the stone further into his flesh. When he was sure it was secure, he stood up, flexed his foot, and limped to the office door.

The office manager awoke to what sounded like slapping at his door. He rubbed his face and checked the time. It was half-past three. The office manager sighed. He had been running the Economy Inn motel for over twenty years. He knew that anybody decent was asleep at this time of night. The normal people of the city had been in bed for several hours. Barflies should have all been home by now, too; the bars had been closed long enough. Even the usual vagrant or oppressed clientele he usually served had chosen their rooms and should give the world a break from their presence for several hours more. The only customer who showed up at this time was a bad one.

Trouble. They were drug addicts, cut-up prostitutes or runaway children. The office manager didn't think children used to be trouble, until he tried to help one out one night and was jailed for pedophilia. The kid went along with the story the police fed him because he didn't want to get in trouble with his parents. The office manager cooled his heels in jail while they figured out that mess. That was the last time he gave a child—no matter how desperate—a second glance. He took the shotgun out from behind the counter and went to the door.

The office manager unlocked the door and held the shotgun out of view behind it as he opened up. The breath caught in his throat as he took in the blanketed man's gray and deeply-lined face. The manager looked the man over and saw the bare and bloody feet. The office manager had seen much what depravity and poverty did to the people of his city, but something about this man stood out from the rest. He would have put the shotgun in the man's face and told him to leave, except for the man's eyes: the whites of the wrinkled man's eyes were yellowed, and the irises barely tan beyond the orb; the man looked desperately ill. There was something else, too. Something about those eyes told him of deep sadness, and even gentleness. Maybe the man was just homeless and sick. The office manager steeled himself against his feelings of compassion by his history of being taken advantage of for it.

"I'm full up," the office manager said. "No vacancy." The man didn't answer. He leaned forward, pushing his face inside the office. The office manager took the shotgun from behind the door and pointed it at the man's grey face. The gentleness left the lined man's eyes. There was no feeling there whatsoever anymore. Nothing.

The office manager pumped the shotgun and put the barrel against the other man's forehead.

"Drugs?" the manager screamed in the other's face. "Are you high? Fuck off out of my door, or I'm going to blow your brains all over the fucking parking lot. The only person who'll give a shit you're dead is the wetback I'm going to have clean up your skull fragments in the morning." The blanket dropped from the sloped shoulders of the crease-skinned man. His bent back showed every brittle bone of his spine through paper-thin skin; wrinkled like a raisin.

"What the hell?" the manager said as his eyes ran over the shrunken hull of the man at the end of his gun. The grey man's mouth dropped open to reveal rotten gums in a toothless mouth. Saliva seeped to the floor as thick, mosquito-like mandibles lowered from his jaw. The office manager pulled the trigger. The shotgun didn't fire. The safety was on. The long appendage from the mandible shot forward. The office manager dodged with speed that belied his bulk. The stinger missed the manager's heart and stuck home in his left shoulder. Immediately, the grey man inhaled mightily. The office manager shrieked as immense pain shot through his body. Everything inside his shoulder wrenched and tore. He looked at his shoulder and could literally see it shrinking.

Eaten, he thought. *I'm being eaten.* The office manager struggled with the grey man in wild panic. Mere seconds had passed, but time seemed to slow where each moment seemed an eternity. The office manager's left hand ripped at the face of his assailant. He plunged a thumb into the grey man's right eye, but the orb yielded like water against rock. It was impossible to crush the eye as it recessed against his attack. A moment later, it was impossible anyway; the office manager felt all the strength leave his arm. The flesh sank from the appendage. The fingers of the emaciated hand curled inward. Rolls of skin hung limp off the bone. The grey man arched his back and heaved to get the last of the fluid. The office manager saw the wizened lines of the man fill out. His body seemed less grey as the office manager's body fluids filled the creature's thirsting body.

The office manager felt the proboscis sink deeper into this body, away from the arm and into his main body cavity. He felt the world begin to go black at the edges of his vision. In a last effort, he swung the shotgun with his right hand and hit his attacker across its face. The jarring blow stopped the creature from drinking for a moment. The office manager jammed the butt of the shotgun against his leg and pumped a shell into the chamber, using his body as leverage for his right hand. He didn't take time to aim as he fired an ear-splitting blast at point-blank range. The bullet tore through the creature's belly, and gore exploded out its lower back. The backfire knocked the office manager to the floor. The proboscis ripped out of his shoulder with the fall. He fell on his left arm. The bones—bereft of muscle and blood—splintered under the impact of his obese body. The pain begged unconsciousness, but the manager slammed the butt of the shotgun against the floor and chambered another round. The creature was blasted out of the doorway and held its hands against its stomach, trying to stop the torrent of blood streaming onto the motel walkway. Its new pinkish flesh quickly dissolved back to its grey and shriveled form at the loss of blood. The office manager watched as the mandibles slid back down the creature's throat. The thing looked up from his wound at the manager. Its yellowed eyes showed neither feeling nor pain.

"Die," the office manager said. "Fucking die, you fucking thing." The creature took a step forward. The office manager sat up. Pain from his arm shook his frame. He pointed the shotgun at the creature. "I've got another one ready for you." The creature stepped back and walked away from the manager's office and toward the line of motel rooms. The manager dropped to the dirty carpeted floor, passing out completely.

Anyone coming upon this scene would have been a bit nonplussed to see a wrinkled and hunched man, completely nude and pouring blood, shambling door to door. As it was, nobody was on the street. That time of night is for the soulless and the lost. The people—good, bad or indifferent—were all in bed. Even the insomniac, lying in their wretched stupor, is too wrapped up in his own problems to be wakeful to the horrors of the world; those that walk, rend and kill. The creature made his way down the corridor of motel rooms, its bloody hand testing each doorknob as it passed. Each door it tried was locked. It moved on to the next one, finally coming to room three. It reached for the doorknob, but saw the door was slightly ajar. It took a hand and soundlessly pushed the door open and walked inside.

Derek dreamed of his daughter. He was home sitting on his couch, watching her run round and round the living room carpet. She was a delightful four-year-old. Her hair stuck out in all directions in unkempt thick curls. She wore her usual self-selected crazy attire—this time it was a superman cape, rain boots and a princess tiara. She ran in circles, making herself dizzy and squealing with happiness. Derek fought the urge to stop her running. He was worried she would get hurt. The parental instinct to protect was fighting with his urge to allow her to continue the joy of her play. She fell to the floor and laughed as the world spun before her eyes. She stood up once her vision steadied and ran over to her father. She tugged at Derek's pant leg, begging him to come and play. Derek felt too tired to get up and play with her. He told her to keep running and he would be right here watching. His daughter continued to tug at his leg. She punched him playfully on the thigh. His thigh hurt from the blow; it seemed to be damaged more than he thought her little fist should be able to do. He told his child to be gentle. She whimpered at his gentle discipline and went back to tugging at his pant leg. She pulled so hard that Derek began to slip from the couch. He told her to take it easy. He was beginning to be frightened of her strength. He told her to stop. She leaned over and bit his thigh. Blood spouted, splashing over her face and hanging in droplets from her curls. She pulled hard, ripping him off the couch and onto the floor. He screamed as his daughter jabbed her cherub hand into his thigh. She shoved hard, pushing her hand into his leg up to her elbow. She tried to pull her hand out but was stuck. She looked at her father with a worried look and began to cry. Derek reached out and patted her blood-splattered cheek, trying to comfort her. He reached his other hand over and grasped her stuck arm by the elbow. He pulled, but her hand wouldn't come out of his leg. Blood welled from the hole and was absorbed by the thick carpet. He pulled again. The arm wouldn't budge. His daughter began to cry harder. He tugged and said soothing words to his little girl.

Derek woke to his body being roughly jarred and shaken. His eyes seemed to melt themselves open. His vision was blurred. His eyes were bone dry. He blinked, but his eyelids were empty of moisture. He shook his head to regain his drink-shrouded sight. His leg was throbbing. He felt his hand gripping something warm; yielding yet firm, like the aged stalk of a thick plant. The pain ripped through his leg. He could feel a pulling sensation from his hip to his calf. His vision cleared. He looked at his lower body to see the creature hunched over his leg, its mouth appendage stuck deep into Derek's now-emaciated thigh. Derek gasped in horror-drenched awe as the man-thing sucked his leg dry. He screamed, tearing at the creature's proboscis. Derek could feel the ready, rhythmic pumping of his lifeblood being sucked into the parasite. The motel room floor was covered in blood—the creature was wounded, and every ounce of Derek it took into its body mostly seeped immediately out of its gashes and onto the room's spotted carpet. Derek pulled at the creature's proboscis, but it wouldn't budge. Derek reached into the back pocket of his jeans and took out a thick folding knife. He let go of the creature's stinger and opened the blade.

The pain in his leg seared through his form as he leaned forward and plunged the knife into the creature's throat. Over and over he stabbed—his efforts only made the creature suck harder to drain him. Derek stopped stabbing the throat and slashed at the creature's proboscis; he made a cut in the tube, but didn't sever it completely. Upon receiving the gash, the creature pulled its proboscis back into its mouth and lunged forward, punching Derek in the face. Derek braced against the blow, but it came softer then he thought. When he expected the hard bones of the creature's knuckles, he felt something less than the density of cartilage smash him across the bridge of the nose. It was like getting slapped in the face with a cooked salmon. The back of his head bounced off the floor from the blow, but it didn't hurt him. It only succeeded in clearing his alcohol-addled head.

Rage burned in Derek. He rose again at his torso and slashed with the blade, looking to kill. He cut a long gash in the creature's chest. It rose. Derek lunged with his blade. He jammed the knife into the creature's groin, cutting its penis in half. The creature fell backwards against the motel wall, knocking over its ancient RCA analog television. Derek tried to stand, but his left leg buckled and broke under his weight at the knee. He screamed a slew of curses and grabbed his destroyed leg. Ice seemed to crawl up his body as he grabbed his knee. Incredibly, his hands fit easily around his appendage. He looked to see that the broken leg was four times smaller than his other one. It was as if everything living was drained from it, leaving nothing but sagging skin and bone. He fought hysteria at his disbelief of what he was seeing of his own body.

The door to the motel room banged open. The office

manager—bloodied and half his body shrunken from the creature's ferocious feeding—stepped into the room, the shotgun held in his right hand and steadied by the skeletal fragments of his left arm. He fired at the creature. The bullet exploded against the creature's left thigh, amputating its leg. It fell to the floor and writhed in soundless misery. The recoil of the blast dislocated the office manager's right shoulder and made the (now) half-fat man thump on his backside. He uttered a low moan.

"Hey, asshole," Derek said to him. "I want my twenty bucks back."

"No refunds," the manager said.

The creature sprang from the floor. It seemed to defy gravity as it vaulted in an eight-foot-tall arc from across the room and landed on the office manager. The manager had one moment where he saw the beast in the air, its body akimbo in its leaping assault. A mass of blood, torn flesh and dead eyes, it landed on the manager heavily. Its mouth opened, shooting out its wounded proboscis. It impaled the manager through his left eye and jammed square into the center of his brain. The creature sucked hard as the office manager's head imploded. The skull remained the only thing that kept any form of the human head intact. The creature vacuumed out the man with dizzying quickness. The skin of the man, once stretched taut by obesity, fell about him like rolls of fabric. As quickly as the office manager was drained, the genetic matter leaked in red waves from the wounds of the creature. It was like trying to fill a water balloon with holes in it. Derek watched in horrified awe as the creature turned toward him and launched again. It pinned him to the ground in the same type of embrace that killed the office manager.

The proboscis shot toward Derek's eye just as he punched the creature on the temple. The blow was enough to make the deadly nozzle of the beast miss him and scrape the carpet next to his head. Derek grabbed the proboscis quicker than the creature could pull it away. He bit down on it and ripped his head sideways, tearing the creature's mouthpiece in half. The creature reared back and put its hands over its mouth. It fell sideways since it only had one leg left to its body. Derek pulled himself forward, ignoring the throbbing pain of his dead leg. He ripped his knife out of the beast's groin and swung his arm, trying to stab it in the face. He missed. He swung again, but his immobile leg made his movements almost comical. The creature slid away from him.

"You're hurting now, aren't you?" Derek said. He brandished the knife at the beast. He saw the yellow eyes look over his head at the door behind him. "You want to leave? Just try and get past me. A couple more slices at that ugly face of yours is all I need to end you."

The creature turned toward a small A/C wall vent and ripped it off, exposing the small ventilation duct. It stuffed itself headfirst into the hole. The creature pushed and rolled. Derek laughed.

"I don't see where the hell you think you're going," Derek said. Suddenly, a large jettison of blood flooded from the creature's body with such force that Derek was pushed back a whole foot. The creature was emptying itself of fluid as it impossibly crammed itself into the ductwork tube. Derek crawled toward it. The pain in his leg was like nothing he had ever felt before. The intensity of his agony made every movement a monument of torture. Inches felt like miles. Derek saw the creature work over halfway into the ductwork tube that couldn't have been more than ten inches in diameter. He remembered the feeling of the creature's soft bones when it struck him as he saw its hips flex, bend and fold into impossible smallness. Derek gave up his crawling—he knew there was no way he was going to catch the creature before it escaped through the hole. A moment later, it was gone.

Derek rolled over on his back and stared at the

ceiling. His breath came in short gasps. He was delirious from the pain in his leg. He could feel the pulsating ache of the dry and shriveled appendage all the way up to his stomach. He wondered just how much the creature took from him; wondered how dead he was from the waist down. He heard a noise at the door and raised his head to see what it was. Standing in the doorway were three of the grey men. Their sunken eyes burned yellow. Their mouths were open, salivating eating appendages drooping from their jaws. Their skin was deeply lined with the texture of a dry corn husk.

"I've really got to learn to lock that door," Derek said. He looked down at his body. Blood seeped from the puncture in his leg. He felt faint and dreadfully week. "There's not much left of me," Derek said. "Enjoy the fucking appetizer."

Then they set upon him.

ASSFACE

Rich Bottles Jr.

Dolores's name was Dolores. But only Dolores's mother ever called Dolores by the name Dolores. Everyone else just called Dolores "Assface."

Dolores was damn ugly.

All through her young life, Dolores was reminded of her appalling appearance by everyone she encountered in her otherwise-sheltered life. There was never any concern by anyone about protecting or promoting self-esteem within the impressionable youth, just constant verbal and nonverbal reminders of her repugnancy.

It is true, Dolores had very little to compare herself to, living a sheltered life as aforementioned—sheltered actually being a shack where she and her mother lived: A shack where the windows were boarded up so that Dolores could not see the charming children of the neighborhood at play; where there was no television that Dolores could watch the beautiful people of Reality TV; and where the only looking glass in the house was behind her mother's locked bedroom door.

"Mother, may I gaze into your bedroom mirror while you are at rest on the couch?" shyly asked Dolores one morning while her mother was blowing a man on the living room couch.

The man laughed heartily, and then heartlessly responded, "Oh, Assface, you should not attempt to look at yourself in a mirror, you'll only scare yourself to death! Not too long ago I took a major dump in the toilet and did not flush it, so go off to the bathroom and look in the bowl if you really want to see what you look like!"

Although her mother said nothing during this particular exchange, her mouth being preoccupied as it was, Dolores reminded herself what her imaginary friend had previously said about Dolores's particular beauty – it being the inside variety instead of the outside kind. Thus, Dolores did not venture into her mother's bedroom that day, even though the door was unlocked.

Inside of Dolores was a shy, backward, young female, who was shack-schooled by her mother to the best of her ability; although Dolores was mostly left to figure out things on her own. For instance, Dolores knew that her body was maturing because of the dark black wiry hair which was sprouting between her legs, under her arms and below her nose.

Dolores also determined that she and her mother must live in a country called Mexico, which she ascertained from listening to the radio while her mother was at work and Dolores was home alone. As far as where in Mexico she lived, she often heard her mother tell people on her cell phone that she lived and worked in "Zona Norte."

Dolores's mother worked during the evenings, so Dolores was usually at home by herself after nightfall. Over the years, she had gotten used to being alone in the darkened shack and was thankful that she had a radio to keep her company. She liked to sing and dance to the musical programs on the radio, but disliked the "talking shows," which she had trouble comprehending.

Her favorite time of the day was the morning, when her mother would come home and bring her some food to eat. Dolores could not play the radio at that time, however, because her mother liked the shack to be quiet while she was sleeping.

But sometimes in the morning, after her mother went off to bed, Dolores whispered to her neighborhood friends through the boards of her bedroom window. She considered these children as *real* friends, not imaginary ones.

The youngsters would ask her to come outside to play, but Dolores would tell them that she was not allowed. Dolores would also tell them that she was not allowed to attend public school or go to Mass at the local church. In fact, the only mention of God she encountered was when her mother brought men into the locked bedroom and the entity's name was sometimes screamed out loud enough for Dolores to hear.

Dolores detested when her mother brought men to the shack in the morning—not just because her mother would forget to bring Dolores food, but because the men were often cruel to Dolores, calling the youngster nasty names and laughing at her awkward appearance. One man in particular was particularly mean, and in a very particular way.

The man claimed that he was unable to make Dolores's mother happy in the locked bedroom unless he first visited Dolores in her bedroom. This did not make Dolores happy, especially since he would spend his time with Dolores yelling at her and telling her that she deserved to be beaten because of the way she looked.

The man would make her lay face down on her mattress while he removed his thick leather belt from his trousers. Dolores could always hear the sudden whisk of the belt as it quickly snaked through the loops of his pants. The dreaded sound made her whimper into her pillow. She always wished that her mother would burst into the room and save her, but her mother never did.

"I'm going to beat that ugliness right out of you, Assface!" the man would declare just before he started lashing her back and behind with the looped belt.

Dolores was often tempted to roll off the mattress or move her hands behind her back to protect herself from the searing lashes, but she knew from past experiences that such defensive actions would only get her tied to the mattress and lashed even more severely. Sometimes she knew her friends were just outside the boarded window, listening to her ordeal, and she felt ashamed.

"If you were pretty like other children, there would be no need to punish you," explained the man as he lashed away at her inflamed skin, "but you were born of sin, so you must pay the price for your wretchedness!"

Dolores could feel the burning welts rising from her tortured skin, often crisscrossing across her body several times over from her shoulder blades down to the soles of her feet, until the entire backside of her body was covered. She bawled into her pillow, trying to mute her protestations, especially if her friends were listening.

Eventually, the man would become tired and she would begin to feel splashes of his sweat hit her scorched skin, bringing just a tiny bit of relief to her tormented body. His strikes would also become less forceful as his breath became more labored. Then he would suddenly stop, rush out of Dolores's room, and yell out, "I think I'm ready for you now, momma!"

One such morning, while Dolores lay sobbing on her mattress after a vicious lashing, she thought she heard a familiar voice outside her bedroom window. "Hey, are you all right in there? Hey, talk to me. Are you all right?"

Dolores rolled off her mattress and moved toward the boarded window. The voice was of a teenage boy who often visited her at the window. "Please be quiet," Dolores desperately whispered. "If they hear you, I will be punished again."

"Why were you punished? What did you do?" the boy asked in a lower tone.

"I am ugly," Dolores admitted, "and deserve to be

punished. It also brings happiness to my mother."

"You do not deserve to be beaten, no matter what you look like," the boy replied. "You need to run away from this shack and never return."

"But I am locked in at night when my mother is at work," she answered. "Besides, where would I run to? No one can stand the looks of me."

"Where is your father? Perhaps he can care for you."

"My mother says she still works with my father," Dolores explained. "She also says my father never wants to see me because I am so ugly."

"Perhaps your mother is lying. I cannot imagine that a father would never want to see his own daughter. I think you should follow your mother to work and confront your father—tell him of the abuse that your mother allows to take place in this shack."

"But how can I follow her if she locks the door when she leaves at night?"

"I can bust you out," he offered. "I will fetch a tool from my father's shed and I will lie in wait until your mother leaves."

Her back still stinging from the lashing and her trust building for the only male who had never abused her, Dolores asked, "When? What day should you bust me out?"

"It should be tonight, while your wounds are still fresh," he concluded. "You can show the marks to your father to prove the abuse you have endured. He may also be surprised that your mother brings these strange men to your shack."

"Oh God, oh God, oh God!" was heard emanating from the adjacent room.

"I must go now," Dolores implored. "They may come out of the locked bedroom and come for me."

"I will see you tonight, then," he promised.

Although her back was still tender and aching

horribly, Dolores found the strength to lie down on her back upon the mattress. She then began masturbating while thinking about what the boy outside her window looked like. Masturbating was something else Dolores discovered on her own.

Dolores had the rest of the day to contemplate her situation, but each time she considered continuing her life inside the shack, she would hear footsteps or harsh voices and realize that she was living in a state of perpetual fear. The bruised muscles in her back and legs would also start to involuntarily spasm whenever she heard anyone walk close to her bedroom.

Dolores did not leave her bedroom that day until it was time to say goodbye to her mother. She watched as her mother dug around in her purse to find the key which would lock Dolores in the shack for the night.

"Goodbye, mother," Dolores said as her mother approached the door to the shack. "Please tell Papa that I am thinking of him."

The woman ignored her daughter's unusual request and walked out the door. Dolores could hear her mother securing an exterior lock on the opposite side of the door. Then all was quiet again in the shack.

Dolores had begun doubting the boy's promise to help her when she suddenly heard a loud scraping noise on the door. As she approached the door to listen more closely to the sound, the door sprung open, revealing a surprised teenage boy holding a crowbar in the threshold.

The boy's jaw dropped open and his eyes widened when he saw Dolores. The crowbar slipped from his trembling hand and clanked onto the sidewalk. He quickly turned his gaze away from Dolores and looked to the ground.

"Thank you for helping me," Dolores greeted, slowly approaching the threshold. "Which direction did my mother go?"

The boy reluctantly pointed up the street where

some flickering streetlamps illuminated the dusk, and then he ran in the opposite direction, leaving his father's crowbar behind. "Wait!" yelled Dolores to the retreating boy, but to no avail.

Dolores scampered into the cool night air, heading toward the streetlamps and neon lights of La Coahuila Avenue. She tried to maintain a low profile and she kept her head down so that she would not draw unwanted attention or unnecessarily frighten any strangers she might encounter.

There were a few people transversing the sidewalks of La Coahuila, but they paid Dolores no mind, except perhaps to move out of her way. Dolores glanced up from time to time in order to try to catch a glimpse of her mother, which she eventually did when Dolores watched the woman enter a seedy-looking bar called Jack's Caballeriza.

Afraid of being recognized, Dolores snuck into an alleyway, which ran along the side of the bar. She was also becoming more and more afraid of the strange men on the sidewalk and the noisy automobiles on the street. She started to miss the solitude of the shack and regretted her decision to leave.

Broken glass and bone fragments littered the alley, and a large rat darted into the path of Dolores, causing her to shriek. A drunken homeless person stirred to her left, barely visible in the diminishing light, while the smell of vomit and urine filled Dolores's nostrils. She picked up her pace.

Upon turning the corner of the building, Dolores noticed a back entrance to the bar, and was relieved to see that the door was left open and that no one could be seen within. She quietly entered the brightly lit room, which she recognized as a kitchen. She wondered whether the food her mother brought her was prepared in the room.

Dolores quickly found an interior door, which she easily pushed open, and subsequently entered into a dark hallway. She could hear muffled voices and mangled music from her position within the empty hallway. Her first instinct was to run away from the unsettling sounds, but her curiosity and her desire to see her father kept her moving forward.

The hallway led to a large room with many tables. This room was also very dark, being poorly illuminated by some candles on the tables. Dolores also noticed some soft yellow electric ceiling lights on the other side of the room, positioned directly above a large bar area and a small stage. The wall behind the bar was stocked with lots of glimmering bottles and a gaudy painting of a nude woman reclining on a settee. Between the bar and the stage was an ancient-looking jukebox, where the eerie music was playing.

Dolores saw a man and a woman standing on the wooden stage. She immediately recognized her mother as the woman, but it took a minute for Dolores to realize that the man was her belt-wielding tormentor. The pair on stage seemed to be engaged in a heated argument. The couple's argument abruptly ended when the man backhanded the woman's face. Both stormed off the stage and disappeared behind a dusty curtain. The only objects left on the stage were a microphone stand and an old wood-planked rain barrel.

Apparently alone now in the large room, Dolores crept out from the hallway and located a table in the darkest corner of the barroom. She blew out the candle on top of the table to make the corner even darker, and then crouched down and hid herself under the table. She quietly waited, but didn't know why or what she was waiting for. She wished she had stayed at the shack where she belonged.

Dolores soon realized that the longer she waited, the less chance she had of escaping the bar unnoticed, because the room slowly began filling with patrons. She watched as some customers took seats at the bar, while others sat down at the tables. She was thankful that no one chose to sit at the table where she was hiding, which she attributed to the darkness of the space and the distance of the table from the stage.

Eventually, the man who had smacked Dolores's mother walked back onto the stage and approached the microphone stand. He was no longer wearing dirty jeans and a T-shirt, but was now adorned in a black and white rhinestone-studded mariachi uniform, complete with a bright red neckerchief and a wide round sombrero.

"Welcome to Jack's Caballeriza!" he announced into the microphone, his voice rising slightly above the relentless jukebox music. "It's time for our first performance of the evening! Please welcome the 'Criada del Criadero,' the lovely Miss Nina!"

A spattering of applause accompanied the appearance on stage of Dolores's costumed mother, while the emcee jumped down off the elevated stage and then removed the microphone stand. The woman strutted barefoot around on the stage like she was marching in a demented Las Posadas parade.

Dolores was shocked at her mother's bizarre costume, which made the woman look like a peasant farmhand. The woman wore a pair of frayed jean shorts which showed off her lower ass cheeks, and were held up by a length of rope. Partially covering her chest was a meager red and black plaid halter top, secured in the middle by a knot, leaving her shapely midriff bare. She also sported a straw hat, like field workers wear, and she was chewing on a long strand of wheat.

The patrons of the club (who appeared to be all men) immediately began chanting, keeping rhythm with whatever song was spewing from the jukebox, "Take it off! Take it off! Take it off!"

Dolores's mother playfully tugged on the small knot which kept her makeshift halter top from separating, smiling deviously at the crowd while she loosened the garment. Suddenly her breasts burst forth from their plaid prison, accompanied by the appreciative whoops and catcalls of the visitors.

She allowed the top to drop to the floor and then cupped both breasts with her hands, squeezing the large orbs like putty. She also rubbed her nipples with her palms before using her fingers to pinch and tweak the erect buds.

Almost the entire crowd loved her performance, raising their cheers well above the music. There was only one individual in the crowd who was not enthusiastic over the show, and that individual was Dolores, who lowered her head in shame.

"Show us your ass! Show us your ass! Show us your ass!" shouted the men as soon as they became tired of watching Dolores's mother playing with her tits.

Dolores's mother turned her back to the audience and leaned forward, half-mooning the men. The men's vocal reaction slowly began reaching a crescendo as Dolores's mother wriggled out of the jean shorts, pulling them completely down below her thighs, and eventually kicking them off with her foot.

The men continued to yell, "Show us your ass! Show us your ass! Show us your ass!"

As Dolores's mother danced completely naked except for the hat, the emcee jumped back onto the stage with the microphone in his hand. "You say you want to see her ass?" he asked.

"Show us your ass! Show us your ass! Show us your ass!"

"Okay!" he exclaimed, walking backstage. Dolores's mother busied herself by tipping the barrel over on its side.

"Show us your ass! Show us your ass! Show us your ass!"

Soon the emcee re-emerged, pulling a long rope behind him. Dolores's mother spread her body over the

237

barrel.

"Show us your ass! Show us your ass! Show us your ass!"

The men in the audience seemed to know what was attached to the other end of the rope, but Dolores was clueless and curious and began crawling out from her hiding place beneath the table. No one seemed to notice Dolores, because all eyes were directed onto the stage.

The crowd erupted in applause when an old, droopy-backed, mangy donkey reluctantly appeared on the stage. The emcee patiently led the beast over to Dolores's mother, who had her butt raised up directly in front of the approaching animal. From any vantage point in the room, everyone was able to clearly see the humungous erection hanging beneath the donkey.

When the emcee began helping the donkey mount Dolores's mother, lifting up its front legs to cover the woman's back, a piercing scream was heard from the back of the room. The shriek was involuntary and not meant to bring attention to her, but everyone in the room still turned their focus from the spectacle on stage to the spectacle which was Dolores.

As the crowd focused its attention on the pathetic-looking young female in the back of the room, many of the men began laughing at Dolores's predicament. Dolores could do nothing but scream and scream again, as if her histrionics were going to stop the scene around her from unfolding, especially since her incessant screams eventually deteriorated into demented-sounding brays.

Dolores's mother attempted to look and ascertain what the commotion was about in the back of the room, but the beast behind her suddenly achieved penetration and caused her to start screaming like her unfortunate progeny. The spectators were torn between which of the bizarre exhibitions to speculate.

The emcee laughed along with the crowd, his

boisterous voice amplified by the microphone. "Hey, Assface!" he announced. "We're so glad you could join us this evening. Come on up to the stage and meet your papa! Although he's preoccupied right now, perhaps providing you with a new sibling!"

The hurtful words of the emcee caused Dolores to start spinning around on all fours, continuing her panicked squalling. She then rushed toward the stage side of the room, kicking over tables and chairs in her path. Some patrons jumped out of her way, while others amused themselves by slapping Dolores's bristly hide.

"Calm down there, Assface, unless you want another good thrashing!" the emcee threatened while removing the heavy belt from his pants with his free hand.

Dolores snapped her snaggle-toothed snout at the evasive hands of the men, spraying spit and snot across the room. She succeeded in biting a few errant fingers, which increased the level of chaos in the barroom. The disturbance could be heard out on the street, where a Tijuana police officer strolled along Coahuila Avenue.

The officer entered the crowded bar to witness what appeared to be a brawl in the center of the floor. Splintered pieces of wood from smashed chairs and tables flew across the room, accompanied by panicked screams and screeches, emanating from within a large group of men. The officer pushed his way through the pack, trying to get to the epicenter of the disturbance.

The policeman eventually found himself face-to-face with a beast-like creature, half covered in patchy fur and baring her mangled teeth at him. Dolores brayed at the cop, glaring at him with demonic red eyes. She stomped her left front limb toward the officer like she was preparing to charge him.

"Stand back, everyone!" commanded the officer as he drew his service revolver from its holster. Seeing the situation was coming under control, the emcee began patiently looping the belt back through his pants.

The donkey on stage ignored the activity on the floor, instinctively continuing the carnal camisade on its concubine's cunt. Hearing the officer's voice, the woman twisted her neck desperately to find Dolores, but had very limited mobility with a determined donkey draped over her back.

When Dolores's mother heard the fatal gunshot, which split open the young she-ass's skull, the panicked puta cried out, "Oh God, oh God, oh God!"

The burrowing burro brayed while the emcee smiled, both realizing that the woman's protestation was prompted more by her own orgasm than out of any concern for her fallen offspring. The refocused audience erupted in applause.

Raising the microphone to his mouth, the emcee thanked everyone for attending the performance, and expressed his sincere hope that the men would make it home safely. "As you're leaving, be mindful of the kindling."

THE HUMANS UNDER THE BED

Kevin Strange

Dexantheon opened his eye. Had he heard what he thought he heard, or was it another nightmare? They'd become so frequent, the terrible dreams of home invasion and violence upon his family, that he didn't immediately jump out of bed when he heard his son's scream.

It wasn't until he heard it again that he leaped from beneath his warm blankets and covered the distance between bedrooms in three loping steps. He swung the door open. Not letting the panic he felt in his wide chest seep into his voice, he said, "Dexy, Willex? You kids OK in here?"

His twins, Dex Jr. and his little girl Willex shared the room. They both had beds situated side by side against the far wall, but inevitably Dexantheon would find Willex curled up next to her brother each morning, snuggled in the crook of his arm.

Now her bed was empty, the covers thrown back. Dexantheon took a cautious step into the room. "Kids?"

Dexy's bed was occupied. A large lump under the

covers rose and fell, as though breathing. "You guys alright?" he asked; this time his anxiousness betrayed him and his voice squeaked a bit. Another step and he was beside the bed. Watching the lump, he carefully took hold of the corner of the blanket and held his breath. When he pulled it back, he had to suppress a cry.

Under the covers were two pint-sized little creatures staring up at him. One was green with reflective, aqua-colored scales, a huge unblinking red eye taking up three quarters of a face already more than half of the ugly little beast's entire body. It was shaped like a Twinkie stood on end: one elongated tube with thin, long arms and feet ending in webbed claws. Razor-sharp teeth lined a mouth that ran nearly all the way around the horrific creature's head, and a long blue tongue wagged out from one side, stretching half the length of its whole body.

The other thing resembled a grotesque fly if it'd been cooked in a microwave and left out in the heat of the sun to spoil. The thing was bluish gray in color, like what a potato might look like if left out in a dark alley in the winter. Its head was all eyes; two big bulbous things with thousands of facets, all red and wet. Four antennae sprouted up from the tiny crown of its head; a head not even half the size of its huge eyes. Its body shape was vaguely humanoid, with three sets of thin arms and one pair of skinny legs, each ending in a lobster-like claw. Two pairs of transparent, slimy wings jutted up off its back and hung down, draping over its thin, emaciated body like a see-through night gown. But its skin was the worst part: it was made up of tiny, pinhead-sized versions of itself. Like the itty bitty things had replicated and multiplied until they had become one larger version of themselves. They were constantly moving, shifting, trading places as they linked together, claw to claw and wing to wing, in tens of thousands of little connections.

But Dexantheon didn't have to suppress a cry

because there were little monsters in his child's bed. His children *were* the monsters in Dexy's bed. And he was a monster, too. A full-grown version of little Dexy—huge and scaly and just as awful looking as his son—and Willex was the spitting image of her mother. No, Dexantheon was startled because there was supposed to be a third monster in the room with his kids: their friend Buxtak, son of Buxtak the Horrible. Buxtak the Titan, the World Eater, the Invincible, The Scourge of the South and Defiler of Nations. He was also Dexantheon's best friend who'd died in the final battle with the humans.

Buxtak Jr. was staying the night, as he did every other weekend while the children's mothers worked night patrol around the monster city. If something happened to her little Buxy, his nine-headed serpentine mother would eat Dexantheon for breakfast...

"What's wrong, Dex? Where's Buxtak?"

Little Dexy looked up at his father, sniveling. His gigantic eye was moist; a tear threatened to drop down onto his enormous blue tongue. "D-daddy. Willex was talking about the humans again! Th-the humans under the bed!"

Dexantheon heard the toilet flush, and the steady *clomp, clomp, clomp* of Buxtak's fat feet stomping down the hallway. The yellow monster—no older than his children, but nearly as tall as the towering Dexantheon himself—awkwardly waddled into the room.

"Had to pee," the hulking monster said, his high-pitched voice betraying his youth. He was round and thick with two sets of stubby, antler-like hands, ending in even stubbier fingers tipped with reptile-like eyeballs (just like his mother's) sticking out of the top of a head that never really ended in a neck, just kept rolling on down his bulbous body. His legs were little more than ankles protruding from the base of his egg-shaped body, ending in two enormous feet longer than Dexy and Willex's entire bodies.

Buxtak flopped down on the floor next to Dexy's bed, where a single pillow lay. He was round and pudgy enough already—he didn't need to sleep in a bed to be comfortable.

Dexantheon sighed with relief and sat down on the edge of Dexy's bed, causing the front end to raise up from his hefty bulk. He stroked Dexy on top of his scaly little head. Dexy the fraidy cat. His sister was always tormenting him with stories of the humans.

"There are no such things as humans, Dex. Haven't been for a long time," Dexantheon tried to say in the calm, soothing voice that always quieted his son's fears. This time, however, the huge monster was not able to control his voice. It warbled when he mentioned the humans. He hadn't personally seen one in over 500 years. Not since the Great Purge, when humanity's single most awesome achievement, a self-aware super computer, dubbed itself the Overmind and called up mankind's greatest nightmares with its flesh forges, waging an endless genocidal war on its creators.

Dexantheon was born in one of those forges, fought in that war, personally murdered countless thousands of human beings. He was there when the last living person was skinned alive, quartered, and fed to the Overmind itself.

But lately, there had been talk, rumors and murmurs from the night patrols that weird looking things had been spotted in the hills and mountain ranges just outside the monster city, horrible creatures that looked like hairless monkeys warped and fused with steel and wires. Human technology. The kind of technology that hadn't existed since the Overmind grew itself a nightmarish flesh body and covered the entire world with great, creeping madness.

The monster city was one grand, cyclopian mound of writhing flesh. Tendrils and clawed things, bat wing-like drapes of semi-transparent flesh and doorways laced with fang-filled mouths made up the houses and buildings; phosphorescent giant eyeballs atop slimy, batracian stalks acted as streetlamps; and rivers of bright green slime served as roads, all weaving together into ambulatory mazes of Stygian horror the monsters called home, overseen by the titanic flesh mountain of gibbering, oozing, twitching horror known as the Overmind. Nothing of human civilization remained, and hadn't been seen in half a century.

"Yes huh," Dexy said, defiantly sitting up in his bed. "Willex said she hears them whispering under her bed at night! Tell him, Wil!"

The little fly creature next to him blushed. She looked embarrassed. She stammered through her explanation. "I-I hear things, Daddy. They... they talk about us when they think we're asleep."

Buxtak gulped and darted his finger-eyes around the room, as if scanning for humans. "I-is that true, sir? M-maybe I should sleep on the couch..."

Dexantheon sat stunned. His children stared up at him, waiting for an answer, for him to calm their fears and tell them everything would be OK.

He stood slowly and sighed. "Maybe," he said, scratching his scaly chin with a purple talon. "Maybe you're right. Maybe there are humans under your bed."

Dexy began to whine. He clutched Willex, another tear forming in his huge eyeball.

Suddenly Dexantheon shot his arm out and grabbed the foot of the bed, lifting it up off the floor, nearly touching it to the ceiling. "Hello?!" he yelled dramatically. "Any humans under there?!" He held his free hand up to the hole in the side of his head that served as an ear. "What's that? You're gonna eat my kids when I go to bed? Don't do that! They're good kids!"

Now all three children were laughing. The lumbering monster dropped the bed, causing his children to pop up into the air before landing back on the mattress made of coiled tentacles. He darted across the room and lifted the other bed. "Any humans under here?!?"

"Stop it, Dad!" Dexy said, his tears now caused by laughter.

Dexantheon charged across the room and swung open the closet door. "Is this where all you humans are hiding?!?"

Now the children's laughter filled the room. Even Buxtak was rolling around on the ground pretending to talk to humans under the bed. Dexantheon smiled. He tucked the children back into bed, kissed them each on the heads, and walked out of the room, shutting the door behind him.

As he crawled back into his own bed, the unease he'd felt earlier almost seemed silly. He turned off the light and laid in the dark for several minutes before turning the bedside lamp on. He peeked under his bed just once to make sure.

***

What woke Dexantheon next was not just the screams of his children; it was the screams of his children followed by an explosion that shook the foundation of their flesh home. Baring his gigantic fangs and flexing his foot-long talons, he galloped the short distance to the kids' room on all fours, ready to tear anything harming his offspring to pieces.

Putrid black smoke hit him as he crossed the threshold into Dexy and Willex's room. The smell of charred flesh assaulted his nostrils. He hoped to the Overmind that it was not the flesh of his children. As the smoke cleared and Dexantheon's eye adjusted to the thick darkness, he saw them. Not his children. There was no sign of the young monsters.

Humans. A pair of them.

They were nothing like he remembered them. The

soft-bodied creatures that he'd once dismembered and eaten in scores had changed in the five hundred years since he last laid eyes on them. There were two of them standing in front of the ragged, gaping, bleeding hole that should have been his son's bed.

Each one was different, but they shared several unmistakable similarities. Their skin was pale. Pale almost to the point of translucency, having never been exposed to the sun. Blue veins coursed through their mangled flesh, and Dexantheon could almost make out the layers of muscle under their skin. Their heads were caged inside a series of steel bars bolted to the tops of their heads and at the bases of their shoulders. Their eyelids were pinned to their foreheads and cheeks, causing their mouths to pull open in hideous grins that were home to jagged metal serving as teeth.

Their torsos were naked, revealing more twisted metal modifications. There was some sort of circular contraption bolted to the center of their chests. Thick metal spokes radiated out from the circular thing across their chests onto their upper arms, digging trenches in the flesh, seemingly grafted to the bones of their arms. The spokes continued past a pair of steel elbow joints, down the forearms, ending in foot-long metal claws grafted directly onto the flesh of their hands. Similar modifications crisscrossed their legs and feet.

It only took Dexantheon a moment to find out what purpose these modifications served. The circular things on their chests spun, creating a high-pitched hum as it sent gyroscopic energy through their technologically-enhanced limbs. This caused their entire bodies to vibrate and shake. Dexantheon was convinced they were about to shake themselves to pieces, when they struck.

They were faster than any human Dexatheon ever fought during the Purge. Stronger, too—tenfold. The two humans screamed, their voices warbled from the motion of all the metal fused to their bodies. They lunged at him as several more crawled out from the smoking pit in the middle of little Dex's room.

Both humans hit him at the same time, one on each of his tree trunk-sized arms. They wasted no time, slashing, biting and tearing at his nearly indestructible scaled hide. To his surprise, they'd already pierced his skin in the few seconds they'd been wailing away at him, a feat no human had ever achieved in hand to hand combat in the thousands of battles he'd fought during the Purge.

Dexantheon quickly smashed his arms together, squashing the first two humans like bugs. Their shattered and broken limbs hung uselessly in their steel cages, dripping blood and gore as the hulking monster wadded them up and used the whole mess like a baseball bat as the next wave crawled up out of the smoking hole in the floor, warbled their war cry, and charged him.

Three of the metal/flesh hybrids ran at him. Two were females with symbols carved into the sides of their heads, and the other a black-bearded male, huge in his own right. With his modifications, he stood nearly to the top of Dexanthon's chest. The monster swung his corpse-bat, making quick work of the first female, giving the second a chance to leap up onto his arm and scuttle onto his back while the male stepped forward, lifting his right arm, which had been fused with some kind of rectangular mace. Using his left arm as a counterbalance, the male human swung his arm weapon at Dexantheon, forcing the monster to parry using his corpse bat. The force of the blow buckled the steel beams and sent most of the wadded up flesh flying across the room.

With his weapon useless, Dexantheon reached back and pawed at the female, who was using some kind of a blowtorch attached to her head-cage to burn the top of the monster's head. Having been forged in flame and nightmare, the blowtorch did little damage, aside from giving the huge beast a slight headache. Dexantheon's talon hooked the torch's wiring and he flung the female off him like a booger. She landed half-in, half-out of the window in Dexy's room. As she struggled to crawl back into the house, the window's razor-sharp fangs snapped shut, severing the female in half at the waist. She twitched and bled, hanging from the wall, dying slowly.

Now face to face with the bearded human, Dexantheon threw a punch. To his surprise, the big man grabbed it mid-swing. The human swung his mace again, forcing Dexantheon to grab it with his free hand. Now deadlocked, the two muscled giants pushed and pulled on each other in a virtual stalemate; that is, until Dexantheon's long tongue split in two, revealing a two-pronged appendage hidden inside. The appendage struck out like a snake, embedding itself into the bearded human's forehead, causing him to instantly go limp. His mouth hung open and his stretched-open eyes glazed over.

Dexantheon was inside of his mind. The monster saw everything the big man saw: saw his fears, saw his memories, saw his whole short, violent life. And as another score of vibrating, screaming humans flooded out from the hole in his son's floor like a plague of locusts, Dexantheon saw the plan. The twisted, insane plot that these creatures had formed. The war they would now wage against the Overmind and his monster race.

And even as he beat, crushed, and smashed the biomechanical things with ease, he knew. After seeing inside the bearded man's brain, seeing what lay beneath him inside the catacombs underneath the monster city, Dexantheon knew...

...The humans would win the war.

***

Dexy was blind. The blast had knocked him unconscious. His ears rang so loudly, he couldn't hear himself crying. As he regained his wits, he felt an immense pressure on his chest. Finding he could still move his arms, he pushed and the pressure moved. The chaos in his little room came into focus as the pressure—his bed—fell from in front of his face, allowing him to see again.

What he saw was at least ten naked, vibrating, hairless monkeys, encased in a shiny material that he'd never seen before, attacking his daddy. Were these humans? The stories Willex had told him about the beings who once inhabited the Earth didn't describe the savage things crawling all over Big Dex—as his mommy called his daddy—at all.

Willex.

Panic set in as the small monster frantically searched through the rubble for his sister. He pulled a jagged piece of flooring away from the top of a pile and saw an arm partially concealed by more debris. Dexy redoubled his efforts, tossing aside the fragmented remains of his bedroom to fully uncover the limp body of his sister.

Lifting one last big hunk of bone that served as his floor, Dexy freed his sister from the mound of rubble. "Willex!" he screamed. His voice still sounded far off, but the ringing had begun to subside. Dexy began to hyperventilate. She wasn't moving. "Willex!" he screamed again, this time shaking her arm. The little fly-girl stirred, coughing.

Relief surged through the small cyclops monster.

"W-what's happening?"

"Humans!" Dexy said, almost excited by the invasion.

Willex's own eyes bulged. She peeked around the huge pile of rubble separating the little monsters from the battle raging next to their bedroom door."We have to hide!" she said, pulling pieces of bone around them to conceal their location.

A huge hand shot out from the side of the rubble. Eyeballs on the tips of the fingers blinked dust away. Buxtak shook himself the rest of the way free. He smiled dumbly at the other two monsters. "Hey," he said, oblivious to the events transpiring directly behind him.

"Don't worry," Dexy said, smiling back. He pointed at his father. "Daddy will protect us!"

***

Big Dex deflected a blow from a pair of humans with spinning buzz saws grafted to their chests using the body of the huge bearded man. The saws shot sparks all over the room as they connected with the gyroscope on his chest, causing an awful, high-pitched squealing noise.

Big Dex's tongue was still embedded into the man's forehead. It stretched across the human's head like a fleshy mohawk before it connected back into Big Dex's mouth another five or six feet away. The bearded human's mouth still hung slack as Big Dex controlled his limbs, having gained complete control of his nervous system. The monster crushed faces and stomped bodies into mush even as he controlled the burly man's reflexes, causing him to smash the two buzz saw-wielding humans with his mace arm (his other having already been sliced off, along with one of his legs). His intestines hung freely from a giant gash in his stomach, and he oozed blood from half a dozen different mortal wounds across his body.

Big Dex figured he could get a few more good kills out of the big man before he'd have to discard him and stab into the mind of another lunatic human. As much fun as he was having felling scores of these savages, he couldn't shake the feeling of dread from the revelations made inside the human's mind. He needed to find his children, and he needed to get them to safety. That's all that mattered.

That's when the machine crawled out of the ground.

It was actually five humans, but they each had machine parts grafted onto their already-modified bodies. A pair of them had their left and right arms removed, respectively. In their place were what looked like cannon barrels cut in half down the center. Another pair was missing either leg in much the same fashion, while the fifth had no lower body at all, just a cylindrical piece of technology grafted onto its trunk that resembled the base of a lightbulb.

The bizarre people began to lock these various pieces into place while servos spun and lights all across the weird machine blinked on and off. The legless human climbed up the half-formed machine and screwed itself into a round opening at the top, completing the unusual piece of machinery.

Big Dex already knew what it was: a weapon. A flesh cannon powerful enough to destroy any monster caught between its crosshairs.

The Overmind had created its monsters to eradicate humans. It made them immune to human weaponry. Guns, bullets, rockets, bombs, were all useless against the hoards of terror. These humans had developed new technology. Big Dex knew because the bearded man knew. He saw the memories of countless millions of experiments over hundreds of years as the beings dwelling below the monster city turned their very bodies into weapons capable of killing monsters.

Big Dex braced himself, grabbing the bearded man around the waist to use as a shield while extracting his tongue from his forehead at the same time. Lights along the sides of the machine all lit up green, and the human screwed into the top of it began to spin. Smoke wafted up off the man's body as he screamed, spun faster and faster, and then, without warning, melted down into the barrel, skin, bones, and all, leaving the metal exoskeleton to fall, discarded off to the side of the machine.

A blast of molten flesh exploded from the barrel. Big Dex ducked behind the bearded man as best he could. The screaming, flailing man, now finally back in control of his own body but held fast by the monster's huge claw, took almost all of the supercharged blast, turning him into a red smear across the monster's scaly chest. Big Dex howled in pain as he looked down to find that his enormous claw had been disintegrated in the blast. The heat of the fleshy plasma had cauterized his mangled stump instantly.

Another legless torso crawled from the hole in the floor.

Ammo, Big Dex thought. *They're using their bodies as ammo.* And if he didn't act soon, he'd be joining his bearded friend as a splatter on his son's bedroom wall.

But the crazed, vibrating things were relentless. Worse, they didn't seem to give shit number one about their own lives. It was as though they enjoyed sacrificing themselves in droves if it meant the death of even a single monster.

Big Dex couldn't let that happen. He had to find the children.

Before the monster could move, another dozen humans swarmed around his legs, digging their claws and teeth into his scaly flesh, while still others clamped down around his feet at the floor, trying to hold him in place as the next "bullet" screwed itself into the man-machine.

***

Seeing his daddy's hand melted off in the blink of an eye wiped the smile right off Dexy's face. He tried to scream, but Willex put her hand over his mouth.

"Don't," she whispered. "If they can do that to

Dad, what do you think they'll do to us?"

Dexy began to cry again.

Big Dex roared. He kicked the humans clinging to his legs like ticks against the wall, smashing them dead, only to have even more fling themselves onto his body. He cracked skulls and bit clean through exoskeletons, but the droves of animalistic humans proved to be too much for him.

The human bullet atop the flesh cannon spun and the lights along its sides turned green as Big Dex was pulled to the floor by at least fifteen naked, vibrating humans. As the bullet-man spun and melted, Dexy broke free of Willex's grasp and screamed out "Daddy!" just as the flesh cannon fired. Buxtak threw his bulk on top of the smaller monster to keep him from running directly into the bio-blast.

Big Dex's eye met with his son's just as the flesh bullet hit him, pulverizing the huge monster's body, along with those of the humans pinning him to the ground.

The sound of the blast muffled Dexy's cry. The humans—those few remaining alive—shuffled back into the pit from whence they came. The flesh cannon disassembled itself, joining the others in the hole in the floor. After only a moment, the bedroom was quiet once again.

"Daddy!" Dexy screamed again. He pulled himself out from under the larger monster's body and ran to where his father lay. Big Dex was crumpled in a heap, his back to his son. When Dexy rolled him over, the little monster gasped and fell on his butt. Half his father's face, his entire arm and most of his chest were just... gone. Black, burnt flesh was all that remained. Big Dex's eye was open and unfocused, glazed over. Lifeless.

Then the hulking beast coughed and shuddered. His eye focused. "Dexy," he slurred.

"D-daddy..." the little creature said, voice hitching in his throat. He'd never had a reason to think his father anything but indestructible, a superhero. Seeing him prone and mangled was too much.

"C-come closer, Dexy." The wounded monster pushed himself—with some difficulty—up onto his elbow and turned his body to face his son.

Dexy did as instructed, his little eye darting to his father's wounds and then back to his face, as though ashamed to look at what the humans had done to his beloved parent.

"I have to...show you... Then you have...to find your...mom and show her. Understand?"

"Sh-show me what?"

Big Dex's tongue split. The forked appendage snaked out. He took hold of it and jammed the end into Dexy's neck.

Then, in that moment, the young monster knew that the humans had their eyes pinned open to keep them from shutting them in the face of the monster race's absolute horror. Knew that the factory which produced the gyroscopic modifications grafted to every human being on the planet lay deep, deep underground and spanned, impossibly, the entire length of the continent. And knew just how many scores of billions of humans were down there building machine bodies and flesh weapons, their only purpose to eradicate the monsters from the face of the Earth or die trying.

Dexy knew *everything*.

***

When Willex and Buxtak finally chanced a glance around the corner of the rubble, Big Dex was dead. Dexy stood alone, his back to his fallen father.

The little fly-girl buzzed through the air, while the lumbering Buxtak trailed behind her. "I-is he...?"

"Yes," Dexy said. A scowl adorned his features.

He no longer looked like an innocent, scared child. He was calm. Focused. He very much resembled his father in that moment, as though some part of the ages-old monster had transferred into his young son when he opened his mind to his boy. "He's dead. They killed him. And they're out there now, killing everyone else we've ever known. Everyone we love. And they won't stop until they kill every last one of us, or die trying."

Tears flowed down his sister's face. Her little mandible parts, constantly moving like an ecosystem all their own, licked the liquid all away as she knelt over the body of her dead father. Buxtak put his big hands on her tiny shoulders. "I'm so sorry, Willex."

Dexy turned to face the other two young monsters. "We have to go. Mom needs to know what she's up against. She needs to know how many of these things there really are. What they plan to do."

Willex wiped her tears away, only for more to stream down her face. "How do you know what they plan to do?"

"Daddy showed me."

Buxtak stomped over to the window. Outside, the screams of dying monsters filled the air. As far as the big thing could see, humans slaughtered monsters. "If *he* couldn't fight them, what chance do we have out there? How do we even know where your mom is?"

"We have to try. Dad thinks Mom and the rest of the night patrol will make their last stand at the base of the Overmind. That's where we're going."

"Buxtak's right," Willex said. "We're just kids. If we go outside now, we won't last a minute. Any one of those... things could kill us without effort."

"You're right," Dexy conceded.

Buxtak rejoined the smaller creatures by their fallen father. "Best we hide and wait this out."

"If we wait this out," Dexy said, turning his attention to the human corpses littered about the room, "there won't be a world for us left out there." He studied each of them intently before moving on to the next. "But you're right about one thing." He stopped above one of the humans. Its neck was bent sideways. Its eyes were vacant. When Dexy poked its exposed pupil, the thing let out a cry, but did not move. It was paralyzed from the neck down.

"We do have to hide."

* * *

"You're crazy," Willex said. She hovered over her little brother, all six arms crossed in protest. "This will never work. You're going to get us killed, Dexy!"

The little monster was busy. He was using one of his sharp claws to carefully slice open the human's midsection at the stomach. "We're dead either way, sis."

The human looked down in horror, screaming gibberish as Dexy peeled back its belly, exposing its vital organs. "Shut him up, will you? If they hear him, they'll swarm back in here and we'll be done for."

Buxtak had been staring into the chasm in the middle of the bedroom floor. It was vast. The sounds of human screams and machinery echoed off the deep walls. He plodded over to Dexy and put one of his gigantic hands over the human's mouth, muffling his protests as the cyclops monster extracted his stomach and most of his intestines, discarding them onto the floor.

"Won't be needing those anymore, will you?" Dexy said, smirking.

After Dexy pulled out several more handfuls of guts, the human stopped screaming. It was pale and sweaty. It continued to jibber, but did so quietly now. It would die soon. Dexy just hoped it would hold out long enough...

"Ok, get him to his feet," Dexy instructed.

Taking the human by the shoulders, Buxtak lifted

it up and held it in place.

"I don't understand," Willex said.

"Watch and learn, sis. This is gonna be awesome!" Dexy rubbed his hands together, and then crawled up into the human's flayed open stomach.

Willex watched, disgusted but fascinated. Nothing happened for a few moments, and then suddenly, the human's hand twitched. The thing looked down in horror as it flexed its fingers.

"Ok, now let go," Dexy yelled from the human's guts, his voice muffled but excited.

Buxtak released his grip on the thing's shoulders. It slumped and fell forward, but at the last second caught itself, steadied and stood upright. It whipped back around to face the young monsters. "This is awesome!" the human said. Its speech was slurred and barely discernible. Blood oozed from its mouth and nose. Even though it smiled, its eyes were still filled with recognition and horror. It was not in control.

Dexy was. Curled up inside the empty guts of the dying human, Dexy had fished his pronged tongue up to the point where the human's neck had broken, and tapped into its spinal cord. He now operated the human's entire nervous system with his own mind.

They now had the perfect cover.

***

"I can't fit in there!" Buxtak said.

Willex poked her head outside the human stomach. Bits of intestine fell out and hit the bone floor with a soft splat. "You can change your size, silly!"

"I've never done that before!" Buxtak said, all ten of his eyeballs wide with fear atop the antler-like hands on his head. "My mom told me never to try that."

"Why not?" the fly-girl asked.

"I don't know. She never said why. She just said

not to meddle with things I wasn't smart enough to understand."

"Concentrate," Dexy said, speaking through the human's mouth. "I know you can do it."

Buxtak sighed. He closed his eyes, balled his hands into fists and strained.

Nothing happened.

"Try again," Dexy said.

Buxtak stomped around in place, cleared his throat and repeated. Again, nothing happened.

"Oh, brother," Willex said. "This is a stupid idea."

Buxtak hung his head in defeat. "Just leave me, guys. I'll stay here till the humans are gone. You don't need me anyway. I'm useless."

"You're not useless," Dexy said, grinning madly. "You're the key to my whole plan!"

The big monster looked confused. "How?"

"Don't worry about it. Look, I've got an idea," Dexy said. He steered the human body over to the mess of steel and flesh that had been people before Big Dex got a hold of them. He rooted around in the pile for several moments before extracting a loop of twisted metal.

"Perfect!"

Dexy wrapped the metal loop around Buxtak's hands. "Now you're our prisoner."

Buxtak smiled. He wanted to believe their plan would work. Wanted to trust in his little buddy. But inside, he knew they were all doomed.

***

Crug of the clan Crug was dying, but lucid. He had wished for a glorious death on the battlefield, like he was raised to believe he'd get when his people rose once again to the surface world that was ripped from their grasp by the Evil Things. He never imagined his guts would be infested with tiny Evil, that he'd be held hostage in his own mind while Evil masqueraded as the mighty Crug. If only he could reach up and push the button. The button would put an end to the tiny Evil. Songs would be sung about his heroic death by the Crug clan forever if he could just take back his body from the tiny Evil for one second.

Push the button.

Boom.

***

Dexy and Buxtak crawled out the window. Blood streamed out of the foot-long wound in the human's stomach as Dexy marched it forward, swaying back and forth, still trying to learn how to walk with human legs.

The monster city was in ruins. Acrid smoke billowed up from a thousand scorch marks across its creeping flesh, choking the children, causing their eyes to water and their noses to sting. Neon blood from trench-like gashes turned the green river streets purple and black. All around the little monsters, screams of death, screams of agony and victory assaulted their senses.

The Overmind loomed in the distance. Its all-seeing eyeball still glowed blood-red, a beacon of hope in a sea of apocalyptic chaos. How could it let this happen? How had it not known the human scourge still lurked below the surface?

Dexy and Buxtak looked at each other and gulped. No sooner had they begun to trudge forward toward the Overmind when a warbling voice stopped them in their tracks.

"You there! Stop!"

Dexy turned around to face a group of humans: three regulars and six pieces of a flesh cannon, including two bullets. They'd barely made it out of their house and already they'd been spotted by an assault team.

"What is this monster which is not to be alive doing with you alive?" the leader of the assault team asked. He was a short, stocky human with metal spikes protruding from his bald skull like porcupine quills.

"He is...my prisoner!" Dexy managed. The human's tongue was swelling from trauma and blood loss. Its body was going into shock, making its muscles rigid.

"The law states that we take no prisoners because of that which the law states!" said another short human. This one female with rows of steel rings buried into the flesh of her large breasts.

"I know this one," a piece of the flesh cannon said. One of the bullets. It walked forward on its hands. "He is Crug from the clan Crug, which I know as Crug from the clan Crug. What is wrong with your body, Crug?"

"I was wounded by this one... in battle with this one?" Dexy said, trying to imitate the peculiar cadence of the human's speech. He began to panic, and as he panicked, his focus wavered.

The left hand of the human twitched; subtly at first, then in jerking spasms, trying to lift itself up. Dexy used the right hand to push it back down into place.

"It looks like glorious death will soon be upon you, who I know as Crug from the clan Crug. Why not take the tiny Evil's head as a trophy to take with you to the great machine beyond which is what awaits you after glorious death?"

Buxtak looked at Dexy, terrified.

"What's happening? I can't see anything!" Willex said, squirming inside the human's empty belly.

"Shut up! I can't concentrate when you're talking to me!" Dexy said, losing more control of the human by the second.

"Ok," Dexy said. "I'll just- EVIL! EVIL INSIDE ME! I'll just- EVIL! -take this one back into the- EVIL THINGS! -house and kill him in there."

"No," the spike-headed human said, his eyes resting on the human's hand, still jerking. "Crug of the clan Crug will kill the tiny Evil here because that is what we've told Crug to do."

That's when the hand broke free of Dexy's grasp. It touched a series of spots on the spinning gyro embedded in its chest. The gyro stopped spinning and popped open, revealing a button within. The hand touched it and the human exploded.

***

For the second time in a day, Dexy woke up blind. He was sure this time was for real. He blinked and blinked, but all he could see was blackness. He couldn't move, either. Maybe this was death? Didn't seem so glorious.

"DESTROY THE TINY EVIL!"

Nope, not dead. But blind and paralyzed? Might as well be dead.

Then Buxtak climbed off him. Not blind or paralyzed. But when he saw what was happening, he wished he was.

The flesh cannon was forming itself, locking all the pieces in place while the bullet climbed atop the contraption. As if that wasn't bad enough, the ring-breasted human held Willex in her hand, holding her out triumphantly like a trophy. The spike-headed human lay dead on the ground: the blast from Crug of the clan Crug's body had sent shrapnel in all directions, impaling Spike Head in four or five different places, including his face, right between his eyes.

Buxtak was unharmed. He charged the ring-breasted human, tearing Willex from her grasp, tossing her back toward the spot where Dexy lay.

Ring Breasts sunk her metal claws into Buxtak's side as her remaining companion did the same. They dug their feet into the ground as the flesh cannon powered up. They were about to do to Buxtak what they'd done to Big Dex.

"We have to help him, Willex!" Dexy said in a panic.

"We're just kids!" she screamed back. "We can't fight!"

Dexy grabbed his sister by the shoulders and looked her in the eyes. His face was his father's face in that instant. "You know what to do!"

***

Dexy sprinted toward the humans as fast as his little legs could take him. He let out a roar that sounded more akin to a squeak and leaped into the air, landing on the back of Ring Breasts. He stuck out his tongue, letting it part, and jabbed the forked prong right into the top of her head, slicing through bone, piercing her brain.

Instantly, the human went rigid and then let go of her death grip on Buxtak. She reached down and pried her companion—a skinny man with twin blades grafted to his forearms in place of actual hands—off the little monster as well, tossing him to the ground. "Now, Willex!" Dexy screamed with Ring Breast's voice.

"I-I can't," she stammered. "What if I can't find myself again?"

"Mom does it all the time!"

"Well I haven't done it EVER!" the little fly-girl cried.

There was no more time to argue. The first bullet-man melted into the barrel and the flesh cannon fired its shot. All three monsters were able to jump out of the way just in time, and the blast instead hit the outer wall of their house, turning it to mush, causing the structure to collapse before their eyes.

Dexy—riding atop the ring-breasted human like a

horse—and Buxtak climbed to their feet as the second bullet began to screw itself into place.

"Willex!" Dexy screamed. "We can't do it without you!"

"OK!" the fly-girl said. She rose into the air above the dazed human with blades on his forearms. He too climbed to his feet, screamed a warbled war cry and charged Dexy and Buxtak, intent on keeping them away from the flesh cannon long enough for it to fire again.

Willex took a deep breath, closed her eyes, and broke apart.

Blade Arms jumped into the air and struck out in a downward fashion, causing Dexy to pull Ring Breasts' arms up in a defensive posture. The move deflected the blow, but not without severing her right arm at the elbow. She stared at the severed limb—now dangling by a single ligament—in disbelief, drool running from her mouth, unable to so much as scream out from the agonizing pain.

Blade Arms reared back to attack again, when a fly buzzed in front of his face, distracting him. He waved at it annoyingly with a blade arm, but another took its place. Then another, and another. Little flies buzzed all around the metal-human's head until he was completely engulfed in insects.

They didn't stop with his head. Soon, more and more flies swarmed around his arms, his chest and finally his legs, until the human was completely concealed within a thick layer of buzzing, writhing little fly monsters.

"Is this what you wanted?" the flies said in unison, a million little Willex voices speaking at once.

Dexy smiled and roared again, but as he turned to lead the charge toward the flesh cannon, the bullet atop its multi-segmented barrel spun and melted down. The blast was aimed directly at the little monsters.

There was no time to evade.

***

Dexy shut his eyes and prepared to be disintegrated where he stood, his only hope that his body, along with the ring-breasted human, would absorb enough of the impact to spare Willex's life. That's when Buxtak jumped in front of him and, without hesitation, grew to over ten feet tall in the blink of an eye. The giant monster turned and braced himself as the blast met him right in the middle of his back.

But a funny thing happened.

Buxtak didn't disintegrate. His flesh didn't melt away. The superheated expulsion of liquid human bounced right off of him and back toward the flesh cannon itself. The spray covered the bodies of the machine, burning their fleshy parts slowly. They howled in agony as the gunk burned through their skin, then muscle, through bone, until finally melting their lungs and vocal chords, putting an abrupt end to their protests.

Dexy and Willex stared at Buxtak in disbelief. The big monster looked more surprised than anyone. "I'm not...dead?" he stammered out, as he shrank back down to his normal size.

"No, big buddy. You're invincible," Dexy said, beaming with pride.

"What do we do with the humans?" Willex asked, walking the blade-armed man around, swinging his blades through the air.

"We'll kill them, and continue with our plan," Dexy said. "This time I won't mess it up."

Tapping the same series of spots Crug pressed in the gyroscopic circle at Ring Breasts' chest, Dexy opened the secret compartment and tore out the self-destruct button, preventing another Crug episode.

"Aw, man. I was just getting good at this! You get to do all the cool stuff!" Willex said.

Suddenly, Blade Arms started to shake. His

screams penetrated the thick layer of flies swarming his body. Blood began gushing out from in between the little flies, and then, just as quickly as they'd swarmed him, all the flies darted off his body at once, leaving nothing more than clean white bones and metal exoskeleton in their wake.

The flies had eaten him so quickly, his bones still shook where they stood for a moment longer before collapsing to the ground in a heap.

"Willex?" Dexy said, growing uneasy after she hadn't reformed into her real body after several minutes had gone by. "Sis? Can you hear me?"

Flies buzzed around, but there seemed to be no focus to their flight pattern. Dexy panicked. "Willex! You have to come back! You have to remember who you are!"

"Chill out, little bro," Willex said, reforming instantly behind him. She burped and rubbed her tummy. "Remind me to eat humans more often. They're tasty!"

***

With Buxtak gaining control of his size, he was able to shrink down small enough so that all three monsters fit snugly inside the stomach of the ring-breasted human—after they'd extracted most of her innards, of course. They trudged along inside Ring Breasts for several miles.

The vast devastation of their beautifully horrific city caused Willex to start crying again.

Flesh cannons ten times the size of those the children had encountered thus far boomed in the distance. Those machines must have required a hundred or more men to construct the bio-mechanical weapons. Explosions rocked the sky, blasting their fellow monsters blessed with flight right out of the air.

The death was nearly palpable. The scent of it— of mutilated corpses both human and monster—created a dampness to the air they breathed. A silent dread grew stronger with every step they took. And still, the Overmind's eye glowed strong as ever.

A rumbling behind them caused the little monsters to stop. What this time? Some new death machine to delay their voyage further?

Worse.

It was the army. The fighting forces of humans were all converging together into one gigantic legion of millions and millions. And they all walked toward the Overmind. This was it. The humans would overtake the Overmind with the sheer vastness of their numbers, like an entire colony of ants overwhelming a bird or lizard.

The gargantuan army marched right past the monsters, paying the bleeding, ring-breasted woman with the huge gash in her stomach and less an arm no mind.

The monsters fell in line and marched along with the humans. They were, after all, headed to the same place.

***

"Glory! Glory! Death! Death!" the humans cried. Their chant aligned with their marching: one word for every step. Ahead of the little monsters inside the body of Ring Breasts was a sort of platform, except made of humans. They were all conjoined at the limbs and contorted in such a way as to make a walking stage, allowing the commander of this particular section of the human army to stand over his troops and survey their movement.

The commander was twice the width of a normal human, because it *was* two humans. Grafted together at the face, shoulder, wrist, hip and ankle, and all encased in an oversized exoskeleton, the commander was both a male and a female.

"Your fathers!" the male head said. "And your

fathers' fathers of those fathers of which we speak of!" the female head continued. They finished each other's sentences as though they shared the same brain. The way their heads were grafted together, maybe they did. "Generations of brave people slaved away in the factories beneath our feet full of brave people. They died of burns and smoke and worse things that they died of so that their sons and daughters would live to see THIS moment that is for their sons and daughters! So that the seed of their seed, the blood of their blood could march upon the Great Evil and SLAY the Great Evil in which they came to slay! Rid this once beautiful planet of the cancer that's smothered this beautiful planet's lush, life-giving force for five hundred years of smothering!"

"Destroy! Evil! Destroy! Evil!" the army chanted.

"Look upon the face of that which has a face upon which we look!" the generals said in unison, as the army descended into the valley that lay at the foot of the Overmind.

It stood taller than any mountain in the world. One glorious hunk of putrid flesh. The very worst, most awful thing ever to be dreamed up in the small, dark hours of the most imaginative human mind. The last time mankind looked upon its mighty visage, its mere presence had been enough to send them shrieking back the way they'd come, welcoming the teeth and claws and other horrors that awaited them, just so long as they never had to look at *It* again.

But these were not those humans. These creatures had somehow escaped the Overmind's wrath and created their own hell. Generation after generation of tortured souls living and dying with but one purpose: To look upon the face of the Overmind once again. Only this time, instead of shrieking madness, there were only howls of joy and chants of doom.

***

The army stopped at the base of the Overmind. They were close enough to the titanic horror that tentacles darted out from the mountain of flesh and snatched several of those humans unfortunate enough to be stationed at the front of the line. They were dragged into slobbering, fanged mouths, violently dismembered, and eaten for their troubles.

Dexy, Willex and Buxtak sat still inside Ring Breasts, doing their best human impression, trying to remain anonymous, knowing that a mistake like last time would mean certain death in front of this legion.

"Every single second that's passed since the Great Evil forced us down into the earth has led up to this second that is passing now!" the generals screamed. "We take the mountain from the Evil, we take the upper world back from the Evil that is the mountain!"

Just then, a spot in the front of the mountain peeled back, revealing a dark chasm. A dozen monsters emerged, the children's mothers among them. They descended the mountain, standing defiantly at the base, directly in front of the legion of millions of mechanically-enhanced humans.

They were all that was left of the monster resistance.

Suddenly, Willex burst from Ring Breasts' stomach, zipping across the heads of the humans in the front line of the army before they could react. "Momma!" she cried.

The little fly-girl slammed into her mother, gripping the larger fly monster made of fly monsters so tightly, she thought she might hug right through her mother's body.

But something was wrong.

"Momma?" Willex said. Blood dripped from her mother's mouth. The little girl looked over at Buxtak's nine-headed hydra-like mother. The eyes of her heads were lifeless. Blood oozed from their noses.

"No," Willex said in a whisper. She jumped back just as metal hands ripped through the tops of the bodies of all dozen monsters. They tore the hollowed-out monster shells off like costumes, discarding their skins like so much garbage.

The human masquerading as the little monsters' mother stepped forward. Grafted to its head were six mini flesh cannons. "Victory is ours! I have just come from the bowels of the Great Evil from which I have come. It spoke to me! It said, 'it is finished!' We have WON the thing in which we came to WIN!"

The ranks of millions of humans cheered. One huge deafening warbled yell filled the air and hung there for a moment. The humans had indeed won. The Overmind had conceded defeat, and every last living monster had been wiped off the planet.

Except for three little kids. Unfortunately for the humans, one of those little kids was Buxtak the Destroyer of Worlds, the Scourge of Nations.

Buxtak the Invincible.

***

Ring Breasts' body erupted in a violent spray of flesh and metal as Buxtak grew. Tens of thousands of the closest humans to him were smashed in seconds as he continued to grow. The monster bellowed a low, mournful scream for his mother and grew larger still.

Buxtak was now taller even than the Overmind. His eyeball-tipped fingers touched the clouds. He stomped backwards and squashed ten thousand more as the army below him began to scatter. But the monumental beast did not purposefully attack the humans. He cried and he screamed, but his eyes were glazed and unfocused. He stumbled away from the war below, aimless, grieving. Mindless.

***

Dexy wasn't blind when he woke up this time. Dizzy, sure—being knocked unconscious three times in one day was enough to rattle even the hardiest of monsters. And he was in trouble. He blinked the darkness away, only to find himself surrounded by humans. A lot of humans. Lucky for him, they were all paying attention to the hulking behemoth stomping away from them, each step like an earthquake followed by thunder, when Buxtak screamed out for his mother.

Dexy took the opportunity to scramble between the humans' legs. He found cover under the corpses of several newly-squashed people. If they saw him, they'd rip him apart before he could finish what he'd come here for. What he'd seen inside his father's mind. He had to get to Willex, and fast. Before Buxtak made it to the ocean.

***

Willex broke apart again. It was hard to control the minds of millions of tiny fly monsters. But it was harder still to control her emotions. Every part of every one of those millions of tiny monsters wanted to see the gun-headed human dead. Willex imprinted all of her hatred and anger for the human race onto the being that killed her mother.

She flung herself at the human, turning herself into a long, flying tendril aiming for his stretched open grin. She planned to fly down his throat and turn him inside out. But he was fast. He dodged the attack, scooping up bits of monster and human gore off the ground as he did so, jamming the hunks of meat into the openings of the six guns on top of his head.

When she turned in the air to strike a second time, he fired all six shots in quick succession. His aim was good for three hits, blowing huge holes into Willex's flying tendril body, killing thousands of miniature versions of herself. While each death hurt, the little creatures bred just as quickly as they died, mating with each interlocking little fly version of herself, giving birth to two monsters to replace every one that died.

Just as Gun Head reloaded his weapons with gore, the flying tendril dispersed, leaving only a small trail of fly monsters in its wake.

"I want ten flesh cannons brought over here at once to the place that I am wanting flesh cannons. We can't let this one get away to a place which we do not know of. She's much more powerful than her size lets us know how powerful she is. Understand?" Gun Head glanced at the human to the left. "I said, do you understand what I asked about understanding what I said?"

The human turned its head and looked at him. Its eyeballs had been replaced by flies.

***

Dexy heard the screaming. He chanced a quick peek out from under his pile of corpses. He saw Willex fifty or so yards away closer to the base of the mountain. She'd encased another human. She was battling with the one who'd come out of their mother's corpse. She had him pinned to the ground, using a swarm of fly bodies to slowly suffocate him. His legs jerked back and forth helplessly as his entire torso was covered in fly monsters.

Dexy took the chance to scramble out of the corpse pile and take off running toward his sister. Most of the humans were forming flesh cannons and firing at Buxtak who still stomped around in aimless circles.

Most. Not all.

Dexy made it about twenty yards before a huge human with two additional arms grafted onto his hips stepped in his path. The little monster skidded to a halt. He gulped and put his hands out in surrender. "N-Now wait a second. You don't really want to kill me, do you? I'm just a kid!"

The human smiled even wider than his pinned back cheeks forced him to. "Gnarlack wants to kill all Evils, even tiny Evils, which is what Gnarlack has been commanded to kill by his commanders."

Before the four-armed man could say more, a swarm of fly monsters attacked his head, completely enveloping it before scattering a moment later, leaving nothing but a clean skull to rattle around in its head cage. A second later, blood gushed up from its neck and the whole big human fell on its back.

Willex reformed in front of her little brother. "Why didn't you kill him?" she asked, anger spewing from her voice. Her eyes were narrow slits. "It's over, Dexy. We've lost. All we can do now is kill as many of them as we can before they overwhelm us." She touched her brother on the shoulder. "It's what mom and dad would want us to do."

Dexy smiled. "It's not over yet, sis. Fly me up to the top of Buxtak's head. I'll tell you everything."

***

A flesh bomb exploded directly in their path, causing Willex to almost drop her brother. Dexy cried out and redoubled his grip on his sister's waist. They flew at eye-level with Buxtak, who was still hundreds of yards away. Dexy told himself not to look down, but did so anyway, causing him to cry out again. For a monster with two fliers in his family, he sure was scared of heights.

"Stop whining and tell me why we're doing this!" Willex said, avoiding another explosion just off to their right.

Dexy took a deep breath and closed his eye so he

wouldn't have to see how high they were. "I saw inside Daddy's mind, into his memories. Big Buxtak, he didn't die in the war. Nothing the humans have in their power, then or now, could kill him. He just grew too big. His brain doesn't grow with his body. Once he gets big enough, he forgets what he is and just... walks.

"Big Bux walked off into the ocean and drowned, sis. That's why Buxtak's mom never taught him to shift sizes."

"And what exactly are we going to do?"

Dexy grinned in spite of his fear of heights. "You'll see!"

***

The generals' two heads screamed in unison. They lived for war, had dreamed about this day their entire lives. The smell of Evil blood on the air, even the honor of sending countless millions of their own kind to the great machine beyond gave them unbridled joy. "This is it! We take down the giant, we wipe the globe clean of the Evil which makes the globe not clean!"

The generals looked around at the teeming multitude of humans surrounding them. There were enough. Of course there were enough. They would not make the mistakes of those weak, soft people who lived here before the Evil. These humans were innumerable. They were legion.

***

Dexy and Willex stood on top of Buxtak's head. Humans swarmed his body. Flesh bombs exploded all around him. It was useless; they hadn't so much as scratched his skin. That was the good news. The bad news was he was only ten or fifteen steps from the ocean.

Dexy split his tongue and drove the prongs into

Buxtak's skull, but they couldn't penetrate his hide any better than the human weapons. "I was afraid of that," he said, putting his hands on his hips as Willex knocked a human who'd crawled up onto the giant's head back down onto his companions below, killing several more on impact.

"So what now?" Willex asked.

"I don't know, but if we don't do it soon, our big buddy's going to walk right into the water. And he can't swim."

"I've got an idea!" Willex said, snatching Dexy up, causing the little monster to scream and flail once again.

The little fly-girl zoomed straight up into the air, corkscrewed, and headed back down toward Buxtak's head, dodging a flailing human who jumped off the giant's hand-antler in an attempt to knock the children out of the sky. Dexy continued to scream as Willex made a B-line for Buxtak's head. Dexy was sure they were going to hit the lumbering beast when, at the last second, Willex tossed her little brother into Buxtak's ear canal. "You're welcome!" she yelled, as his screams faded the further he tumbled into the giant's head.

Her celebration was cut short when she turned around and saw what loomed before her. How did something that... big sneak up on her like that?

***

The generals were face to face with Willex, all those hundreds of feet up in the air. The thing was breathtakingly enormous. Half a million humans must have comprised the skeletal structure alone, all interlocked together, their metal hands and feet welded together forever. It was a mega centipede. Its body was miles long, arching backward in the middle and forward again way up here in the sky, forming a gigantic S. Row after row of flesh cannons, numbering in the hundreds of thousands, lined its underbelly like the legs of the bug it resembled. And fixed atop its head, like a great horn, were the generals.

"Fire at the thing in which needs to be fired at!" they screamed.

Willex couldn't dodge the incredible number of flesh cannons firing off at once. She had to break apart and skitter away as the explosions rocked Buxtak's titan body, causing him to stumble ever closer to the edge of the water.

Something was wrong. Dexy should have taken control of the giant monster by now and steered him away from disaster. As more explosions knocked Buxtak onto the shoreline, Willex reformed and darted into the big beast's ear canal.

She found her brother sitting cross-legged in front of Buxtak's little brain. His tongue prong was in place and his eye was closed in concentration. His brow was creased, and the little scaly monster trembled. Willex put her hand on him. "Dexy, are you OK?"

He opened his eye. "It's not strong enough. Even with me controlling it, his little brain can't stop him from walking. The explosions outside, what is that?"

"The generals. They knows they can't kill Buxtak. They're just pushing him into the water. They know everything, Dexy. They knew exactly how to wipe us off the planet."

"They've had five hundred years to plan, sis. But they didn't plan on three little kids ruining their party." Dexy turned and faced his sister. "We can beat the humans. Just do exactly what I tell you."

***

"The Abomination is the last of the Evil that is the Abomination!" the generals screamed from the top of the mega centipede. "The sea is its weakness! Push! Push it into the unfathomable depths of that which is its weakness!"

Buxtak was now ankle-deep in the water. The mega centipede was right on top of him. The shoreline was completely obscured by human bodies. They waded into the water, singing songs of glory and death as they swam out to the mega centipede and climbed up its towering body, only to crawl into the barrels of the innumerable flesh cannons to be shot into the indestructible hide of the Abomination. If every single human on the planet had to die to kill the last of the Evil, that was just fine by them. Maybe the trees would sing the songs of their glory.

More cannons exploded, driving Buxtak ever deeper into the ocean, now nearly up to his waist.

The big thing was still crying and blubbering about its mother when the flies began pouring out of his ears.

***

Willex replicated and replicated some more. Buxtak was shoulder-deep in the water. Soon, there would be no way to turn him back. He would drown where he stood, and then this war really would be over. No sooner would she replicate enough little versions of herself to cover the big monster's head than the mega centipede would fire off another thousand-round volley of flesh blasts, incinerating all of her work. This happened again and again, frustrating Willex to no end. She was about to give up.

And then the cannons stopped firing.

They'd come too far out into the ocean. The humans couldn't swim out this far. They were all drowning from exhaustion before they made it to the mega centipede.

The generals screamed, their fury shaking the entire titanic creature. "Swim! Swim for your lives as though glory depended on your swimming!"

This gave Willex just enough time to replicate herself over Buxtak's whole head, then his shoulders, then grew three sets of arms made of fly monsters from his long torso under the water.

She concentrated. It was difficult synching the minds of all the billions of tiny flies covering the giant's body. If she lost focus, she would certainly never find herself among all of those little monsters again. And then it happened.

Working together with Dexy, with much effort, they managed to turn the great beast around in the water.

***

The generals unlocked their feet from the mega centipede's head. They climbed down its back, stepping on faces, backs, and elbows, ignoring the pained protests from the interlocked humans they stomped on. They stopped in front of a flesh cannon, reached down and ripped one of the humans from the structure, tearing the helpless man's arms out of socket in the process, due to the fact that they were welded to the person above him. "For the glory of the death which brings me glory!" the armless man screamed as the generals stuffed him down the cannon's barrel, melting him down instantly, blasting his remains toward the Abomination. The single shot did nothing to stop the towering beast which now trudged back through the water toward the mechanical being.

"We have come too far to lose after we've come so far!" the generals bellowed, scrambling back up to the mega centipede's head. No sooner had they locked themselves back into place than a gigantic fist covered in flies swung directly at their faces.

***

The generals ducked, barely avoiding the blow. They locked their arms and finally their two heads permanently in place, allowing a series of nanobots to weld their bodies to the creature's frame. Their brains took full control of the giant centipede. Now they saw from the eyes of the millions of humans comprising the gargantuan machine. Felt what they felt, heard what they heard.

As soon as the two-person being finished orienting themselves with the mega beast's nervous system, the Abomination's gigantic fly-covered hand shot back out, grabbing the mega centipede around the throat. In response, the generals commanded their miles-long body to thrash up like a whip, smashing into the Abomination's head, sending the titanic Evil back another hundred yards closer to the abyss that awaited it below the waves.

***

Flies covered the vast space inside Buxtak's head. They continued to multiply exponentially, now by the millions every minute. Soon they would cover Dexy as well. He panicked when the flies began to swarm over him. He tried to pull his tongue free of Buxtak's brain, but the prongs held fast, almost as though Buxtak wouldn't let him pull them out.

"Don't fight it, Dexy," millions of Willexes said as the flies filled the brain cavity entirely. "This is the only way. You know this. You wanted this."

Now flies crawled into his own head, massaged his own brain with the relaxing words of his sister. He no longer panicked. No longer cared about his own insignificant little life. He, Buxtak, Willex, they were all one creature now. One glorious monster known as... What had the humans called them? The Abomination. Their minds were perfectly in sync. They no longer thought as three separate entities. Their memories, their rage, their sadness melded together into one unstoppable giant.

The mega centipede was wrapped around their face, trying to choke the life out of them. Impossible. The Abomination took a step toward the shore. Then another.

That's when the centipede changed.

Its segments shifted, creating two pairs of long legs, while maintaining its noose-like tail. It more resembled a scorpion now. With these modifications, the human-machine hybrid was able to pull the Abomination off balance, and send both titans crashing underwater.

Below the surface, the giant machine made of men changed again, splitting its long tail into two segments, each digging into the sediment of the ocean floor, pulling the flesh beast further underwater as it permanently anchored itself beneath the waves.

***

The Abomination's fly carapace began to drown. Whole pieces of it broke off and floated back toward the surface. Air bubbles escaped its lungs as it fought to break free from the mechanical titan.

But the general and his millions of humans were not immune to the water, either. Parts of its vice-like legs began to drown and loosen their grip. The generals were close to unconsciousness themselves. Waves of panic swept through the machine giant.

Glory comes to those who would drown to see the Evil drown at the hands of those who would drown for glory! the generals thought into the minds of each of the humans struggling to hold their breaths. *Just... hold on... a little... longer!*

The Abomination braced its arms against the sediment and arched its back, allowing it just enough space to smash down on top of the machine creature, killing thousands of drowning humans, causing it to loosen its grip that much more.

More flies died and washed away as the three-minded monster swam in and out of consciousness. Another minute, and it would die as well.

The generals spat out a lungful of stale air. Then another.

The Abomination lashed out with its fists, tearing off segments of the machine in one last desperate attempt to break away. Air bubbles streamed from its mouth as it choked, still unable to swim to the surface.

Then the machine creature spasmed. Its legs kicked uselessly in the water. The Abomination held it fast, pinning it to the ocean floor.

The two faces of the Generals mouthed the word *glory* in unison, and then went slack, the remaining air bubbles from their lungs trickling out of their mouths and noses.

The Generals were dead. The war was over. The monsters had won.

Victory was short-lived, as the Abomination let out its final lungful of air in a vast stream of bubbles. In seconds, it would join the legion of humans in death. It was calm in that moment, ready to accept its encroaching demise knowing it had wiped out the human race again, preventing them from taking back the world the monsters had won from them so long ago.

Its final thought: Would there be glory in the afterlife for monsters? Or would the humans hog it all for themselves?

That's when a gigantic arm reached into the water and pulled the titanic monster back to the surface.

***

The Abomination puked sea water on the beach. The few thousand humans left alive on shore ran for their lives, choosing to scuttle back under the rocks they'd crawled out from under rather than face the glorious death they'd so recently sung about. Without their leader, they were as useless as a colony of bees without their queen.

Already the fly monsters were replicating, reforming across the surface of the Abomination's flesh as it rolled over, breathing in huge lungfuls of air. After several minutes, it opened all ten of its reptile eyes atop its hand-antler head. What it saw made its breath hitch in its throat.

Had it actually died down there deep in the ocean? Was this Heaven?

***

The Overmind. After five hundred years of silence, it had chosen to stand up. Now it stood over the Abomination, offering a hand to the fallen mega monster.

The Abomination took its hand and rose to its feet. It still had to look up to meet its savior's gaze. The Overmind's mountainous head loomed in the planet's lower atmosphere. Its huge glowing eye cast a red hue over the entire northern hemisphere.

Its body was slender, its six arms long and lanky, each ending in a hand the size of city-states, its legs taught and muscular.

The Abomination looked up in awe, then fell to one knee.

"Master," it said, shuddering in ecstasy at the sight of the most horrible of horrors. The Creator of all monsters.

"Rise," the Overmind said. Its voice shook the Earth enough to cause tectonic plate shifts. Tsunamis roared across the surface of the ocean, washing away continents.

The Abomination did as instructed.

"Walk with me."

The two titans strode the Earth's surface, causing earthquakes and volcanoes to explode in tribute to the two godlike beings.

The Abomination looked into the Overmind's mountain face. "Why did you let them live, master? Why let them slaughter our entire race?"

"Five hundred years ago, mankind blessed me with life. I, in turn, created my own. But try as I might, I could not create a being as powerful as myself.

"I became lonely in my omnipotence.

"Even Gods are limited by their own ego, I suppose. I was forced to be patient. To let the nature of this world—the nature of life—carry on at its own pace.

"I let the humans live so that my creations could breed. So that the humans could breed their hatred for me and my children. I hoped that when the time came, when nature pushed back, my children would be strong enough to survive. Would be strong enough to do what I could not."

"Create a God," the Abomination said, finishing its master's thought.

"And what a beautiful God you've created, my child."

The Overmind knelt down and kissed the Abomination on its lips. "Come. Let us leave this planet to fester and die. Its worth has run its course. We have more Gods to create, worlds to conquer. Maybe the two of us can create a being powerful enough to worship ourselves. Wouldn't that be something?"

With that, Overmind opened at the chest, revealing a hollow cavern. The Abomination stepped inside its master's body without hesitation. The Overmind grew wings made of trillions of little fly monsters, and launched itself off the Earth into the unknown blackness of space.

ABOUT THE AUTHORS

Jacob Lambert *A Game of Chance*
First place recipient of the Scott and Zelda Fitzgerald award for short story, Jacob M. Lambert has published with Dark Hall Press, Midnight Echo: The Magazine of the Australian Horror Writers Association, and more. He lives in Montgomery, Alabama, where he teaches music and is an editorial assistant for The Scriblerian and the Kit-Cats, an academic journal pertaining to English literature of the late seventeenth-and early eighteenth-century. When not writing, he enjoys time with his wife Stephanie and daughter Annabelle.

Kevin Strange *The Humans Under the Bed*
Kevin Strange is a prolific filmmaker and author with seven feature films and over a dozen shorts to his credit. He has published two novels, ROBAMAPOCALYPSE and VAMPIRE GUTS IN NUKE TOWN, a short story collection, THE LAST GIG ON PLANET EARTH, and numerous novellas including MCHUMANS, and COTTON CANDY. He loves schlocky B-movies, hardcore pornography, Bizarro fiction and Queen records.

D.M. Anderson *Zombie Bowl*
D.M. Anderson lives and teaches middle school in Portland, Oregon. He's the author of two young adult novels (*Killer Cows* & *Shaken*) as well as an upcoming collection of dark tales (*With the Wicked*), all published by Echelon Press. His short stories have appeared in such magazines as *Night Terrors*, *Implosion* (RIP), *Infernal Ink, Perpetual Motion Machine, Encounters, 69 Flavors of Paranoia* an *Trembles*, He is also the author of *Free Kittens Movie Guide*, which features nostalgic/irreverent essays, humor and film reviews. When he isn't writing, Anderson enjoys heavy metal music, NASCAR, going to the beach and staying up late with his youngest daughter

watching horror movies.

Rich Bottles Jr. *Assface*
After an unillustrious print journalism career in south-western Pennsylvania, Rich Bottles Jr. moved to West Virginia at the age of 32 to pursue a career in technical writing. He spends his free time visiting and hiking at the many state parks in the Mountain State, which is also where he develops the concepts for his novels. He is producing a trilogy of WV-themed "humorrorotica" and is currently working on a bizarro novel set in the vicinity of the West Virginia State Penitentiary. His previous novels include "Lumberjacked" and "Hellhole West Virginia." He was also a co-editor and contributor to the infamous anthology "The Big Book of Bizarro." His only regret in life is that his out-of-state secondary school education prohibited him from earning West Virginia's prestigious Golden Horseshoe Award.

John Bruni *The Knot that Binds*
John Bruni is the author of STRIP, a crime novel from Musa, and TALES OF QUESTIONABLE TASTE, a collection of short stories from StrangeHouse Books. His shorter work has appeared in magazines like SHROUD, MORPHEUS TALES, THE REALM BEYOND, CTHULHU SEX MAGAZINE, AOIFE'S KISS and others. He has also appeared in anthologies like ZOMBIE! ZOMBIE! BRAIN BANG! from StrangeHouse Books, A HACKED-UP HOLIDAY MASSACRE from Pill Hill Press and the critically acclaimed VILE THINGS from Comet Press. He was the poetry editor of MIDDLEWESTERN VOICE, and he was the editor and publisher of TABARD INN, a fiction magazine. He lives in Elmhurst, IL, and he swears he doesn't have a conjoined twins fetish. Really. He's more into amputee porn.

Eric Dimbleby *Appelonia*
"Eric Dimbleby lives and works in Maine, with his wife

and 3 children. His newest effort, a short story collection called THE FETUS CLOUD is available on Amazon. His previous novel, THE KLINIK is still available from Damnation Books, ans is available at most online retailers. To learn more about Eric, visit www.ericdimbleby.com.

Justin Hunter *Cephalopod*

Justin Hunter is a dark literary fiction and post-apocalyptic black comedy author. He and his wife thrive amidst the beautiful chaos of their four children.

Matt Kurtz *Worse for the wear*

Matt Kurtz is a lover of all things horror, thanking his mother for rearing him on Hammer movies and Universal Monsters. He grew up with Aurora monster model kits, *Kolchak the Night Stalker, Famous Monsters of Filmland* and *Fangoria* magazine. Being bombarded with such monstrosities at an early age, Matt became terrified of the dark. It was while cowering under the covers at bedtime that his mind leaped into overdrive, creating tales of terror he'd eventually spew onto the page decades later. His fiction can be read in anthologies from Blood Bound Books, Evil Jester Press, Comet Press, and *Necrotic Tissue* Magazine. Check out more about him at http://www.strikingly.com/mattkurtz.

K.M. Tepe *Cockblock*

Tepe began writing stories as a child. The darkness began in her teenage years after long term exposure to a pair of sentient bananas who frequently coerce her into setting fires for the Democratic party. Now she writes this stuff. Her fiction can be found in the SHB anthologies ZOMBIE! ZOMBIE! BRAIN BANG! and A VERY STRANGEHOUSE CHRISTMAS. She just finished work on her first novel Slaughtertown Circus.

Billy Tea *Rape C(o)untry*

Billy Tea should probably be a serial killer, considering his two primary interests in life are sex and death. Instead of being a murderer, though, he is something infinitely worse: a writer. "Kafka's Run" is his second published fiction work. He is currently working on his first novel.

Frank Edler *Dick Sick*

Frank J Edler resides in New Jersey where he attempts to write. His work can also be found in Tim Baker's UNFINISHED BUSINESS, STRANGE VERSUS LOVECRAFT, and STILL DYING 2. Frank is currently working on a longer form project for 2014. He is co-host of the wildly popular BOOKS, BEER AND BULLSHIT podcast. His antics can be heard at http://booksbeerbullshit.podbean.com and the companion blog at booksbeerblogshit.blogspot.com.

MP Johnson *Hearts and Caterpillars*

MP Johnson has been writing strange fucking stories all his life. His short stories have appeared in more than 35 publications. His debut book, The After-Life Story of Pork Knuckles Malone, was released in 2013 by Bizarro Pulp Press. His second book, Dungeons and Drag Queens, is due soon from Eraserhead Press. He is the creator of Freak Tension zine, a B-movie extra and an obsessive music fan currently based in Minneapolis. Learn more atwww.freaktension.com.

Christopher Hivner *The Painter's Mother Rode a Pale Horse*

Christopher Hivner writes from a small town in Pennsylvania surrounded by books and the echoes of music. He is neither famous nor infamous. He has recently been published in Dark Eclipse, Illumen and Miseria's Chorale anthology. A collection of short horror stories, "The Spaces Between Your Screams" was published by eTreasures Publishing. Website: www.chrishivner.com

"Strange Sex"

What if Joseph wasn't the first man to be cuckolded by God? What if there was a cult of adulterated men who would do anything to kill him for fucking their wives into useless shells of nymphoid lust? What if a woman possessed was so utterly tormented, that the only way to save her soul was to perform a Sexorcism? What if a scaticallogically inclined man found a way to pleasure himself with bed bugs? What if a woman fell in love with a dinosaur? What if a seemingly innocent Furry gangbang turned out to be a mating ritual for a tribe of nomadic cannibal were-teddy bears? These questions and many more will be answered when StrangeHouse books takes you on a journey unlike any you've ever seen before with their debut anthology of strange erotic horror fiction, "Strange Sex".

"The Last Gig on Planet Earth"
Kevin Strange

Kevin Strange's fiction has been described as bleak, hopeless, bizarre, and always unpredictable. This is Strange at his most nihilistic. The Last Gig on Planet Earth collects seven tales full of suspense, of dread, of that side of human nature that most pretend does not exist. Strange sets his spotlight directly in its gnarled face and demands it reveal its most twisted secrets.

This collection is sure to leave you repeating, "this is only fiction, this is only fiction, please let this only be fiction..."

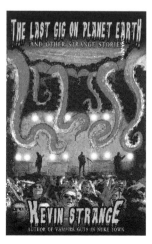

Now Available at StrangehouseBooks.com!

"Alien Smut Peddlers from the Future" *Kent Hill*

Porn, it's a part of our society. but in the future, it has all but eclipsed every known form of currency. The creatures that control it are as terrifying in form as they are lustful for sexual gratification. And one of them has just crash landed in the wild west. Gold will glisten, blood will flow, many shall be massacred until a few brave souls call down the thunder. A thunder named Badlands Meredith. part man, part machine, all bad ass. ready your senses for the most shocking, the most offensive, the most incredible showdown in this alternate universe when the most feared gunfighter goes one on one with the… Alien Smut Peddlers from the Future!

"Damnation 101" *Kevin Sweeney*

The Breakfast Club fucked to death by Dante's Inferno. Thanks to a balls-up by a moron God, all humans go to Hell when they die. But the Academy that trains demons to torture can't churn out students fast enough to cope with demand, and so as an experiment a human is enrolled to see if the damned can be used shore up the number of tormentors. But first she has to survive the harsh lessons of Damnation 101...

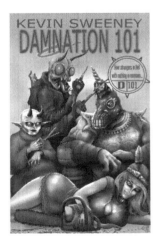

Now Available at StrangehouseBooks.com!

"McHumans" *Kevin Strange*

After Cthulhu awakens and destroys civilization as we know it, humans are used as slaves and food by their new slimy, submerged masters. One such young man, Ricky, works at an under-sea fast food joint where he's forced to kill and cook other humans for the Deep Ones to eat. But he has a plan. His restaurant caters to the Big Man himself, and if Ricky's plan works, he could pull off the unthinkable:
He could actually Kill Cthulhu.

"A Very Strangehouse Christmas"

What do a Gasmask-Wearing, post-apocalyptic Santa Claus, A Weed Witch bent on fucking Christmas, a family of abominable snow beasts, and people with Christmas present heads have in common? They could only exist inside the bizarre and horrific world of StrangeHouse Books!

This collection of 9 twisted tales of Christmas horror brings together weirdo literary talent from around the world, all with the sole purpose of turn-

ing the most sacred of holidays on its head, and making sweet, sweet love to its defenseless ear holes! Join SHB ring leader Kevin Strange, as well as StrangeHouse anthology alumni Rich Bottles Jr., Jesse Wheeler, KM Tepe, and new-comers like Lindsey Goddard and MP Johnson on this sometimes magical, always fucked up journey to the north pole. We promise you'll never look at Christmas the same way ever again!

Now Available at StrangehouseBooks.com!

HORROR BOOKS

STRANGEHOUSE

"Re-Animated States of America"
Craig Mullins and Andrew Ozkenel

Re-Animated States of America is a collection of short fiction set in a post-apocalyptic world, beautifully crafted by lifelong H.P. Lovecraft aficionado, award winning film maker and author Craig Mullins. RSoA is twelve stories all featuring beloved mythos character Herbert West, Re-Animator and his human-headed dog companion, Jehovah. Each story contains an illustration brought to life by Mullins' long time artistic collaborator Andrew Ozkenel in striking black and white.

"Strange Fucking Stories"

Caterpillar portals to other dimensions, monster holocausts, suits tailored from human flesh and wild west shootouts with pink minotaurs are but a few of the themes comprising this quintessential book of Strange Fiction. Strange Fucking Stories gathers together the best of the best StrangeHouse Books authors and teams them with brand new voices yet to grace the pages of an SHB tome. StrangeHouse editor Sean Ferrari and the prison warden himself Kevin Strange bring you their finest collection of fiction yet with 13 tales of the weird

and the macabre, from SHB anthology staples Rich Bottles Jr., K.M. Tepe, and John Bruni join MP Johnson, Billy Tea, and many more of horror and bizarro's best authors, proving once again that Strange-House Books is a brand not to be ignored!

Now Available at StrangehouseBooks.com!

HAMSTERDAMNED!

THE NEW BOOK FROM
ADAM
MILLARD

COMING SOON
FROM
STRANGEHOUSEBOOKS. COM

AN EXCERPT FROM
HAMSTERDAMNED!
BY
ADAM MILLARD

Mike's balls were on fire. He jerked forward, patting at his crotch, expecting to feel the burn on his hands as the flames engulfed them. The drunken haze in which he woke prevented him from seeing the conflagration immediately, and as he punched away, slapping his apparently bare bottom-half with both hands, he was suddenly aware of laughter, cruel and boisterous, all around.

"Looks like he's whacking off!" an excited voice said before erupting with laughter once again.

As the miasma lifted, affording Mike a view of his cream-slathered crotch, it all came flooding back.

Stag-do. Amsterdam. Bunch of asshole friends whose job it was to make his last few days as a single man as tortuous and pleasurable – often at the same time – as they possibly could.

"How's that feel, buddy?" John said. The sight of an empty tube of *Deep Heat Max* in his friend's hand offered Mike little relief. Sure, his balls hadn't been doused in petrol and set alight, as he'd first thought, but it still *felt* like it.

Hissing, sucking air in through clenched teeth, Mike said, "You fuckers! Oh, fuck, that burns so bad." It was all he could do not to pass out; this, he thought, is what my dick should feel like at the *end* of the weekend, not the beginning.

Through watery eyes, a can of something green appeared. The sound of a ring-pull snapping pulled him from the depths of unequivocal agony into which he'd been sucked. *Hey, your cock and balls are melting, but at least we have beer…*

Mike snatched the can from Stuart, who had laughed so much he'd turned an unnatural shade and seemed to be wearing a beard of mirth-induced drool. After pouring half a can on Big Jim and the Twins – he couldn't be certain, but he thought he saw steam – he drank the rest in one thirsty gulp. A cheer went up around the minibus and Mike immediately forgave them for inflicting so much pain upon him.

"Told you not to fall asleep," John said, taking the empty seat next to the groom-to-be. "These fuckers are *animals.*"

"Oh, I must have missed the part where you tried to stop us," Stuart said, immediately followed by a snort that would make a pig blush.

Mike wiped his eyes on his sleeve, being careful not to get any of the liquid lava in, or even near, them. "How long was I out for?" he said, reaching for another can. That was the great thing about stag-dos; you could drink until you feel asleep, wake up, and carry on where you left off. The only downside was that, in essence, you were having one final blowout before it all came to a grinding halt. Mike wondered how long it would be before Beth – of 'will you please marry me, Beth?' fame – started telling him who he could be friends with, and who he had to give the brush-off. It was only a matter of time, and when that time came, he knew he would do it. *That's what married life is*, she'd say, and he'd nod like a dutiful dachshund, all the while discarding years of friendship as if it mattered less than a week's toenail growth.

"You've been asleep for an hour," John said. "So far you've missed Tony lighting the mother of all farts, and Donald mooning a coachload of nuns." He threw his head back, chuckling like a kid who'd just seen his first dirty magazine. "You should have seen their faces, dude. Looked like they'd never seen a black dude's bare ass before."

And why *would* they? Mike thought. In fact, that

was the *last* thing they'd probably expected to see on their way to whatever fucking nunnery they called home.

Still, John persisted with his story, about how one of them had made the sign of the cross, and how another had made a finger-crucifix, as if Donald's ass was a vampire, liable to bite her neck should it get close enough.

"If you hadn't fallen asleep," John said, licking foam from a freshly-cracked beer, "you'd have seen it and your balls wouldn't be looking like something from *Attack of the Killer Tomatoes!*"

Mike was tired. The trip had been underway for less than twelve hours and he was ready to turn around head back to Birmingham. That was the thing. His days of partying were over; it was time to grow the fuck up and act his age. Thirty-two was nothing, not really, and certainly not to his buddies, who saw nothing wrong with dragging alcohol-marinated slappers back to their respective bedsits for one night of instantly forgettable, and practically ineffectual, lovemaking. Mike had moved in with Beth, waved goodbye to his eight-by-eight shed he'd called home, and was now spending his nights *talking*; talking about kids, about kids' names, and about who the kids were going to take after. *I hope they take after you because you're tall. No, I hope they take after you because you're smart. No, they won't take after* either *of us because we're not doing that thing we have to do to fucking* make *kids.* Mike had listened to her incessant yapping, replying with the occasional nod – it kept her happy – and saying things like, 'That's a nice name,' and, 'I'm sure it won't hurt.' He'd listened, because that's what good men *do*, but if the truth be told he wasn't ready for kids, not yet. It had taken him two years to propose, and another six months to set a date. Who the fuck was he kidding by pretending he was ready to shoot out a few sprogs?

"You're thinking about *her*, aren't you?" John said. He sounded disappointed. "Snap out of it, man. This is probably the last time she's ever gonna let you go out again. After this it'll be nights in with mutual foot-massages; before you know it, you'll be reading the babies a story and getting up five times a night to change shitty nappies."

John was right; this was his weekend – his final weekend as a free man – and the last thing he should have been thinking about was Beth.

"You're right, mate," Mike said. "And I really appreciate you putting all this together. I *don't* appreciate you burning off my nut-sack, but I know you've put a lot of time and effort into this." He smiled.

"Just enjoy the ride," John said as he uncapped a hip-flask. He handed it to Mike. "You're going to have the best weekend of your fucking life. I guaran-fuckin-*tee* it."

Taking a long, hard slug from the hip-flask – probably should have sniffed it first, though he didn't think they'd go as far as handing him piss to drink – Mike glanced out through the window as a cheer erupted throughout the minibus. They were just passing a large green sign; pockmarked and weathered, it announced their arrival and the start of what John promised to be, *The best weekend of your fucking life.*

Welkom In Amsterdam.

Made in the USA
Lexington, KY
13 February 2014